Aberdeenshire

COUNCIL

Aberdeenshire Libraries
www.aberdeenshire.gov.uk/libraries
Renewals Hotline 01224 661511

CHANCE

A *Strictly*
NOVEL

ALEX HINES

HARPER

HARPER

An imprint of HarperCollins*Publishers*
77–85 Fulham Palace Road,
Hammersmith, London W6 8JB

www.harpercollins.co.uk

First published by HarperCollins*Publishers* 2011

1 3 5 7 9 10 8 6 4 2

A catalogue record for this book is
available from the British Library

ISBN 978-0-00-742734-5

Printed and bound in Great Britain by
Clays Ltd, St Ives plc

MIX
Paper from
responsible sources
FSC
www.fsc.org **FSC** C007454

For Louis, with whom I
can barely wait to dance.

Acknowledgements

With huge thanks to Sarah Ballard, Matt Gunn and Jessica Ruston.

Chapter 1

Roses on a Monday

As she opened the door Ava could see the floor was covered in flowers: unopened peonies in tight pink balls, crisp white lilies, their stamens bristling with pollen, and a bank of roses, almost mocking in their velvety glamour. Taking a deep breath to enjoy the aromatic mixture their scents made, she stepped over buckets of daisies to reach her desk. She hung up her coat, flicked the kettle on and flipped open her laptop. While the kettle boiled, she flicked through her post – the usual selection of bills and junk mail, along with a flyer for new classes at the Arts Centre. There wasn't really anything worth opening or reading properly before she had a cup of tea on the go, so she stared absent-mindedly at the flowers as the comforting sound of the kettle grew louder and louder. They were lined up according to type and colour, creating an extravagant floral carpet. Ava knew it would take her another few minutes to start to feel fully awake and was glad of some time alone with the shop.

She swirled a teabag around in the water, wondering if Rob was up yet. He had taken to staying at her house more and more lately, although whether his motivation was the prospect of cosy evenings together or being closer to his office was unclear. Either way, he had been dead to the world when she left the house – completely still and snoring lightly, despite the clatter of her Monday morning routine. Ava wondered if he was even awake yet, if he had discovered the cup of tea she left by his bedside, or if he was still curled up in her bed, leaving his imprint on her pillow.

'Morning, Boss!' Matt had arrived and was standing in the doorway, a bucket of flowers already under each arm. 'Had a good weekend?'

'Yes thanks, Matt, nothing special,' she replied. She repeated those last two words to herself: nothing special. 'You?'

'Oh yeah, it was wicked!' Matt was grinning at the memory and it wasn't even nine o'clock yet. Was he immune to Monday mornings? If he wasn't a little sluggish at this point in the week, when was he? 'We went down to the coast for a bit of surfing, had a barbecue – good times, amazing waves.'

Well over ten years younger than her, Matt seemed to have boundless energy and an insatiable appetite for fun. Even a spare half hour would be filled with some kind of sporting activity, an impromptu burst of socialising or a quick trip somewhere. He was no sofa surfer; indeed TV seemed to hold no allure for him at all. Just hearing about his hectic social life made Ava feel slightly dizzy, but he was so good-natured it was hard to begrudge him a moment of it. Truly, he was a gift. She smiled to herself as he put the first two buckets of flowers up onto the highest bracket of the shelving unit, whistling, then immediately turned round to reach for the rest.

'Look at these!' he said as he picked up the roses, holding them admiringly with outstretched arms as if they were Liz Taylor herself, ready to dance. 'They're gorgeous today – I wonder where they'll be ending up …' He winked at Ava and she rolled her eyes. Relatively new to the job, he was still enthused by almost every part of his work at Dunne's. 'Although you've got to wonder – what's a man doing buying red roses on a Monday if he's not a little bit guilty about something?'

'Oh come on, so young and already such a cynic! Maybe some men are just impulsive or romantic. I wouldn't keep ordering them for a Monday if they didn't sell.' She gave him a playful cuff over the head and he ducked, giggling.

'They sell all right,' replied Matt with a wink, 'but to romantic men … or those in the doghouse?'

'Stop it – that's too depressing!'

'Only kidding,' he said, as he finally hung up his jacket. But Ava suspected he wasn't. She shook herself, trying to get rid of the leaden Monday morning blues she still felt.

'Right, you – a cup of tea?'

'Go on, then. I reckon it's going to be busy for a Monday.'

For the next few minutes they worked alongside each other in companionable silence. Matt knew where the usual spots for all of the flowers were and neatly moved bunches from the plastic buckets in which they had been left to the smarter tin pails they were displayed in. More delicate blooms were stacked on wooden shelves across the main side wall of the shop and he took the smaller, almost wine-bucket size pails outside onto the street. Daffodils, sunflowers and sturdy tulips were all arranged on the pavement beneath the shop window, with Matt whistling along to the radio as he worked. Ava made his milky tea and handed it to him before checking off deliveries against the invoice left three hours earlier.

'Something's missing,' said Matt, as he nodded to thank Ava for the mug she had just passed him.

'The sweet peas are late.'

Unlike the more exotic flowers that Dunne's stocked, the sweet peas were not imported from abroad, but delivered sporadically by a local farm. They tended to swing by and drop off a supply whenever they felt the shop needed them, paying little heed to such trivialities as whether or not Ava actually needed them, or had indeed ordered them. But Ava couldn't bring herself to start ordering them from elsewhere. She loved the area, having grown up just outside of Salisbury, and stocking local flowers was important to her. It made no sense to have spent her childhood playing in the fields of the West Country and then to import absolutely everything from elsewhere once she had her own business in the area.

When she left college and headed off to London with dreams of a career arranging cutting-edge displays for celebrity events and society weddings, she had wanted little to do with the gentler countryside flowers such as blowsy roses, peonies and sweet peas. After over a decade of providing breathtaking arrangements for corporate

4

receptions only to watch city brokers and their nonchalant PAs walk past completely oblivious to their beauty, she began to tire of wasting her best work on an audience who cared so little. The breaking point had been the week when she worked her fingers raw on a series of jaw-dropping displays for the awards ceremony of a glossy magazine, held in an echoing warehouse somewhere near Docklands. She had led a team spending eighteen-hour days to transform the imposing concrete structure into a venue where pop princesses, rock icons and supermodels alike would be happy to pose and party against a backdrop befitting them. Exhausted, but aglow with the satisfaction of a job well done, Ava had left the building only to wake to a series of charmless tabloid photographs of a well-oiled soap starlet flicking her cigarette into one of her red ginger and anthurium arrangements before collapsing into another – apparently fuelled by a lethal combination of four-inch fluoro heels and limitless free fizz.

'At least your work has been in the papers,' was her ever-pragmatic younger sister Lauren's response. 'Other florists would kill for that kind of exposure.' Ava was convinced Lauren herself would probably be first in the queue, but still wondered if her fee for the work could ever make up for the body blow that seeing those pictures had provided. And then came the second punch: later that very same day Ava received an email from a woman in which she explained that she had been having a six-month affair with Mick, the darkly handsome but elusive and unreliable boyfriend with whom Ava had just spent the last three years of her life.

Already living together, they had been saving to buy a property while making do in a tiny one-bedroom in East London, above a bone-shakingly noisy main road. Devastated by how her dreams of urbane adulthood had panned out, Ava decided to leave London for a year and spend some time in the area where she had grown up, trying to decide her next move.

Initially concerned months spent within 'popping by for a quick cup of tea' distance of both her parents and Lauren would leave her suffering a nasty dose of claustrophobia, Ava soon realised the opposite had happened. Now she breathed a deep sigh of relief at being away from the capital's eternal hamster wheel of marriage–career–babies, even if those possibilities still preoccupied her mother. Slowly the pain of soured romance faded, as did the stress of working for her dictatorial former boss, Nigel, Bespoke Florist to the Stars. Of course she missed some of her friends and occasionally daydreamed about walks along the river or shopping in department stores with proper cosmetics departments, but largely, she realised, she was not a Londoner.

When that first year of working at the charming little garden centre in the grounds of a local stately home ended, she knew she couldn't go back to her old life. Instead she chose to invest her savings in buying a small place in Salisbury and setting up a business of her own. If the 'finding eternal love' column on her life plan was to take a little longer than planned, she was damned if she would waste time on the 'enjoy your work, and be the very best at it' column. Thus Dunne's of Salisbury, her pride and joy, was born and quickly became a fixture in the market town. Ava found she was far more quickly integrated into the local community than she had ever been in London, where the idea of borrowing a cup of sugar always remained a faintly ridiculous fantasy. So what if life was quieter, less glamorous and or dramatic in Salisbury? It was the path she had chosen and what would make her happy. Just like Robin, with whom she had now been for five years. Lovely dependable Rob – he would never let her down, of that she was sure.

Ava's two cups of tea had hit the spot by the time she followed Matt outside with the large wooden A-board. It had 'Dunne's' written across the top of it, in the classic typeface she had chosen five years ago and still loved as much today. The bottom half was blackboard, upon which Ava leant forward to write 'Peonies – 6 for £5', and beneath that 'Rosemary – £6' in her wide loopy font. After brushing the white chalk off her fingertips, she stood back to check her handwriting and then admired the pavement display.

'Looking lovely,' she told Matt, who was just tweaking some of the last bunches to make sure none were squashed too tightly together. Ava stooped and rubbed a stem of young, oily rosemary between her fingers. She held one hand to her nose and inhaled the fresh scent of clothes and roast dinners.

'As are you, Boss,' replied Matt, with a cheeky wink. He held the door open for her, and as it closed behind them both she turned the 'closed' shop sign over. As the beeps of the 9 o'clock news began on the radio, Ava rested one hand against the sign hanging on her glass door. *Open*. Smiling to herself, she headed back to her desk.

She hadn't even reached it before the bell on the door tinkled, announcing the first customer of the day. But it wasn't immediately clear who it was for they appeared to be entering backwards. It took a moment and a commanding 'EDMUND!' before Ava realised that it was a woman reversing a double buggy into the shop. Readying herself for the potential chaos, she brushed a stray hair away from her face. Matt immediately left the worktop of foliage he had been separating and went to help the customer. As she swung the buggy round, a ruddy-cheeked toddler leant out of his seat towards the brightly coloured strands hanging from reels of twine fixed to the wall. He was wearing a pair of bright blue trousers and a rugby shirt that would have fitted one of Ava's childhood teddies. His hair was soft, with a hint of a curl, and his dimpled cheeks and knuckles gave the impression that he was made entirely from uncooked pastry dough. His sister was asleep in the other seat, wearing a huge overcoat. Her legs, in a pair of bright pink tights with patent leather shoes on the end, were limp; her head was thrown back and she was drooling.

Their mother had the kind of haughty glamour only gained by living in the countryside in a house so big you don't always know who is in it. Almost impossibly thin for someone with such young children, she had long, dark, slightly wavy hair, falling around a face that was horsey and beautiful in equal measure. She too was wearing a rugby shirt, only hers was clearly a women's cut – deep pink, with a pale pink collar. On her feet were flat Converse All-Star Plimsolls, but even so she was as tall as Matt. Entranced by the twine, little Edmund clambered out of his seat and toddled off, causing the entire buggy to lurch forward. Dangling from the handles were an enormous Mulberry handbag and several carrier bags of groceries from the wildly over-priced delicatessen across the square, their weight clearly greater than that of the sleeping young-ster now jolted from her sleep. All three adults leapt to support the buggy as organic baby food and Dorset Knobs tumbled. The child woke with a start, looked around her and then settled back down again once the buggy was secured.

'Hiiiiii,' the woman said, lifting her chin. 'I need some flowers.' Ava wondered why else she might have come in, but smiled patiently. Meanwhile, Matt busied himself back at the worktop.

'Great,' said Ava, brushing her hands on her jeans in readiness. 'What are you after?'

'Dinner party, this weekend, but I'll need them delivered – there just isn't going to be time.'

'That's fine. We do local deliveries.'

The woman seemed neither surprised nor grateful, apparently used to living in a world where she knew she would get her own way, on account of knowing she could afford to.

'Super. Well, we need a couple of large arrangements for the table ...'

'The dinner table?'

'Yah. Like, centrepieces.'

From the corner of one eye Ava spotted the reels of twine spinning wildly as Edmund turned round and round, wrapping himself in coloured strands. She tried not to wince. What good would that do?

'Okay.'

'And then I want, like, something romantic. Something that looks as if, like …' the woman paused, a flash of uncertainty crossing her face for the first time.

'Yes?' Ava continued to concentrate on focusing on the customer, not her son.

'Well, something that will seem …' Gazing heavenwards, she held her hands out in front of her, thinking. It was impossible for Ava not to notice her stunning engagement ring. A huge diamond, surrounded entirely by several other tiny diamonds, it was breathtakingly beautiful. Ava imagined her husband choosing it for her. Someone, somewhere, adored this woman enough to pick out a fabulous piece like that for her. To him she was adorable, not formidable or brittle as she seemed today.

'What I'm after is something that will look as if my husband has bought it for me. Like I said, I need something romantic.'

Ava blinked, momentarily baffled by such a curious statement. Was the woman buying something that she wanted her guests to believe she had had bought for her? The way she was now avoiding her gaze suggested this was exactly what she was doing. For a second the awkwardness hung in the air between them. Then, just as suddenly, the tension left. Ava thought no more of it – if she were to spent her life trying to second-guess people's reasons for buying flowers, she would be quite mad by now.

'Edmund, do stop that!' the woman said with resignation, leaning to take her child's chubby hand. Squealing, he ran across the shop, where he hid behind Matt's legs. 'Darling, behave!'

After rummaging around in her handbag for a scrap of paper and a pen, the woman glanced up at Ava. Leaning on the back of an expensive-looking navy blue wallet, she wrote a name and number.

'Super. It's very charming in here so I'm sure you'll do something appropriate. Why don't you call the house later and talk to Mary about delivery and sorting out payment.' She half-handed, half-threw the piece of paper to Ava, while grabbing her son and attempting to strap him wriggling into his buggy seat.

'No problem,' said Ava. 'So, two dining table centre-pieces and something romantic, and I'll speak to – Mary, was it?'

'Yah, Mary.'

Once again the woman avoided eye contact and then, at twice the speed they had arrived, the family were gone.

As the door closed behind them, Matt looked up with a smile.

'Told you,' he said.

'Told me *what*?'

'Roses on a Monday – they never go anywhere happy.'

'Oh, you are *such* a cynic!'

But deep down Ava felt a prickle of uneasiness as she wondered what was going on in the woman's life. Seemingly she had it all, yet she was bristling with tension.

'Just you wait, we'll have a romantic in before long!' she added lightly, causing Matt to roll his eyes at her.

She walked over to the twine and started rolling.

As Ava returned to her heap of Monday morning paperwork, Matt put together some of the arrangements that they created for local businesses, occasionally stopping to take payment from some passing trade. Ava noticed that he was selecting some elegant lilies and arranging them with some of the greenery he had prepared earlier. It was for Ruston's then – the hairdresser on the corner of the high street. Ava was very fond of Sarah, the manageress there, and the two would sometimes go for a glass of wine after work to discuss business (and end up talking about anything but).

She still felt slightly unsettled by the brittle woman who had been in earlier. Though she had been treated far worse in the past, especially in London while working for Nigel, there was something about the pure invisibility that the woman had caused her to feel: she was so sure of her place in life, so glossy and confident. Ava imagined how sophisticated her dinner party that weekend would be, and imagined her husband thanking her for it afterwards, before they headed upstairs. Someone like Ava was of no interest at all to this woman – there was barely any respect there at all, and certainly no admiration.

Ava made a start on the invoicing, while making sure that her suppliers in Holland and London, as well as locally, were paid, and checking that she had invoiced her clients in the nearby hotels, restaurants and private homes. These were the jobs that brought her financial security, but it was the passing trade that interested her most. She enjoyed feeling like an agent for romance, helping men to make that special gesture, or creating bouquets to celebrate births and weddings. So often it was up to her to sprinkle the magic on a situation, or to encourage communication at moments of extreme emotion for those who otherwise said little of importance to each other. She pushed Matt's conviction that a percentage of her flowers were merely props for cheating hearts to the back of her mind. Yes, she was an agent for romance, not an aide to the unfaithful.

The filing complete, she shuffled through the junk mail that had gathered over the weekend. Pizza delivery, cheap cable TV deals and local taxi companies ... She shoved it all into the recycling bins beneath her feet, thinking of the weekend she had bought the bins with Rob, shortly before the shop opened. They had still been friends then, yet to turn their relationship into a romantic one. Not that they were a particularly romantic couple these days. After all, a courtship spent hunting for recycling bins would never lead to too many sparks flying. But Ava loved Rob – kind and consistent, he might be attractive in a catalogue kind of a way, but he was everything Mick hadn't been. She looked down at the recycling bins again and saw that in with the pizza leaflets was the flyer for the local arts centre. Sarah had mentioned it the last time they met – she was thinking of taking some classes.

'You all right down there?' asked Matt.

'Yeah, yeah,' she replied, absentmindedly. 'What time would you like to take lunch?'

'Ooh, I don't mind, whenever suits. Soon?'

'No problem, and while I remember – I don't have to get to the supermarket tonight as Rob's said he'll cook at mine, so I can lock up.'

'You're kidding? That would be great – I offered to give Amy another driving lesson tonight.'

Ava forced herself not to flinch at the mention of Matt's airily optimistic plans to teach his girlfriend to drive.

'Yeah, it's fine. Honestly.'

'Great stuff, we're both happy! Amy gets her lesson and you get a romantic dinner for two.'

Ava smiled at the memory of Rob promising to make her favourite pasta dish tonight. She had been very proud of the roast she put on yesterday, but hadn't expected him to make such a sweet gesture in return. Cooking wasn't a strong point for him, so she knew the offer was heartfelt and was secretly a little smug about it. Romance didn't have to be all champagne and roses. An image of herself pointing in a mirror and mouthing 'You've still got it, gal' floated through her mind. Obviously there was the mild anxiety about what he might do to her kitchen, left unattended, but she had chosen to overlook this and focus on the loveliness of a meal cooked for her.

'Look at you – all flushed with excitement!'

'Oh, behave,' she muttered, blushing at having been caught out in her daydream. 'Go for your lunch now, then, or I might change my mind about tonight.'

Within minutes of Matt heading out to get his sandwich there was a sudden lunchtime flurry: a cheerful woman of a certain age who spent ten minutes looking at each of the bunches of Dutch tulips to check she had chosen the best, a retired gentleman after a bay tree for his garden, an unnervingly over-familiar woman who seemed to relish telling Ava exactly how much she knew about each and every one of the bunches on offer, and a brisk, housewifely type who seemed furious that daffodils were no longer in season and out on the pavement for a pound a bunch. Ava did her best to keep everyone happy, while leaning back once or twice to take the odd phone call. Just as she said goodbye to the final customer, she heard the shop door go again. She turned around, mildly frustrated that a Monday lunchtime had turned so chaotic, and saw the back of a man's head already bent over the lowest row of flowers.

'Hi there, can I help?' *Fake it till you make it*, she told herself. *He'll be gone in a minute.*

'Yes, please – I'd like some roses, please. The most gorgeous you've got …'

Smiling, he turned to face her. His eyes naturally turned down on the outer corners, lending them an air of gentle sadness despite his broad smile. Dark brown, the irises melting into the pupils, they were hard to look away from. He was wearing a cornflower blue shirt – un-ironed, but expensive-looking – and navy blue trousers; he also had on a smart pair of brown brogues, well worn but good quality. Ava walked towards him, one hand held to her lips in thought. Once she was standing next to him she realised even over the scent of the flowers in the shop that he smelled of a combination of leather, expensive soap and perhaps a hint of vetiver. She took a deep breath.

'Well, we have some wonderful ones in today,' she began, pointing at the red roses Matt had been discussing earlier.

'No, red's a little ... Well, it's a little Argentine Tango for me.'

Ava blinked. She knew exactly what he meant. For an inexplicable reason she suddenly imagined herself, her fair hair mysteriously dark, tied back in an elaborate, glistening bun. She was wearing a dress the same deep red as the roses, split to the thigh. In between her rouged lips was one of the roses.

'What else do you have?' he asked, staring at her curiously.

'What else do I have?' Ava nodded seriously, playing for time. *Wake up, woman, you're serving a customer!* 'Well, we have all sorts.'

'What would you recommend?'

'*Me?* Well ...'

'Yes, you don't look like you really do tacky bouquets ...'

'Thank you.' Blushing. Again.

'So why don't you put together something you'd like to receive.'

'*Me?*'

'Well, I don't know what I'm doing and clearly you do, so why don't you choose something you think someone like you would love to receive.'

The thought of this man bringing her flowers made Ava bite her lip very hard.

'But it's my job – no one brings me flowers. Bit of a busman's holiday, I suppose.'

'Oh, come *on*! Surely someone presents you with a bouquet from time to time?'

'Not really.' She was blushing again, remembering the delicate and awkward conversation that she had once had with Rob, where he firmly explained that he could never buy her flowers as she would always know better than him what she liked – and get a better price. Suddenly being an agent for the romance of others seemed less enchanting.

'In that case I'm going to have to rely on your imagination.'

All Ava wanted was for her imagination to slow down a little ...

'Okay, what's your budget?'

'Ooh, £40?'

'I'd choose something less formal than roses – perhaps more rural, local flowers?'

'That sounds perfect.'

'Softer ...' Ava's eyes seemed to have locked with his again.

'Perfect.'

She smiled, then began making up the bouquet. The man stood against the wall opposite her and watched as she plucked a selection of gentle late-season tulips and sweet peas, some of the gorgeous cabbage roses that had arrived earlier in the day, then various foliage, and tied them together with plain, straw-coloured twine. Both were silent during this process, Ava doing her best to concentrate on her task, all the while conscious of his gaze on her hands and the back of her neck. He seemed comfortable in the quiet, unlike a lot of her customers who so often wanted to talk about the weather, the latest celebrity gossip or how business was going. When she was finished, Ava lifted up the bouquet to show him.

'It really is perfect. I can't thank you enough.'

'It was nothing – I'm so glad you like it.' She glanced at him again, then quickly dropped her gaze to the floor, suddenly shy. The man took two £20 notes from his wallet and passed them to her. She put them in the till before presenting him with the flowers.

'I do hope you receive the bouquet you deserve soon,' he told her.

'Honestly, I'm more of a chocolates girl,' she replied, suddenly tiring of his constant gaze on her, flustered by his assumptions about her life. 'I am surrounded by flowers all day.'

'It's not so much the flowers as the gesture, though, is it?'

He was at the door now and turned as he said this, before winking and heading outside.

Smug, thought Ava. She wondered what sort of man goes to buy romantic flowers and can't help but flirt with the florist? As for the assumptions he had made about her lack of romance ... Charmless. She reminded herself of her romantic Monday-night dinner as she swiped the trimmings from his flowers into the bin: *Flowers aren't the only way to express yourself.* As she slammed the bin lid shut, the image of herself dressed for the Argentine Tango once again flashed before her.

Chapter 2

Summer Strictly Feeling

On the dot of 5.30 Ava waved goodbye to a cheery Matt and indulged in some Olympic-level pottering once he'd gone. She gave the easy option – simply locking up thoroughly – a swerve, instead indulging in a little time in her shop. Polishing the brass handle and plaque on the door as if it was a fancy hotel, twisting the coloured twine neatly on its reels and all the while enjoying the silence of a closed Dunne's the Florist. She made sure all of the paperwork for the next day was in order, closed her laptop properly instead of just hitting 'sleep' and slamming the lid, then gave the mugs by the kettle a little tidy. Sure, a women's magazine would have advised heading home early for a luxuriant, candle-surrounded bath, but this level of A-grade faffing about relaxed Ava and she loved every minute of it. Once more she watered the cornflowers, the tall, lonely-looking bay trees and the herbs now inside on the shop floor. She picked up one of the rosemary plants and inhaled the refreshing scent again, before popping it in her canvas bag to take home. Yesterday's roast, cooked with rosemary from the same delivery, had been such a success that she decided to take another pot home and plant it. First, a nice terracotta pot on the windowsill to keep an eye on, and then in the garden in the spring, for future roasts. After a day filled with hassle and hustle, anything seemed possible in this stillness.

She felt a sudden surge of affection for Dunne's. It was her safe place, one created by her, *for* her. A place where she had made her dreams and those of others come true. The haughty woman from that morning seemed a distant memory, an irrelevance. Ava was happy to have left it to Matt to call her housekeeper, the elusive Mary, and she was right to do so for he had charmed her in no time at all and the order had been smoothly made. The majority of the red roses had been bought by an exhausted and exhilarated new father who turned up towards the end of the day, who clearly hadn't slept since Saturday night and was covered in a thin sheen of nervous sweat. He stared manically at Ava, while explaining in at least forty words per sentence more than he needed that he had driven in from the hospital on the recommendation of one of the nurses as his older brother once told him that garage or hospital flowers would be a mistake he'd come to regret for the rest of his life. Ava listened calmly, letting his manic stream of too much information wash over her while Matt smirked to himself in the background. Twenty long-stemmed deep red roses ... Exquisite, they had been the high point of her day apart from the doe-eyed flirt, whom she hurriedly pushed further to the back of her mind.

Before she put on her coat, Ava texted Rob to tell him that she was now on her way home and to ask if she could pick anything up *en route*. She knew he'd probably be back by now and would have let himself in. Maybe he'd even got to work on her meal. As partner in a small local web agency, his work was largely portable, which meant that he usually finished work very promptly. When she first met him she had recoiled at the mention of him working for a web agency, imagining soul-sapping London-based companies named 'Obtuse' or 'Slap Tha Truth'. But Rob's agency was considerably less cutting edge: named after himself and his business partner Laurence, it was simply Collins & Cook – creators of websites for local businesses, data companies and a couple of regional artists and authors. The whole thing sounded mind-numbingly dull to Ava, but as he had pointed out to her when they were still friends: 'It's how I make my money, not who I am.' To be fair, he had gone on to win her over in that first year of friendship with trips to the local playhouse, the cinema or museums. He liked to read, he enjoyed similar TV shows (within reason) and he was also enthusiastic about discussing all of this, as well as her growing business.

Rob's punctuality was a real bonus when it meant long romantic evenings in together while his portable, self-employed ways seemed a modern, cutting-edge way to live, but it was less enticing when he started tinkering around with his phone late at night, checking up on things in the second half of a film, suddenly jabbing at the touch screen in a frenzy. In fact, it pushed Ava to the very limits of her patience and reminded her of how glad she was to have a shop whose well-polished brass-plated door she could firmly shut at the end of the working day. She smiled to herself as she locked up, feeling a small, almost smug glow about heading home to such dependability and love, before crossing the market square towards her car.

Ava walked past the cinema, the butcher's and her favourite shoe shop, pausing to admire a pair of strappy sandals that she was hoping to find the excuse to buy some time soon. After crossing the cathedral square just as the bells were briefly pealing, she walked beside the river, whose banks were delicately lovely in the hazy evening light. She stopped to buy a bottle of crisp white wine at an off licence not far from the river, and as the shop owner handed it to her she could feel the condensation from the fridge chilling the paper he had wrapped it in. She pictured herself peeling off the paper, pouring two glasses and handing one to Rob at the hob. Maybe she could persuade him to give her one of his shoulder massages, too. She was almost hugging herself with contentment by the time she reached her car and began the ten-minute drive to her little house. The roads were clear and she was home in no time, pleased to see that the roses she had spent years encouraging around the front door were now as English and elegant as she had always hoped. Now the sun was dipping over the horizon and Ava could hear a cuckoo in the distance as she reached for her handbag and the wine from the passenger seat, then shut and locked the car door. She peered into the front window – her sitting room was neat, untouched since last night.

* * *

On turning her key in the front door Ava gave it a shove, but it was slow opening, edged on a heap of post beneath the letter box. For the second time that day she picked up an uninspiring clump of bills, direct mail and flyers. She dumped it on the hall table with the wine and started to take her coat off.

'Hellooo! I'm home!'

Silence. She paused. The house was clearly empty. After hanging her coat on one of the pegs above the table, she walked through the hallway to the kitchen at the back of the house. The evening light made the room look so pretty, but it was unavoidably empty. There was a used mug on the wooden surface next to the sink. It was the same one that Ava had left on Rob's bedside before heading to work that morning. Next to it was a half-full milk bottle, gently warming in the sun's rays. And in the sink itself was a used cereal bowl containing the dregs of some old, once-damp muesli, slowly cementing itself to the edges. Ava turned and went back to the hallway, where she placed a hand in her coat pocket to retrieve her mobile phone. She glanced at the screen: nothing. Following this, she placed it on the hall table next to the wine, which was now in a small puddle of condensation, its tissue paper sodden. She picked up the bottle and put it in the fridge. As she did so she heard the buzz of a text on her phone and went back to look at it.

'Sorry darling forgot I had squash with Laurence. Promise dinner tomorrow? At mine?'

Ava glared at the screen, as if she might develop special powers – the ability to rearrange the letters into something a little less rage inducing, perhaps. Stepping into the sitting room, she hurled the phone and then herself on to the soft leather sofa. She slumped, staring into space, with nowhere to vent her frustration. In seconds her evening had transformed from the kind of perfection that justified her every adult choice to an anxiety-inducing pity-party for one. How could he be so casual about it? Why had he only thought to tell her now? Surely they were already at the courts? So why hadn't he suggested coming over afterwards? Why did he care about none of this, and how was it that she suddenly felt so desperately flat?

She took her shoes off, rubbed her feet and then rubbed her shoulders. All alone, an evening in … Maybe she was the woman no one bought flowers for, after all.

The phone buzzed. Ava wriggled a hand back down behind the cushions and glanced at it again. An apology? Not a chance.

'Hey hey you. Can we talk later? Major dress stress coming up. Can. Not. Deal.'

Ava winced a second time. It was not Rob, but Lauren. Ugh, an enticing suggestion for what would inevitably be a half-hour conversation about wedding dresses! What a way to finish the day. More ambitious, tougher-skinned and more inclined to relish a confrontation than her sibling, Lauren often seemed to play the older sister role, despite being five years younger. Relishing every life stage, she sailed through them, competence oozing from every pore. Her career as a property finder for Wiltshire's finest appeared to go from strength to strength, she had a gorgeous and supportive fiancé in Rory and she was also a rigorous athlete, regularly competing in local and regional triathlons. Lauren seemed intimidated by nothing, prepared to take on anything and with the ability to create drama and excitement wherever and whenever she felt like it. Invigorating as she was infuriating, she had thrown herself into wedding plans with the enthusiasm of a woman accustomed to succeeding.

'Just got in. Give me 5 mins' typed Ava, keen to buy herself enough time to open that wine and pour herself a large glass. She'd need fortifying for this particular chat.

To be held at the same stately home in whose adjacent garden centre Ava had been employed when she first returned to Wiltshire, Lauren's wedding was to be one of Wiltshire's finest: a full country-house extravaganza, complete with the dress of her dreams. Only trouble was, Lauren's dream dress wasn't quite coming into line with her dreams. Where her pragmatism and straightforwardness usually served her well, it now meant she was struggling to explain her 'vision' to the dressmaker she had chosen. Tensions were rising. Somehow, Ava had found herself Designated Listener.

Shoulders slumped, she wandered into the kitchen barefoot, casting a dismissive glance at the cereal bowl in the sink on her way to the fridge. She swung open the door, looking for inspiration – or at least a snack. There was a lump of old Parmesan, nearly at the rind, some watery ham in its supermarket packet, the top now curling, and three eggs. *Omelette it is*, she thought to herself. In the shelf on the fridge door was half a lemon, turning green at the edges:

the remnant of a long-forgotten gin and tonic. Next to it was the wine, which Ava opened and tipped liberally into her glass, cherishing the glug that only comes from the first pour. She took a sip and returned to the sofa, where her phone was already ringing.

'Hi there!'

Momentarily confused, she paused. That wasn't Lauren's voice. She glanced at her phone to check: it was Mel.

'Oh hi there! Sorry about that – I thought you were Lauren for a minute. She was about to ring and now you've saved me. Anyway, boring! How are you?' Ava took another big sip, relaxing into the idea of a good gossip with an old friend.

'Marcie, NO! Sorry, Ave, just a minute ...' There was a pause. Mel was one of the legion of Ava's friends from college who was currently knee-deep in homework, scribbled-on walls and bruises from accidents sustained by slipping on Lego. She had two small children: two-year-old Marcie and six-year-old Jake. Ava waited, half-listening to Mel as she reprimanded her youngest, who was at the stage where experimenting with paint while wearing a highly flammable-looking pink princess dress were life's greatest joys. She was mindful never to judge Marcie, though. After all, she spent several hours a week daydreaming about the infinite romance of owning a proper ballroom dancing gown – one with a train, sparkling diamante straps and a skirt that swished with every movement. She realised she would much prefer to talk to Marcie about *her* dresses than to Lauren about hers.

'Sorry, honey, I'm back.' Ava's reverie ended. 'I was just calling for a catch up really, no big gossip. I know it's easier to email, but I fancied a chat. Jake's making a cake for the first time and I'm not allowed in the kitchen for another forty minutes, apparently.'

'Awwwww, sucks to be you!' teased Ava. 'But, um, is he by himself?'

'Ha, yeah! I've just left him to it – Rich is upstairs on the Xbox.'

Their relationship, based on ridiculous teasing, had remained largely unchanged since college, which was exactly how Ava liked it.

'Oh great, sounds wonderful – make sure he cleans up the knife drawer afterwards,' she replied.

'I've got Marcie on it now. For Mummy, it's Wine Time.'

'Tell me about it. What a day!'

Ava pictured Mel at home on her bright pink sofa. She knew she'd be wearing jeans, her Birkenstocks and a hoodie in an eye-wateringly bright colour, probably orange. Her dark hair, of which Ava had been so envious when they were flatmates in London, would be scraped back – the brief period of trying to blow dry it for work long over. Mel had always been scruffy in a sexy kind of way, so the mayhem of motherhood suited her. She was rarely any messier than before, but she was certainly not going to let impending middle age prevent her from dressing how she wanted. Nor was Ava, but whenever they spoke it crossed her mind that it was somehow more impressive that Mel was pulling off motherhood with such verve, especially as she still worked part time.

'You okay, hon?' began Mel.

'Yeah, fine really,' she muttered before beginning to explain Rob's last-minute change of plan, but she didn't get very far without almost being able to hear Mel's hackles rising all the way from London. She could sense her bristling at the mention of him failing to meet her exacting standards for what Ava's boyfriend should be.

'What a charming way to behave!' observed Mel, dryly.

'Yeah, it's not ideal. Fridge scraps for me tonight. You're the one with the kids, I'm the one with the lover, and yet you're at home with your feet up while I'm the one foraging for dinner. This is not what the lady mags tell me our roles are supposed to be.'

'This turn of events is far from usual for either of us, at least you can console yourself with that.'

Certainly it was rare for Mel to sound so relaxed at this time in the evening, but Ava realised with a shiver that this wasn't exactly the first time that Rob had flaked out on plans lately.

'Yes, I suppose so.' Ava bit her lip, thinking.

'It is, isn't it?' Mel pounced on that small pause.

'Yeah, yeah! Let's put it this way, it's certainly not something I'm used to or intend to put up with.'

'Good! Getting used to it would be the worst of all.'

As the words were still leaving Mel's mouth, Ava felt something unfurl within her: the realisation of her acceptance. She *was* getting used to this.

'Anyway, let's park Rob for a minute,' Mel continued. 'I've got a plan – and I want you to hear it.'

'Oooh, go on!'

'I'm going to apply for tickets to *Strictly Come Dancing* this year. We are going to do this ...'

'Oh wow, that's given me the Summer Strictly Feeling.'

'Eh?'

'Sorry – it was Lauren who coined that term, not you. You know what I mean, though – end of the summer, nights are drawing in, you're wondering if the diamante sandals you bought for summer are ever going to get used again this year, but secretly, deep inside, you're thirsting for Saturday nights curled up in front of the telly with a stew, instead of marinating chicken breasts in peri-peri sauce and chopping up endless feta for salads.'

'Oh I HEAR you! I am *dreading* the day I have to accept that the kids will be back playing inside all day instead of using the garden, but still ... winter jumpers, new long boots and *Strictly*?'

'*Exactly*! It's so bittersweet. On the one hand, dark evenings coming up; on the other, dark evenings of Salsa and Waltzes.'

'Oh goodness, you've got me all excited about it now. So – tickets?'

'YES! I want to do this. How come we never thought of this before?'

'You know how it is – new babies, new businesses, you leaving London and deserting me.'

'I suppose. What made you think of it?'

'Emma – she's started taking Salsa classes.'

Ava snorted with laughter. Emma was a particularly pushy mum who lived on Mel's street – albeit the 'smarter' side, as she was always quick to remind her. She had two children the same age as Jake and Marcie, and felt very strongly that Mel would be quite unable to cope without her peerless and never-ending stream of advice. It was always delivered in a stage whisper, with a dead-eyed smile, while Emma's children slept angelically in their expensive double buggy and Mel's threw their shoes – *and* socks – into the hedge. From breast feeding to violent video games and even as far as how to 'keep the spark alive' between herself and Rich, Emma's advice was a constant source of both fury and hilarity to Mel and Ava.

'Wow! Emma. At Salsa classes.'

'I *know*.'

'That I simply cannot imagine. Where is she doing it?'

'Same place as I do Pilates!'

'How do you know?'

'She took me aside to tell me in her special whisper – some things *never* change. I was in the supermarket car park, trying to get everything in the boot and she came over and announced it, as is her way.'

'Well I never!'

'I *know*, I thought I was about to be given a lecture on how spending too much time on Angry Birds gave Jake a 72% chance of being a crack addict by the age of 13, but no – she wanted to talk Salsa.'

'So what did she actually say?'

'She decided it was going to be a good way to keep fit during the winter, when the outdoor tennis courts are closed. Remember, she gets bored terribly easily because of her fierce intellect, so the gym – or running around after her children like a normal person – just isn't enough stimulation for her. She says the instructor is very respectful and he's called Damiano. And you know what?'

'*What*? She's run off with him?'

'*No*! It was the first time she has ever not bragged. She wasn't telling me in a "Now you must do this because, guess what, I've just raised the bar in the being-as-good-as-me stakes", she just seemed to be enthusing about it. I was braced for the "fierce intellect" nonsense, but this time she managed to keep it all in. She says she now has a different relationship with her body – she feels more free!'

'I don't know what to say. I want to take the mickey but it sounds kind of sweet.'

'Yes, it was. For the first time, she seemed … happy.'

'Wonders will never cease.'

'And that, my friend, is why we must make sure we sort ourselves out with tickets this year. I've got the link to the website, and I'm poised like a cat, ready to pounce into action to apply. My children will be playing with knives behind my back as I sit there clicking "refresh". Can't wait! Apparently they allocate for the whole series in one go and we just have to wait and see which show we get tickets for. *So* exciting!'

'That would be great. Not the knives bit, please – I love those kids. But imagine if we got them. I could get Matt to look after the shop for me and make a proper weekend of it – leave Rob to his squash games, and come and see you and the kids for a while.'

'I'd *love* that. It's been too long to be left with only Emma for company.'

'It would be wonderful, cheer me right up.'

Ava didn't realise what she was saying until she had said it. But suddenly, what had been unfurling in her was spreading its tentacles. Loneliness, unhappiness, or was it simply a case of the grass always being greener?

'Do you *really* need cheering up? I'm worried about you.'

'Oh, I'll be fine. I'm just, well … a little bit flat.'

'Because of Rob?'

'No. Well, *yes* – but not just Rob, just a creeping sense of …'

'MUUUUM!' Mel's son Jake was screaming from the kitchen, alarmingly loudly even via Ava's phone.

'Is everything okay?'

'Oh, God! I think Wine Time is already over … It's not fair to leave Rich to deal with this alone.'

Sounds from the kitchen were ominous. Was that a plate breaking?

'No problem, you get back to them.'

'But we'll pick this up in an hour or so when I've dealt with this lot.'

'Sure.' Ava tried to give an audible but reassuring shrug but it didn't work very well. 'You take care, and love to the lot of them.'

Ava pottered back to her kitchen with an empty glass, refilled it and then made what she could of the Parmesan, ham and eggs. She snipped a few needles from the rosemary plant she had left by the door, telling herself calmly that there was no need to let standards slip just because she was unexpectedly alone. After all, it wasn't as if she lived with Rob yet. That was a whole separate discussion.

She sprinkled the rosemary onto the omelette, gave it a final turn, put it on one of her favourite plates and then sat with it at her kitchen table, listening to next door's cat squawking at a blackbird. Soon she saw the bird flap up over the wall and fly away, clearly flustered. She remembered Mel's obsession with feeding the birds in their shared flat at college: she had spent hours staring out the window at birds on the adjacent garage roof pecking away at the stale bread and bird balls she had thrown there for them. It was possibly the most unglamorous and most endearing thing any of her college friends ever did. But the two were firm buddies long before the bird-obsession revealed itself. They met at swing classes in their first year and warily spent time together, each fearful the other was what they considered to be a 'part timer' where their love of dance was concerned. Back in the early nineties being a dance fan had seemed almost subversive and certainly not a regular hobby for 19-year-olds, so their commitment was unusual.

'Ava, as in Ava Gardner?' had been Mel's first words on being introduced to her.

'Yes,' she replied hesitantly. Usually people turned their noses up at such a deliberately retro name, or thought she was assuming a mannered alias.

'Wow! Named after *The Barefoot Contessa*. Impressive … I think my parents had been watching too many Melanie Martin dramas when I was born.'

And then the dancing began. Ever confident, Mel had paid Ava little attention for the next few weeks as she was furiously pursuing a boy whose name neither of them could remember any more. But after a few months of regular attendance at Swing Night and some pretty raucous parties, they formed a close friendship. By the end of the year they were flatmates. Despite the inherent skankiness of their student accommodation, dancing proved an irremovable streak of glamour and romance in an otherwise average student experience, and despite house moves, babies and their impending forties it remained the glue that bonded them. Mel's unstoppable pragmatism needed a friend with Ava's ability to let her imagination fly. And Ava's over-imaginative tendency for anxiety was grounded by the reassuring sense Mel was always able to provide.

The unfamiliar trill of the landline jump-started Ava from her memories.

'Hello?'

'Hi, how are *you*?'

Lauren's sugary, super-kind tone was the one used when she was keen to get the polite practicalities out of the way as quickly and emphatically as possible before launching into a chat that was to involve her getting her own way. It worked like a dream in the property-finding business when she was schmoozing with City players for whom she was commissioned to find idyllic boltholes in which to install their docile wives, movie location scouts who needed country homes that didn't require the guttering to be digitally removed, or privacy-conscious celebrities who wanted a driveway slightly longer than the longest of lenses. But it was too much of an old trick for Ava, who was able to read the signals loud and clear. In fairness, it wasn't always Lauren's tone – Ava did her fair share of whinging too, but tonight this was the last thing she felt like. She poured a further slug of wine into her glass.

'I'm fine, sweetie, just a bit down but it'll pass.'

'Oh, *right*.'

Ava noticed that Lauren didn't ask why she was feeling down – a classic move. 'Rob messed me around over dinner,' she continued, regardless.

'Were you supposed to go out?'

'No, but ...'

'Oh, *right*.'

Another slice of classic Lauren: in her opinion, if it wasn't a smart restaurant in Marlborough or a genteel gastropub with portraits of hunting dogs on the walls, it can't have been a big deal.

'You sound really disappointed, though.'

'I am. It's no big deal, though.' Her tone softened as Lauren showed genuine concern.

'But you're okay, you two?'

'Yeah, I think so.'

Now a pause when Ava would have liked Lauren to ask a little more.

'Great. So listen, about this dress ...'

And that was that.

'Yes?'

'There are big problems with organising this dress fitting. The woman is being totally unreasonable about timings and when I can actually get to see her. She doesn't seem to understand that I'm not at a desk all day like *normal* people.'

Ava wondered what was so bad about being at a desk all day, and if Lauren had ever noticed she wasn't either.

'She is saying she won't cut the fabric without my approval but the times she's giving me are really restrictive. I can't just drive all over Wiltshire on a whim because it suits *her* – I am the customer after all! Honestly, I knew I should have had it done in London, one of those lovely ateliers.'

'Why didn't you?'

'This *woman*,' Lauren seemed to spit the word, 'is some kind of well-kept secret. One of the guys working on *Bishopstone Park* told me about her – she had worked on the costumes and did the dress for Violet Bennett.'

Violet Bennett, breakout star of the country-house drama *Bishopstone Park*, had indeed worn a glorious dress for her well-documented wedding to the romantic hero of a gritty urban crime series. Elegant, befitting of a leading lady, but avoiding the trap of trying to look like a princess, it had been praised by the weekly magazines and the designer had been the subject of much debate but a name had never been released. Sadly, if the tabloids were to be believed, the marriage itself was not enjoying quite the same level of success as the gown.

'If she did that dress or any of the other dresses on the show maybe she *can* call the shots, Lauren. She's clearly a pro – she can probably pick and choose her clients.'

A moment's silence.

'Look, the long and the short of it is if we don't want the whole thing to turn into a total 'mare, I'm going to have to take a half day off work – rearranging a really important client meeting – and I'd like you to come with me.'

Ava, apparently, had no essential meetings with clients.

'Right, when is this?'

'Just under two weeks: Saturday, 3 September.'

'And you'd like me there?'

'Yes, of course – I think it would be less tense if you were there and we could discuss your bridesmaid's dress.'

Ava watched the blackbird circling the garden again, and prayed for a quick, sudden death. She swallowed another sip of wine. Being an adult bridesmaid had long been such a source of complete terror to Ava that she and Lauren had been joking about since long before she even met Rory. It was time to face the music.

'My *what* …?'

'My bridesmaid! Don't say it like that – it'll be fun. I'm not going to put you in a weird prom dress, you'll be in a Viv creation just like me and we can choose it together.'

'I'll put the 3rd in the diary, but I want you to know that I hate you.'

'I know you love me, sis. Honestly, if I'd known getting married was this much stress there's absolutely no way on earth that I would have decided to do it.'

'That couldn't be less true. It simply could *not* be less true! For that ring, sis, you would have agreed to do whatever Rory asked you to do.'

'Oh God, you're *so* right!'

'And you bloody love him ...'

'I do!' And she did. Rory was a godsend, to the point where Ava and her mum had started to refer to him as the 'Lauren Whisperer'. Indeed, the rest of the family was no longer able to imagine living without him. He was gentle and had eternal patience with Lauren's more diva-ish demands, but secretly Ava suspected her sister not only really loved him but still found him wildly sexy and would do more than she was ever going to let on to keep him happy. There was also the engagement ring, which had almost blinded Ava the first time she saw it. Rory, a man who spent all day working with his hands and had been too shy to speak to Lauren's family for the first six months they had been dating, had surpassed all expectation when he surprised Lauren with it. A woman who always maintained she would like a say in any jewellery bought for her discovered in an instant that sometimes not being in control could have its pleasures. And that instant was when she opened the small, dark green velvet box containing a 1920s Art Deco ring: an antique-cut solitaire surrounded by three baguette-cut diamonds on each side. It took her just under a second to say yes. She was as stunned with joy at being asked as she was by the heart-stopping fact that Rory had bought the piece at auction, paid for the history to be written up and presented an elegantly framed version of it to her. Lauren liked to pretend her car – a terrifyingly fast Audi TT – was her favourite possession but she wasn't fooling anyone.

After hanging up, Ava washed up the few things in the sink. Before doing so, she carefully removed the small diamond that Rob had bought her to celebrate the one-year anniversary of Dunne's. At the time it had seemed such a romantic gesture, so respectful of her work and her pride in the shop, but now it was hard not to see it as a friendship ring, a holding pattern to postpone any more serious discussion. Resentfully, she chipped away at the muesli around the edge of Rob's cereal bowl, wondering if they should have a relationship more like her sister and Rory. Trying to impose such a thing would never work, but still, it already seemed as if she and Rob had been married forever and now they might never make it down the aisle. *Was this the worst of both worlds*, she wondered while drying up her plate and replacing it in the cupboard.

Enough, this moping must stop, she then told herself. *A successful independent woman in a contented relationship should not be spending her evenings comparing diamond sizes with a sister she loves dearly. That way, madness lies.* She headed upstairs, had a quick shower and set up *Swing Time* on her laptop to watch in bed. After half an hour, the Fred and Ginger Waltzes and the heavenly frocks lulled her into a dreamy sense of calm. Just as she turned off and turned over, her phone buzzed.

'Sorry again about tonight. Hope you had a good evening. Will make it up to you tomorrow or, even better, Sunday, I promise. I won the squash!'

The thought was sweet, but Rob had clearly forgotten they were going to her parents for lunch on Sunday. As she turned over and curled up, she told herself firmly that it didn't matter, that the absence of kisses on his text wasn't a sign. She replayed the Waltzes in her head until sleep finally came.

Chapter 3

Welcome to Stability

'Sunday drivers!' spat Rob, slamming on the brakes of his somewhat battered Polo as an elderly couple in a dark green Rover pulled out in front of them with no warning. Ava winced, lurching forward and feeling the seatbelt cut into her chest across her necklace. Meanwhile, Wogan chatted chummily on the car stereo. Ava had barely slept, her nerves were jangling and there was a small well of nausea in the pit of her stomach. At this stage it could have been nerves, Rob's driving or that extra Scotch she had had before bed last night causing it. Either way, she just wanted to close her eyes and block everything out. Instead, she turned to Rob, whose face was now puce with rage. A tiny bead of sweat trickled down from his hairline to the front of his ear. His hair seemed thinner than she had realised before, volume masking the areas of scalp that were beginning to peek through.

'Easy!' she said, hands pressed onto the dashboard. She looked back at the elderly couple's heads bobbing away as they chatted to each other, oblivious to their part in the drama playing out behind them.

'We're running late. You know how your parents are about us being late. We can slow down if you like, and then we'll arrive with ten minutes of wise-ass comments about how we're never on time. *Your* choice!' muttered Rob, raising a sanctimonious eyebrow.

'I really do think they would prefer us late than dead …'

'Oh, so I'm trying to kill you now? *My* apologies! I thought I was doing my best to employ my driving skills to get you to your parents' in time. *My* mistake!'

'Come on, I know you're only doing your best. Relax!'

'It's hard to relax, knowing Lauren and Rory will have been sitting there for half an hour already when we arrive, late as usual, turning up like bad pennies.'

'No one minds. They'll be pleased to see us. Dad will make some stupid dig, and then we'll all forget about it. *Jeez*, why are you getting in such a state about it?'

'*You'll* all forget about it – *I* won't! And you *know* why I'm getting into a so-called "state" about it.'

'Don't try and pin this mood on me. That just isn't fair!'

'Well, there's a marked absence of anyone else to …'

'To *what*, to blame this on? Hmm … *I'll* tell you what, how about *you*? How about you take responsibility for this weird, petty fixation you have about my parents not liking you because it's all in your own head! It's simply something you invented and none of us know why.'

The track playing on the radio ended and Wogan piped up again, jolly as ever. His tone was so completely at odds with the mood in the car that Ava almost started to giggle in desperation. Instead she turned her head and gazed out

43

of the window at the fields now whizzing by. She was exhausted at having this fight with Rob again. A couple of years ago, not long after Rory really became one of the family, Rob had convinced himself that Ava's parents did not like him, that they somehow thought he wasn't good enough for their daughter. It was simply not true and based on nothing beyond what seemed like an elephantine chip growing on his shoulder. He had clearly cherished his role as 'the good boyfriend' prior to Rory's arrival more than any of them realised. Having known him for so long, Jackie and Andrew were thrilled when their daughter had 'finally' fallen for him. During those early years of Dunne's Ava felt as if she and Rob were some kind of dream couple – blessed to see the potential in each other. Now, five years on, the cracks in their relationship were deepening, but what really stuck in Ava's mind was that neither of her parents loved Rob any less than they ever had.

'You know, things have changed,' said Rob.

'Yes, I do. But what changed was *you*, not them. All they ever wanted was for me to be with someone who loves me, which you do, so that's fine.'

But this statement was met with further silence and no confirmation of the fact that he loved her. *Welcome to stability*, thought Ava; *it looks a lot like being taken for granted*. Meanwhile, Rob stared ahead, tensing his jaw. Ava watched the muscle on the side of his face flex and relax, and thought of the nights she had lain awake recently, hearing him grind his teeth. *What has happened to us, and how can we undo it?* A tractor turned out in front of them, followed by a small rush of cars coming down the lane from church. Ava saw Rob's hands grip the steering wheel even more tightly. Clenching and letting go … Clenching and letting go.

Of course the glass of Scotch she had had last night was nothing to do with why Ava felt so sick, and in her heart she knew it. She had tried to look forward to the weekend, surrounding herself in a cloud of positivity all week, but the nervous knots she could feel just tightened as doubt and anxiety unfurled themselves. She had tried to pretend to herself that she had had a stressful week at work, but she knew that wasn't true. Matt had worked so hard and with such a sunny attitude that she was actually thinking about giving him a bit of time off to enjoy the last of the summer on his surfboard. He was charming to the female customers and mates with the men who needed a hand in choosing flowers for their loved ones. In so doing he had definitely affected the shop's turnover and been a pleasure to work with.

Only a couple of days ago she had enjoyed a drink with Sarah from Ruston's the hairdresser and their fruitful exchange of local gossip had been as much fun as ever. Ava was sure that other shops and businesses did it too, but she and Sarah always laughed at the way the locals assumed they were all so anonymous – especially some of the fancier wives from the smart villages outside Salisbury. Little did they know their shopkeepers were taking an interest in their lives, noticing their children growing older, their hair getting longer (or greyer), their cars bigger. It was as if a whole local soap opera was running, kept alive by gossip between the shops around the market square, and Ava adored being a part of it. There had been great pleasure in the discovery that one of her clients was ordering flowers to be delivered to herself at work, even going so far as to pen romantic cards to make her colleagues jealous. That joy was even greater when Sarah revealed she had attended school with the same woman, who had a terrible reputation for stealing other people's boyfriends.

No, it hadn't been a bad week at work at all – it was life at home that was behind this sinking feeling. Rob had not taken well to being reminded about the long-planned Sunday lunch and had been making sly little comments about it since Tuesday. The resentments bubbled over this morning, leaving them silent in the car, all the while simmering and unable to find a way out.

It was not how Ava had ever imagined that Sunday mornings with her true love would be. During two long years after she had broken up with Mick – just as all of her closest friends were falling in love, getting engaged or married – she had fantasised about the Sunday mornings they were all having. She would wake with a start, wondering how to fill the next three or four hours until it was acceptable to call someone and not be interrupting anything, while her imagination cruelly filled in the time by picturing her friends in exaggerated romantic scenes. She never went quite so far as the cliché of the single long-stemmed red rose in a slim glass vase on a tray, but there had been bleak weekends when similar images presented themselves and taunted her. The Romantics – wildly in love, sharing the newspapers in bed, their side tables holding smug little cafetières of heavenly-smelling coffee and dainty fruit salads comprised of carefully sliced berries that they would feed to each other between kisses.

Whether or not these scenes had ever taken place was neither here nor there to Ava. Now she could grudgingly admit that when she first got together with Rob there had been very little of that, for he wasn't really one of life's natural relaxers. Enjoying a moment was 'wasting time' and holding hands in the street only meant 'shoving it in people's faces'. By the time they crossed the divide into romance, they had known each other for so long that those early Sunday mornings together had not proved as much of a discovery as they usually were with a new boyfriend. So little heat, so little intrigue. It wasn't that Ava hadn't loved him – in fact, she had been relieved when there turned out to be so little left to discover – thank goodness for none of the nasty surprises she had been dreading! But that stage seemed so far away, as if it had faded with time. If he was so reluctant to show her he loved her at all these days, what did that say?

It's just a phase, she had told herself that morning. *All relationships go through bad patches*. So for the first time in months Ava had gone against her natural instinct and actually tried to be proactive about things. Convinced a bit of a spice was what would rock the status quo, she decided to channel Lauren's effervescent confidence. Rob had been sitting up in bed reading the motoring section of the paper when she rolled over and kissed him, nuzzling right up against him, pushing her head through the crook of his arm. He had smiled, given a little sniff of a laugh and kissed her on the top of her head … then batted her away as if she were a naughty toddler. In that moment it was as if a piece of her had been rubbed away, as if there was slightly less of her.

'Oh, come on! What's motoring got that I haven't?'

'It doesn't want to talk to me about the future – and it doesn't have morning breath either,' he told her coldly.

Ava withdrew at once and perched on the edge of the bed, increasingly vulnerable in her pyjamas.

'I see,' she said quietly. 'Thanks for that.'

He had smirked and muttered that it wasn't personal.

What had been the loneliest time of the week when she was single turned out to be even lonelier now she was part of a couple. Shaking with despair, she pulled on a pair of tracksuit bottoms and an old T-shirt, then went for an hour-long run through the crisp country lanes. As she closed the front door behind her at midday, Rob was there, showered, hair combed, tidying up the kitchen. He smelled of soap and self-righteousness, and greeted her with a tight smile – a masterpiece in passive aggression.

'You know we need to leave in fifteen minutes if we're to have a hope of getting there for 1 p.m., don't you?'

'Yes, yes, I do! I'm just going to have a shower now,' she replied, flustered.

'Well, be quick – we wouldn't want to be late …' and when she headed up the stairs, 'Hope you've got all that pent-up energy out now.' As she turned into the bedroom, Ava could still hear Rob chuckling to himself.

The rest of the journey passed in silence but for the reassuring mutterings of Wogan, which Ava tried laughing at once or twice to make the point she was merely concentrating on the radio and not ignoring Rob. Finally they pulled into her parents' driveway, just ten minutes later than planned. As Rob's car crunched on the gravel, Andrew stepped out of the kitchen door to greet them. He was wearing a pair of slacks and a classic 'Dad' jumper. *There must be a thousand men like that up and down the country*, thought Ava, *and there isn't a golf course in England that won't have someone wearing that jumper somewhere on the premises.* She waved back at her father and wound down the window on her side.

'Hi, Dad!'

'Hello, darling,' he said, as he walked to her door and opened it for her. 'How *are* you? Business good?'

'Yes, thank you, and how are *you*?' She hugged him tightly as he helped her with her bag, then she reached into the back of the car to collect the pudding she had brought with her.

'Everything seems under control here – the courgettes are coming along well. Your mother is *thrilled*!'

He turned to Rob, who was pointing his keys at the car to set the alarm. 'Hello Rob, old chap. *Good* to see you – and on time for once!' At this, he let out a great belly laugh and Rob smiled the smile of a man heading into court.

'I'm fine, thank you, Andrew. And yes, we *are* on time – although if we'd driven at Ava's speed of choice I think we'd still be somewhere on the A303 right now!'

She shot him a glance. *Not right now. Please can we just get through lunch?* Rob avoided her gaze.

All three headed into the kitchen, with Andrew holding the door wide for Ava and Rob to make an entrance. Ava was holding a large pavlova overflowing with the last of the summer fruit. She had painstakingly assembled it the night before and was relieved to see it had somehow survived Rob's driving, safe in the special container her mother had given her for Christmas. Though sagging a little, possibly in sympathy with its creator, it was more than passable. Rob looked almost bride-like, carrying a huge bunch of perfect creamy white calla lilies. He strutted into the room and presented them to Jackie with a flourish as if he had taken the time to organise them himself; that Ava had gone out of her way to get in a few extra of her mother's favourite flowers on the Saturday order seemed of little consequence.

Jackie was standing at the hob, stirring the gravy. She was wearing a ridiculous saucy apron that Rory had given her that Christmas. Beneath the Venus de Milo emblazoned across her torso she had on a pair of black velvet trousers and a bright patterned knit. It was the sort of garment described as a 'crazy hotchpotch weekend sweater' in the catalogue – exactly the kind of thing that made Ava feel quite murderous, but Jackie considered it a 'hoot'. Her ash-blonde hair was perfectly blow-dried and she was wearing a chunky necklace of randomly sized glass beads twisted together. As ever, her lipstick was perfectly applied – she was, after all, a woman who had named her daughters after Hollywood goddesses.

'Jackie,' said Rob, kissing her lightly on the cheek. 'It's a *joy* to see you!'

Going with a charm offensive, thought Ava. *Sly move.*

'Rob, how *are* you?' Jackie's face broke into a crinkly-nosed smile as she stretched up to return his kiss. 'Have you had a dreadful drive?'

'Not at all,' he told her. 'It's been a glorious morning.'

He'd stolen the march on her, and Ava was seething.

'Sit down and let me get you a drink. Gin and tonic?'

Jackie waved to the large wooden kitchen table on the other side of the room, where Lauren and Rory were already sitting, surrounded by newspapers. Rory was clearly wearing cashmere and was working his way through the same motoring section that Rob had enjoyed earlier that morning. Lauren was reading the style pages, effortlessly glamorous in a floral dress that Ava remembered having seen in a boutique a couple of months ago. She hadn't even taken it off the rack as it had looked so odd on the hanger, but now it was perfectly obvious that this was a heavenly 1950s tea dress. Rory looked up and smiled as Lauren got up to greet them.

Ava gently placed the pavlova on the kitchen worktop and gave her mother a huge hug.

'Ava, darling,' said Jackie, holding her arms out to her. 'Words fail! You look *exhausted*. Have you been getting enough protein? You girls work all hours and I don't think you eat properly. Protein's what you need. I read about it online – Penny sent me a link on the Facebook.'

'I'm *fine*, thank you, Mum,' Ava told her firmly. 'And it's Facebook, not *the* Facebook.'

'Yeah, and when did *you* get a Facebook account, Mum?' asked Lauren over her shoulder as she hugged her sister. 'And what are you doing with it?'

'They started organising so many of my clubs via the Facebook, I was getting rather left out,' Jackie explained, while Andrew stood behind her at the kitchen worktop with two glasses full of ice, into which he was hurling large slugs of gin. 'And it turns out it's wonderful! I've joined a group for fans of *Bishopstone Park*, where we can chat about that scandalous gamekeeper business. There's a woman on there who claims to have seen the scripts in the back of a taxi and she says she know how it's all going to end. I can barely cope! You girls should get more involved. I've checked it out and there's all sorts of chit-chat about *Strictly* – different pages about the dancers and the kinds of dance – it would be heaven for you, *heaven*! And as if that's not enough, I've already seen photos of Penny's baby grand-daughter in Australia – she's just two days old!'

She was almost puce with excitement.

'That's wonderful ...'

'But seriously, Jackie, it's called Facebook, not *the* Facebook,' interrupted Rob.

'It doesn't matter, it's sweet,' said Ava, putting an arm around him, eager to keep the peace.

'It's interesting,' said Rory, who had now looked up from the motoring section. 'Because it really was called *the* Facebook to begin with – it only got changed later. So maybe Jackie's the most cutting-edge of us all.'

At this, Jackie shrieked with laughter and clapped her hands together.

'Cutting-edge? *Marvellous*!' laughed Andrew.

Clearly Rob didn't think this comment was at all marvellous, as Ava could tell when she felt him stiffen with indignation beneath her touch.

It didn't take long for the conversation to turn to local gossip. Ava and Lauren, who had grown up in the village, were always keen for an update: who was having a ridiculous argument with whom, how the local farmers had done with the year's crops and what the latest dramas from the village pub were. There was no shortage of news from Jackie, who had a heart of gold but the eyes of a hawk. No petty grudge went undocumented, no late-night shenanigans were unnoticed, and thanks to Dave, her favourite barman from the King's Arms, no drunken indiscretions went unmissed. As it turned out, one of the big local farmers had not only been cheating on his wife but he'd been doing it with the lithe daughter of one of his friends. Just 22, she was fresh out of university and still hanging around at home, with her floppy blonde hair and cardigan sleeves pulled down over her knuckles. Her parents seemed to have been hoping she would simply fall in love with a passing Wiltshire landowner and they might be able to have their house to themselves again. Apparently not!

'It's the oldest story of them all,' declared Jackie. 'Men are all the same – I don't know why anyone would get married.' She chuckled at her own wisdom, seemingly unaware of her audience.

'Erm, Mum,' said Ava. 'We are all still here, you know – your husband and your engaged daughter. *And* her fiancé.'

'Well, I didn't mean *us*,' said Jackie with an airy wave. 'I just meant, you know, generally.'

It was exactly this kind of theatrical generalisation that most irritated Rob. Ava watched his jaw clench and braced herself for his analysis later. Meanwhile, Lauren and Rory chuckled at Jackie's ludicrous statement and started teasing her about whether she thought they ought to be getting married.

'Ooh, that reminds me, Ava! I really want to talk to you about flowers before you go.'

'Oh girls, you must! Flowers are *so* important at weddings.'

'Thanks for that, Mum,' said Lauren, rolling her eyes at her sister. 'More much-needed advice for Ava, who as we all know really struggles with her floral know-how.'

'You lot are so mean. I just want to pass on the wisdom of my great age.'

'Yeah, you're ancient,' Lauren prodded her shoulder, 'practically a crone.'

While they were teasing each other, Ava was wondering exactly what it was Lauren wanted to say about the flowers for her wedding. Would it be advice on getting a good florist, or was she about to ask her to do them herself? Ava was slightly dreading being asked as she knew it would be a fresh new level of stress, but then she didn't want to be deemed not up to the job, or too 'difficult' either. She was about to ask, but the conversation had meanwhile galloped on to an analysis of how much better this summer's village fête had been organised. Unsurprisingly, Andrew had some quite firm ideas, while Jackie had the inside track on who had fallen out with whom by the end of the day.

The meal itself proved as delicious as the gossip. Lauren had brought homemade pâté, which she proudly served on Jackie's favourite Melba toasts before everyone tucked into an amazing piece of roast pork. The crackling was perfect, the gravy sublime and the roast potatoes crisp, comforting nuggets of heaven. Jackie beamed with pride to see them all enjoying it and seemed to puff up like a proud hen as she offered seconds around the table. Ava watched Rob load a second helping onto his plate. He took a mouthful, wiped a trickle of gravy from around his mouth, and then carried on chewing his meat, completely focused on his meal. She tried to imagine how he would look and behave once he was the same age as her dad, who was sitting there with his twinkly-eyed grin and booming laugh. Would she still know Rob when he was that age? Perhaps they'd be sitting like this with their own children one day? Was this where they were heading? It seemed impossible to imagine, but then Ava remembered those years when she had found it unfathomable that they would ever be boyfriend and girlfriend.

Halfway through the meal, relaxed and with the soothing food inside her, Ava felt overwhelmed by tiredness and decided to offer to drive home. She put a hand over her wine glass when Andrew offered her a second glass and whispered over to Rob, 'You go ahead. I don't mind driving back – I really don't fancy drinking.' At this, he eyed her with suspicion. Ava spotted this and felt as if someone had pinched her heart between finger and thumb. 'Honestly,' she told him, 'just enjoy yourself.' This wasn't met with a smile, however, just a shrug and then 'Fine.'

Ava got up to serve the pavlova. Everyone ooh-ed and ah-ed as she brought it to the table, and Jackie and Andrew seized the opportunity to give them all a rundown of how the various fruits in their little garden were coming along. The courgettes had been the stars of the season, the basil almost out of control during the heat of the summer, but the darling fig tree had let no one down either. Ava concentrated on dividing the meringue into equal portions, preventing the fruit from falling too far down the sides of each slice and letting the chatter wash over her. She was at the exact point where sad and relaxed meet, a resigned melancholy. It was as if the room were in soft focus as she passed a plate to each of them, sat back and enjoyed her pudding, half-listening to a conversation Jackie and Lauren were having about how to keep their jewellery clean. So intent were they on maintaining sparkle without causing damage, it was as if they were in some sort of Bling Club.

'That ammonia diamond cleaning stuff absolutely stinks, doesn't it?' said Lauren.

'Oh I know, it's ghastly! Sometimes I have to put my eternity ring in the shed if I'm cooking,' agreed Jackie. 'I just can't bear the smell of it in the house. But then one day I became incredibly nervous that a squirrel or a magpie or some other creature would find its way in there and either help itself to my diamonds or drink the stuff and die.'

'So what do you do now?'

'I make your father clean it when I'm at bridge.'

Andrew raised his eyes heavenwards and nodded.

'It's like a horrible window into my future,' said Rory, with the kind of childlike smile that made it perfectly obvious that he loved all conversations about his finest hour: the engagement ring. As the table chuckled collectively, Ava glanced idly at what she called her 'Dunne's ring', with its simple band and small stone. She felt her father's broad hand pat her leg beneath the table before he leant in and whispered in her ear, 'Your day will come, my darling. I have no doubt.' At this, she stared down at her plate, ashamed to be once again comparing herself to Lauren, for whom she was genuinely happy. She felt the tears well up and blinked fast to do her best to quell them: she didn't care about a wedding or even want a big ring, just a slice of the joy that Lauren and Rory seemed to share – the sense of being in the same boat together was what she envied, not the accompanying accessories.

As Ava looked up, she noticed Rob was staring at her curiously. For the first time all weekend she was completely unable to read what his face was saying. This in turn panicked her, not because she couldn't tell, but because once she found it so easy to do so. She smiled at him and he smiled back, but each looked as if they had just told the other bad news. Tiredness turned to sadness as she stirred milk into her coffee.

The drive home was even more silent than the one there. Rob reached for the radio controls as soon as the car was out of the driveway and they had stopped waving to Jackie and Andrew. Once he found a books show on Radio 4, they listened to it intently for the entire journey, occasionally commenting companionably. The programme provided a conversational buoy that they clung to gratefully. Anything rather than drown in the mire of the things they suddenly needed to talk about. There was none of the resentment of earlier in the day; it was almost as if their situation was something they shared. At last they had found common ground again. Maybe now they could turn a corner.

Ava pulled up outside the house and turned the engine off.

'Would you like me to come in?' asked Rob.

He always stayed over on a Sunday night. They might never have chosen 'their song', but there had never been any doubt that Sunday night was 'their night'. The fact that he even had to ask this question made feel Ava sad. Meanwhile, the sensation of cold, prickly anxiety running through her was increasing.

'Of course, it's Sunday.' She smiled up at him. 'I'm still really full, though. Not sure about cooking.'

'Okay, no problem.' He smiled back, politely.

Their new-found awkwardness continued as they reached the front door, each trying to hold it open for the other: the timidity of a first date, with none of the delicious tension. When they finally entered, both were tired and took their coats off with relief.

Ava went into the kitchen to put the container from the pavlova into the dishwasher and saw that it had not been emptied from last night's curry. She scanned the room; it quickly became obvious that the ostentatious tidying up that Rob had been doing when she had returned from her run had been somewhat superficial. As she noticed this, she heard the insistent mosquito buzz of racing cars in the living room. Clearly Rob had decided to pop his feet up and catch up on Formula 1. Ava took a deep breath. She didn't want to be that woman – the one who whinged on about the housework, only pausing to nag about commitment. That woman was everything she dreaded; becoming her was to be avoided at all costs.

She took a deep breath and went upstairs, where she lay down on the bed for a couple of hours, trying to read a book. It was soon replaced by the remainder of the morning's papers, which she flicked through looking for something to distract her. Eventually she gave up and had a bath. By the time she came back downstairs in her pyjamas and fluffy dressing gown they had been at opposite ends of her admittedly tiny house for almost three hours.

'I'm going to make an omelette,' she said, standing at the living-room door. 'Would you like one?'

Rob looked up, displaying all the signs of having forgotten that she was in the house at all.

'Ooh, yes please! And look – *Morgan & Hughes* is on.'

59

The regional detective show was one of Ava's favourites – second only to *Strictly* in the cosy autumn TV watching schedules. They had spent many happy evenings together, with trays of comforting wintery food on their laps, trying to work out who the unlikely murderer was. (It was always the most famous of the weekly guest stars!)

'But it's already begun.' She glanced at her watch. 'I've missed the set-up.'

'You'll catch up …' He patted the sofa next to him, as if she were a cat.

But you didn't call me, she wanted to say. *You used to call me!* She chose not to say anything – it seemed wiser at this point.

Fifteen minutes later she was snuggled next to Rob on the sofa, their omelettes eaten and an apple shared. They watched the programme in the same companionable silence as they had driven back from her parents', as if they were the best flatmates in the world. Later, Rob had a shower while Ava got into bed and returned to her book. He returned from the bathroom wearing pyjama bottoms and an old T-shirt, got into bed, kissed Ava on the forehead and rolled over before she had a chance to kiss him back.

'Good night,' she mouthed to herself as she leant over to turn off the bedside light. She lay in the dark, staring at the ceiling and listening to the rise and fall of Rob's breathing.

Just before she fell asleep she realised that Lauren had never explained what she wanted for her wedding flowers.

Chapter 4

Those Ballet Girls

Monday. A fresh new day, except it didn't really feel like it after a muggy, restless night's sleep. Ava struggled through the morning as if she were wading in treacle. All of the usual tasks seemed to take twice as long; part of the Dutch flower delivery was wrong when it arrived so they were swimming in an extraordinary amount of tulips. A small child, momentarily unwatched, had silently pulled the petals off several hydrangeas within the first hour of Dunne's being open. She felt stifled in her own shop, her safe place, of which she was usually so proud and felt so at home in. Today it felt too hot, too small for her – it was as if summer had suddenly decided to make its final effort.

By eleven o'clock Ava had dropped a tin pail filled with stale flowery water. She watched with resignation as it spilled out onto the shop floor and all over her feet. The plimsolls she had on seemed particularly inappropriate footwear as she felt the water seep in, knowing they would now stink for a day or two. She remembered standing in front of her wardrobe only a few hours earlier, too tired and defeated to wear anything more sophisticated than the jeans and stripy T-shirt she had opted for. *Why bother?* she remembered thinking. *No one will notice what you're wearing.* Now she regretted not putting on her patent leather ballet pumps.

With her soggy feet and her sour attitude, Ava was less than a ray of sunshine for the customers. She was usually cheered to see Mrs Lambert, an adorable old lady who lived alone in one of the town's smarter houses and often came by to cheer herself up with flowers. Though old enough that she walked with a stick and her voice had softened with age, she was always smartly dressed with her hair in neat curls and her jewellery on display. Unfailingly polite and always interested in Ava herself, she was one of her favourite customers. But today she dithered a little, apparently as tired as Ava was. She changed her mind once or twice about what she wanted in her bouquet and Ava would usually make suggestions and tell her what was fresh in, but today she was forced to bite her tongue to avoid snapping at the old lady and hurrying her along. Flustered by the change in tone, Mrs Lambert dropped her wallet on the shop floor and Ava realised with a jolt that her impatience was not unnoticed.

'Oh, let me get it, Mrs L ...' she bent down on the shop floor, her younger hands scooping up the coins from the slate tiles at twice the speed of Mrs Lambert's arthritic fingers.

'Thank you, dear,' she said quietly.

'I'm so sorry, here we go.' Ava put the coins into the wallet and handed it to Mrs Lambert. 'Don't worry about the rest. I feel I've been rude this morning and I'm so sorry – I barely slept in this heat and I can hardly think straight.' She waved her hand away as Mrs Lambert tried to pass her the few remaining pound coins.

'Really, dear, that's very kind but I'm perfectly happy to pay full price.'

'Of course, please accept my apologies.'

'I was wondering if you were feeling all right – you're usually such a happy soul.'

'One of those days, but I'm sorry you bore the brunt of it.'

'Don't you worry,' said Mrs Lambert, taking her flowers and standing as tall as she could. As Ava held the shop door open for her, she turned and looked at her. 'Just you remember your worth, dear. Don't go letting anyone take you for granted.'

Ava stood in the doorway, looking out across the square as Mrs Lambert walked away. How did she know to say that? Was she starting to look like a woman who was taken for granted, one of those who settled out of fear of being left alone? Despite the heat she shivered at the thought, then noticed Matt making his way back from the bank, having deposited some cheques.

'Hello you, all done!' he announced, as he headed into the shop with her. 'You feeling better?'

'Yes, thanks – Mrs Lambert's so sweet. She's so dignified, isn't she?'

'She's a class act, Boss, no mistake.'

'Isn't she just! I could do worse than end up like her.'

'I don't think you have to worry about that just yet, do you? Anyway, what about old Rob-o?'

'Hmm …' Ava stared into space and Matt quickly looked away.

'Listen, do you want to go early again if I take a bit of a longer lunch break?' she continued. She was suddenly keen to take a walk and clear her head, to be outside for a while and feel the breeze by the river.

'Sure thing! I'll give Amy a text now and see if she's up for another driving lesson.'

'Great! How's that going, by the way?'

'She'll get there.'

'I see – it's like that, is it?'

'Yeah, but you know, patience …' Truly, Matt seemed to have a boundless supply of it.

'She's a lucky girl. I hope she knows that.'

'Aw, she's a doll!'

Ava smiled and reached for the canvas bag under her desk. 'Right then, see you later.'

'Sure thing, Boss.'

Ava walked out into the market square and took a deep breath, determined to turn this suffocating day around. She crossed the square and headed to Marshall's, the deli. The husband-and-wife team who ran it were about her age, but had two small children, yet they still seemed to work all hours, run a great little business and be astonishingly chirpy to each and every one of their customers. She had a ruddy, rosy, classic English complexion and a sturdy, earthy kind of sexiness. He was of similarly generous proportions

– clearly they were a couple that enjoyed consuming their produce as much as selling it. Ava doubted she had ever seen either of them not smiling, and she had caught him pinching her bottom more than once. There was something of a modern-day Ma and Pa Larkin about them.

'Morning, Ava!' boomed Jeff Marshall as she entered the deli. 'Glorious day, gorgeous! How can we help?'

Ava selected some fresh pasta as a bit of a treat, knowing she wouldn't feel like proper cooking when she got home in this heat, and asked for a box of eggs from the Marshalls' hens, as well as a bunch of enormous-leaved basil.

'How's business then?' asked Sandy in her soft West Country burr, as she bustled up to the till with Ava's goodies all wrapped in neat paper packages.

'Not too bad. It's been a lovely summer. You?'

'Yeah, can't complain. And that sister of yours has her wedding coming up?'

'Not for a few months yet – it's exciting, though. We're off to meet the dressmaker in a few days.'

'Cutting it a bit fine, aren't you?' asked Sandy with a small frown.

Ava gave a small wince. 'Well, yes. But you know Lauren, nothing but the best for her. She has a fancy dressmaker doing her dress and mine – she works on telly stuff like *Bishopstone Park* and this is her last wedding dress slot of the year. We're very lucky, apparently."

'Goodness! And what about you? Been waiting a while!' Just as Sandy spoke, it seemed the rest of the lunchtime hubbub in the deli went quiet. For a moment even the air seemed a little more still. Why did people care so much? Just because Lauren was engaged, or did they think something was wrong with her because she'd been with Rob for five years without them so much as living together, let alone getting engaged? For a moment Ava longed for the anonymity of London. She blushed and ran a hand through her hair.

'Oh, you know. No rush!' Her voice, intended to be breezily casual, sounded shrill and insincere.

'Right you are, then.' Sandy seemed to realise that she had overstepped the mark and gave Ava a big wink as she handed over the goods.

Ava left the shop and headed for one of the benches on the riverbank, looking forward to sitting in the sun with her sandwich. So what was the Marshalls' secret? Why did they always seem so delighted by one another? Their youngest was easily four, which meant they must have been together for at least as long as Ava and Rob. The chances were they had been a couple for significantly longer, and yet they behaved like newlyweds. Had they ever collapsed into a rut, or did they genuinely find each other deliciously gorgeous every single day? Were their standards lower, were they more realistic, or did they simply manage to put on a better show in front of their customers?

These unanswerable questions swam around Ava's head as she sat by the river, sticking her feet out in the sun to dry off. What was making her feel so paralysed was the nothingness of the situation with Rob: he had committed no great crime, no unforgivable acts of cruelty, but neither had he done anything to convince her that theirs was a romance worth sticking with. Were they going anywhere, or were they simply, irrevocably, in the doldrums? *Time for action*, she told herself. *Something has to be done.* She took another bite of her sandwich and watched a family of ducks eating some bread crusts thrown by a passing toddler and her exasperated-looking mother. As she wondered what to do, Ava's phone buzzed in her handbag. She pulled it out and saw a text from Mel.

> Applied for Strictly tickets first thing – am beside myself with excitement. Cannot WAIT to hear! Am also convinced Emma is having an affair with Damiano, she's like a different woman. Polish your dance shoes, babe, we're heading to Strictly. I know it! xxx

Ava was thrilled when she saw the message. The idea of getting to see *Strictly* live seemed impossibly glamorous compared to her current humdrum daily routine. Seeing the dances up close, and as for the dresses … it was impossibly exciting! She was halfway through a reply when her phone rang – it was Lauren from her car, clearly bored.

'Hi, Sis!' Ava could hear the crackle of the in-car speaker system. Lauren had a habit of calling when journeys were longer than ten minutes, or if she found herself stuck in traffic. Ava found it endearing that it was conversation she turned to in those instances, not music.

'Hello, you.'

'I wanted to check that you were okay – you seemed a bit down yesterday. I couldn't tell if you were just tired or what and I know we talked about the wedding for ages so I thought I'd check in and find out about you.'

'Okay, I am a little down but nothing major. No specific thing has happened.'

'But what's up?'

Ava explained a little about Rob – the rut, the sense of nothingness. 'I suppose we need to decide to move in one direction or the other,' she concluded.

'Why are you so "we" about everything?' asked Lauren.

'Ha! Hark at the woman getting married in a few months!'

'It's not *that*. It's just … well, you don't do enough for you. Do you know why Rory tries so hard to please me? Because I please *me* the most.' Listening, Ava knew she was right. 'You need to do something for *yourself*, stop making your happiness dependent on Rob.'

'I know …' began Ava.

'I know you know! But sometimes you need someone to say it out loud. Don't forget you're a successful, creative, romantic woman. Rob's lucky to be with you and maybe he needs to remember that, too. Has he stopped making an effort with you? I'll kill him if he has!'

'I suppose he has a bit, but now I find myself wondering if I …'

'If you've stopped making the effort with you too? Stop making your life so much about *him* and pleasing *him*! Remember what you're proud of in your life.'

'Urgh, stop getting so motivational speaker on me! I just want my business to do well, to be kind to people, to get on with things without feeling as if I'm being a bit left behind by life – you know what I mean.'

'Your business does do well, but the worst thing you can do is to start moping around in that shop. Who wants to buy romantic gifts from someone who looks as if she has a heavy heart? No one. *No. One!* You know what? At this point I think the kindest thing you can do, for you and for Rob, is to be good to yourself. Take a little of the pressure off. Do something you like doing – he clearly does, what with his squash matches and Formula 1.'

'I suppose …'

'Yeah, yeah, and if you want to win points for still being a good person you can do something nice for him too. Cook him a bloody pie or something! Jeez – relax, Sis!'

Sometimes standing in the full force of Lauren's advice was a bit like standing under a power hose on a warm summer's day – refreshing and exhausting in equal measure.

'Okay, *okay*, you're right. Thanks, doll. Well, you'll be pleased to hear that Mel and I have applied for tickets to see *Strictly* live. Can you imagine, we might get tickets and go up to the studio – the works! Anyway, how are you? Aren't you supposed to be the stressed one?'

'I'm fine and I really must talk to you about the flowers for my wedding, but I'm sitting outside of a property now so I can't chat any longer. I do want to hear all about this *Strictly* business, though. It sounds amazing! Let's have coffee before we go to see the dressmaker, shall we?'

'Sounds great! We can hatch a plan for maximum efficiency.'

'Oh, *relax*! We'll just have coffee.'

'Okay, *okay*!'

She could hear Lauren laughing as she said goodbye and hung up. For every inch that was terrifying about her sister's personality, there were two of good-heartedness. Ava wriggled her toes, noticed her plimsolls seemed to have survived their dunking and headed back for the shop.

As soon as Ava was back behind her desk with a smile on her face, Matt popped out to get himself something to eat. Typically, the moment he left there was a sudden flurry of customers and then Ava had the shop to herself once more to do a little tidying up. She was standing inelegantly on a chair, trying to reach into one of the highest pails, when she heard the tinkle of the doorbell and looked down to find out who it was. The sun beaming through the shop front meant that she could only see a figure in silhouette, but she knew who it was in an instant. That curious combination of leather and vetiver drifted over the scent of the flowers again: it was the man from last week, the Argentine Tango man. As she stepped down from the chair, she brushed the hair from her face and for the second time that day wished that she had made more of an effort with her outfit. She swiftly dismissed that thought, however, remembering Lauren's wise words that she should do more for herself, not other people.

70

'Hello there,' she said with a smile, brisk and professional.

'Hi. Me again, I'm afraid.'

This time Ava noticed that he was not as young as she had thought him last time. He looked crisp and fresh, though, and carried himself with none of the defeated slouch that Rob had lately acquired, but he was unmistakably her age, or maybe even slightly older. This time he was carrying a classic Harris Tweed overnight bag. An umbrella was lying across the top of it, along the zip between the two soft leather handles.

'How can I help?'

'I'd like something gorgeous again.'

Ava blushed and quickly looked away.

Stop it, she told herself.

'Last time you did a perfect job.'

Why did everything he say sound so outrageous? She must stop thinking like this.

'Thank you,' she mumbled. 'You liked the cabbage roses, didn't you?'

'Yes, and those sweet peas are rather lovely too. Where are they from?'

'They're local, from a farm near Alvediston.' Ava was proud to have been asked – and also relieved that for once the sweet peas had actually arrived when she'd been told they would.

'It's wonderful down there – I love that valley.'

He had taken a bunch of sweet peas from the pail and was now holding them up to glance at them against the

71

light of the window. The petals looked translucent, almost glowing.

But Ava wasn't looking at them.

He probably had a little more girth than he should beneath that bright blue shirt, and in profile she could see that his dark, slightly curly hair was greying a little at the sides, just the beginnings of salt and pepper. His hair was perhaps an inch longer than someone her dad's age would have approved of and it certainly wasn't a cut that Rob would have deemed businesslike, yet he carried it off. His clothes, especially his brown leather shoes, were pretty smart and his bag was clearly expensive. He had a lovely nose, and as he turned back to her she could see how dark his eyes were, almost black.

'That's where I grew up,' said Ava – at exactly the same time as he asked, 'Could you do me something with these, then?'

There was a confusion of apologies and gesticulation while each did their best to let the other be heard.

'You ...'

'No, you ...'

'Go ahead ...' and eventually, 'So, you grew up there? Me too – well, Bower Chalke.'

'Really?'

Suddenly the shop felt extremely hot again. Why had she told him this? She took a fresh posy of sweet peas from the pail and started on the bouquet.

'Yes, I used to go to ping-pong club in your village hall.'

'So did I! Well, I did ballet – just after the ping-pongers.'

She looked away. *Stop telling him this stuff …*

'Oh, those ballet girls! The 12-year-old me used to dream of catching a glimpse of them on our way out of ping-pong. Wow, I was a real dork! I'm sorry, you don't need to know any of this.' He laughed sheepishly. Was he embarrassed too?

'It sounds like it!' Ava laughed. 'We ballet girls were not impressed by the ping-pong dorks! We thought we were the bee's knees. In fact, I'm pretty sure I thought I was Ola Jordan at the very least. By the way, we could see you looking in the window at the end of our lessons – none of you were very subtle.'

'Busted!' As if wounded, he put a hand to his chest. 'So cruel, the ballet girls! And it turns out even today they remain heartbreakers. That's my childhood you're trampling all over.'

Ava giggled again. For a moment she was unsure what the noise was before realising with sadness that she had become unaccustomed to the sound of her own happiness.

'Suck it up, Dork – the ballet girls rule!'

Her exuberance was bubbling over, she had to catch herself and remember he was there for flowers. Now she set about making the bouquet, carefully selecting the stems, greenery and twine. She put it together deliberately, concentrating on each movement, proud of her art. The man watched as she did so, silent as last time. There was no sulky tension here, though – he seemed perfectly comfortable without speaking, happy to watch her work without

73

needing to comment on it or to make polite chit-chat. It was a sort of collaborative concentration. Ava remembered the silences that she and Rob had shared over the weekend, how they seemed so leaden, as if their words had been locked in an airtight room. This silence was very different: the longer it lasted, the more nervous she became about saying the wrong thing. All weekend she had been afraid the wrong words would appear too heavy and crush the mood, now she was afraid words would be too ephemeral, too unknowable, fizzing with uncertain electricity.

Whatever else, she mustn't ask who the bouquet was for.

When he came to pay Ava, the man patted down his trousers and realised his wallet wasn't in one of his pockets before bending down to search for it in his overnight bag. Ava made a point of looking away, not wanting to see a flash of his boxer shorts, or an intimidating scrap of some other woman's silk négligé. Then she looked back immediately, eager to see exactly that. Her desire for clues as to who this mysterious – yet local – charmer was now consumed her. But she saw nothing, and he paid for the bouquet in cash. Denied a glimpse of either his name on a bank card or the contents of his bag, she was none the wiser. Should she ask?

She picked up the bouquet, ready to hand it to him and by now convinced there might be an actual crackle if they touched.

This is a man with an overnight bag, who regularly buys flowers for someone else. Don't ask, she told herself. *Just don't!*

'Thank you,' he said, with a gracious sincerity that unnerved her more than the lighthearted flirting ever had. He took the flowers but there was no crackle. 'They're beautiful,' he told her. He looked up, smiled at her and then left, quietly.

Ava watched him go, noticing how broad his shoulders were, really lovely and broad. Not in an ironic superhero way, just capable-looking.

She sat at her desk, staring ahead and strummed her fingers a couple of times. *Something good, for me*, she thought to herself. It had been so long since she had considered this that she really didn't know what she wanted. She glanced down at her nails, stared around the shop again, uncomfortable with this moment of deliberate self-examination, then looked for something else to do. Anything. She reached for the pile of junk mail that had been below the door when she had opened up and idly flicked through it. There was another flyer for the local arts centre. She plucked it from the pile and turned it over, knowing she had thrown away an identical one last week. They were advertising dance classes: one week Latin, another ballroom, twelve-week courses.

Uptight, judgemental Emma, who had made Mel's life such a misery at times, crossed her mind. She remembered Mel's exasperated reports after discussing *Strictly* with Emma at the school gates – always she had some arch comment about how she could do better than the celebrities, they just weren't training hard enough. 'Why can't she just enjoy it like the rest of us?' shrieked Mel one evening.

Always keen to impress some imagined external adjudicator, Emma had apparently bitten the bullet and was now by all accounts a model of relaxed womanly confidence, whether or not she was up to no good with her dance instructor! Ava remembered the fun she'd had with Mel over the years, so much of it on a dance floor. She thought of the times she had tried to dance with Rob at various weddings or Christmas dinners but he wasn't at all interested, thought it faintly ridiculous. Ava realised that for as long as she'd been with him she had barely danced. This was it, this was what had to change: her ladder out of the rut.

She glanced at the website address running across the top of the flyer, above an image of a tanned man swirling a blonde, smiling woman round on his waist. Eagerly leaning in towards the screen, she typed it into her laptop. The website was very bright. Couples dipped and twirled across the page, while boxes with times and prices opened and flashed. There was more information than it was possible to absorb, but she quickly realised that she would have to start as a beginner; the embarrassment of trying to keep up with lithe young dancers might be too much. Ava chewed her lip in a moment of hesitation – did she really want to do this? Of course she did! She imagined herself floating across the dance floor, supported on shoulders as wide and capable as those belong to the sweet pea man. Or dancing a Samba, out of her dreary jeans and T-shirt, wearing something short and bright, her skin glistening with tan and sweat, thighs like Beyoncé. She thought of the jaunty

Strictly theme tune and how it brought a smile to her face even when she was entirely alone in the house.

These images alone were enough to cheer her up. She brought up the music selection on her laptop and changed the track in the shop to a CD of something Brazilian sounding – as close to Samba music as her personal collection could provide. Then she whacked up the volume, grabbed her wallet from her bag and started to fill in the details for the course. Grinning and jiggling her legs in time to the music, she bent over her desk, tapping away at the laptop. The door to a world of possibilities had just been thrown open, it seemed. *I will force a large spoke of dance into my Wheel of Tedium*, she chuckled to herself. She flicked the music another notch louder, fingers almost tapping the keyboard in time to the beat now.

'We really must stop meeting like this ...'

The voice was next to her, just as the familiar scent of vetiver wafted towards her. She looked up. The music in the shop was comically loud now – no wonder she hadn't heard the bell above the door.

'Hello.' She leaned in towards her laptop, aware that the contents of her screen could be seen in profile, in all of its flashing glory, from where he was standing. Her pose was awkward – she was too far from where she was trying to lean, which made her look as if she was standing at a bar, drunk.

'Yes, we really must!' Her voice appeared as a whisper. *Why was he back? What could he possibly want?* Despite her faux-nonchalant pose, Ava felt as if a jolt of electricity was swimming through her. 'So, why are you here?'

'My umbrella – I think I left it in here.'

'Oh, I see.' Her voice would have been barely audible, even if it hadn't been for the pulsating music. 'Well then, I'm sure it's here.'

After adjusting the volume on the music, she slammed her laptop lid shut in as casual a manner as she could muster. She scanned the room and at once spotted the umbrella leaning against the wall between two pails of flowers, exactly where he had been standing earlier. Large orange Birds of Paradise flowers were slightly obscuring it, as if to provide a protective screen. She had always hated Strelitzia, with their garish colours and sinister lobster-claw shapes. They were just about acceptable in the hotel lobby of an exotic Caribbean hotel, but why UK customers would ever want to buy them was beyond her. She was always suspicious of anyone who requested them, but today she felt strangely fond of the flowers for hiding the umbrella and bringing him back.

'There you go.' She pointed at the umbrella, then reached over to get it for him. Turning it, she held it as if it were a knife and handed it to him, wooden handle first.

A pause. They were each holding the umbrella, him grasping it, leaving it parallel between them, while she held on for a moment more than necessary. She was convinced she felt a crackle this time.

'Thank you,' he said. 'I'm glad you've changed the music.'

Then he kissed her, just a brush on the cheek. And he was gone, leaving her to the Samba.

Chapter 5

Hollywood Goddesses

Ava was in the passenger seat again, watching the world go by. This time it was Lauren's Audi, being driven through the Wiltshire countryside to Cirencester. The car smelled clean, almost antiseptic – expensively valeted. It was the scent of an adult life successfully lived. Lauren herself smelled of fresh coffee and delicate perfume that had no doubt been bought for her by Rory. It was Saturday morning. Ava had left Matt in charge of the shop with his girlfriend Amy and was accompanying Lauren on a visit to Viv the dressmaker. Yes, the time for the wedding dress had arrived.

'She has told me three times now that she doesn't see people on weekends.'

'Lucky us,' ventured Ava.

'Except, she clearly does because she's seeing us.'

'How did you persuade her?'

'I don't know, really – I think I just kept asking …'

'Until you'd worn her down?'

'That might have been it!' Lauren grinned and looked over. Ava smiled back, an eyebrow raised. '*What*? If you don't ask, you just don't get!'

'But did you ask? Or did you ask and ask, and ask and ask?'

'What does it matter now? We're on our way, and you're with me so she'll think I'm nice!'

Ava smiled at the unexpected compliment. It felt like a light, carefree kind of day. She had had a great week at the shop; just knowing she'd booked for her dance course had cheered her up, and she'd had an unexpectedly lovely Friday evening at the cinema with Rob. The sun was at its most beautiful: the light crisp and clear as if summer was shedding its final rays before embracing the comforts of winter. This change in seasons was more beautiful to Ava than spring ever was.

Clearly a step ahead in her enthusiasm for autumn, Lauren was wearing a slim-fitting sweater-dress in charcoal grey with a chunky belt and long boots. Ava could tell she was too hot in it, though, as she kept fiddling with the car's air conditioning, running her hand through her hair and pulling the wool away from her chest in an attempt at ventilation. The dress was new and Ava wondered if it was being worn to impress the dressmaker. 'I am a stylish woman, do me proud' might have been her chosen look for today.

Ava herself wasn't experiencing quite such a style win, having considered it most sensible to wear loose-fitting clothes that she could remove easily for changing into things. She was comfortable but there was an undeniable pyjama-ness to her outfit. Her priority had not been to give the impression that she understood the finer points of pattern cutting, but to be able to change quickly and without drawing attention to herself. Now, a slightly more elegant option looked as if it might have been preferable.

'How are the plans going otherwise?' Ava knew this was a 'Day to Discuss the Wedding' and that veering from the script simply wouldn't do.

'Things are really shaping up now. Only four months to go! I can't believe how much there is to do, though. You just don't realise it until it's happening to you. And Rory is powerfully disinterested in it. Mum and Dad are being great, but Dad's a bit weird about Rory's parents chipping in.'

'That's a good thing, though. Isn't it?'

'Yeah, for me, but I think Dad feels a bit uncomfortable.'

'Suppose.'

'He's just traditional – he wants to be able to give us the moon on a stick.'

'It'll be an amazing day, I'm sure.'

'Oh yes, I know.' Apparently Lauren had never doubted this. 'I want it to be a wonderful day, but I also want there to be incredible photographs, for it to be memorable.'

'Of course it will be.'

'I know. But to make sure, I'm being quite specific about the look. Because it's winter, the classic English Country Wedding theme will look a bit different. The last thing I want is for people to think I'm just a Kate Moss and Lily Allen wannabe.'

'Who are these "people" that you're referring to? Surely you're only going to have people who love you there. We'll

81

all know you'd never be doing that, and whatever we thought it wouldn't affect our love for you both.'

'The guest list has grown a bit big now, though. I've a handful of work contacts coming, and then I invited a couple of clients – only the nice ones, but still. And I invited the Finches from The Grange.'

'How come?'

'Well, they put a lot of work into trying to persuade us to have the wedding there, and we're spending our wedding night there. And they're lovely.'

The Finches, the charming middle-aged couple who ran the area's smartest boutique hotel, were indeed a lovely pair but they were undeniably work contacts. Ava had had the contract to supply their flowers for a couple of years and Lauren often pointed people in their direction while they were house hunting. It seemed the wedding was not just intricately planned but a minor networking event as well. Ava adopted her best 'politician's face', her carefree mood of ten minutes ago starting to fade.

'Sure, they're lovely. But do you really want that kind of people at your wedding? People who didn't know you growing up, who won't get Dad's jokes and aren't invested in your relationship? Mrs F standing around in one of her powder blue or baby pink suits, casting a style eye on everything and thinking how they could have done it better?'

'For starters, even Rory didn't know me when I was growing up and he's going to be there, so that just isn't the criterion I'm applying to the guest list. And I don't care if they cast a style eye over things because I'll have made sure everything is perfect. You see?'

Lauren was smiling brightly. In another light it might have looked as if she was smiling manically, but Ava decided to go with brightly.

'Okay.' Ava felt the soft crunching of eggshells beneath her feet. 'That sounds ...'

'For example, I spent two hours online last night looking for the perfect ribbons to tie on the back of the chairs that the vegetarians will be sitting at, so that the staff don't even have to ask. It will be seamless.'

'Ooh, what are *we* eating? Something that will offend the veggies?'

'Dinner will be like a medieval feast – Hog Roast & Winter Vegetables. And instead of having a wedding cake, we're having a stack of wheels of cheese.'

'Wow, can't wait! And what are the veggies having?'

'I haven't got to that yet.'

'Right-o.'

'I will think of something, though and it won't involve filo pastry or feta cheese, I promise them that. I just want it to be a great day when people come together. An event, a celebration.' Lauren's shoulders suddenly slumped. 'It will be good, though – won't it? I so want it to be perfect.'

Truly, with all her heart, Ava believed her.

'Sis, it will be *incredible*.'

'Oh, and Mick's invited.'

Ava tried not to let her sister see her flinch. She knew that Lauren had stayed good friends with her ex-boyfriend

– after all, it was through his younger sister being her friend that they had met. But Lauren hadn't couched the news as delicately as she might.

'*What*?' It seems the flinch hadn't gone unnoticed.

'Nothing – I didn't say anything.'

'You didn't *have* to.'

'Lo, it's fine! I'll be with Rob – it was years and years ago. There's absolutely no problem.'

However much they wanted to pretend this was true, both girls knew seeing an ex at a wedding was never that simple. Even if the time for pain or guilt had passed, that uncomfortable competitive moment of 'who's happiest now?' never would.

'Good. I knew you'd be wonderful about it.'

Ava suspected this was not the only time she would be hearing those words.

'Now then, these flowers … So will you do them? You're clearly the best in the country, let alone the area. Anyone else would feel weird, and I know you'll be amazing. I'll pay you, of course.'

This at least was a conversation Ava had prepared herself for.

'Don't be silly! You absolutely don't have to pay me.'

'No, honestly, I will have to. It's going to be a lot of work. I want the church covered – a Winter Wonderland and a slight 1930s theme. I don't know what 1930s flowers are, but I want you to find them. The atmosphere is to be as if it's between the wars and we're all partying and celebrating as if we know that we might die by the end of the year.'

'Goodness, that's rather dramatic.'

'It's just something from my mood board.'

But Ava didn't know about the mood board – and part of her wished she still didn't.

'Lo, I'm not your hired hand. You don't have to pay me to do your flowers.'

'But if I'm not paying you then I won't be able to be as demanding as I might need to be.'

No one could deny Lauren was honest.

'So you're paying me so that you can be rude to me?'

'Demanding, professional ...' She smiled – the smile of an assassin.

'Let's just see how you behave in here first, shall we?'

Lauren had turned into Viv's street and they were looking closely at the numbers on the house doors. It was a quiet road, with houses that looked as if they might be deceptively large at the back. Lauren spotted the number and turned into the driveway.

'Yes, let's just see,' she replied with a wink.

A smiling woman in her late forties opened the front door and welcomed them in. The house looked extremely ordinary: large-ish, yes, but not glamorous. As they entered the hallway they could see through into a kitchen, which contained the evidence of a large family breakfast not long finished. Ava immediately stiffened, wondering if this set-up would be 'special' enough for Lauren. Where were the clear Perspex chairs, the reception piping non-specific atmospheric beat music, offers of champagne from obsequious staff? Those were the details that were fuel to Lauren's ambitions for style, yet here they were largely absent.

'Wonderful to meet you, ladies! Don't you look similar? And which of you is the bride?' Viv's hands were clasped in front of her and her smile was broad and open. Her blonde, slightly greying hair was tied back in a loose bun. She was wearing a symphony of oatmeal and biscuit colours, lots of layered jersey. Though she gave little of herself away, she seemed eager and confident about meeting them. Ava could immediately see the challenge that she might pose to Lauren's ego.

'I am,' said Lauren, stepping forward as if at school assembly.

'Wonderful.' Viv shook her hand warmly as if there had never been so much as a cross word between them. 'It's a pleasure to meet you, and congratulations. And you're the sister?'

'Yes,' said Ava, 'that's me.' She really did feel as if they were meeting a teacher.

'Could I get either of you a cup of tea, or coffee?'

'No, thank you, I'm fine,' replied Lauren, and Ava followed her lead.

'Splendid. That means we can head up. Follow me.'

Viv lead the way up a wide wooden staircase lined with family photographs. Ava was feeling a little uneasy about heading up to the family bedrooms, but as they turned to the first floor they realised the entire front of the house had been converted into a large, airy studio. Upstairs were the ominous thuds of teenage offspring, but this floor was a haven of calmness and designer chic. Viv opened a small fridge in the corner of the room and pulled out a couple of bottles of sparkling mineral water, which she set on a coffee table next to the padded bay window area where the sisters were sitting. The room was flooded with light from the window and across the facing wall stood several dressmakers' dummies in different styles of dress.

One side wall was entirely fitted with shelving units, filled with huge bolts of fabric and row upon row of rolls of trim, fluff, jewels, feathers and boxes of buttons, bobbins and reels of thread. Facing it was a huge worktop area, on which were two industrial sewing machines, which looked as if they could do serious damage in the wrong hands. The entire room was either white or cream, and every surface was spotless. Ava watched the tension drain from Lauren, whose confidence in her choice of dressmaker looked to be being restored by the second.

'So,' Viv unscrewed the lid from one of the bottles of water, poured it into a chilled glass and handed it to Lauren. 'Where shall we start? I'm not sure we were really communicating properly on email …'

Ava turned to Lauren, before babbling: 'No one comes across that well on email, do they? It's so great that we're all able to meet like this. Thank you for seeing us on a weekend. So, it's a winter wedding, obviously.'

Lauren shot her a look, clearly still in business mode, where she felt she operated best. Ava looked into the middle distance, hoping no one would notice she was there at all.

'Yes, but the church is heated and I'm not hoping for photographs out of doors, so it doesn't need to be an especially warm dress.'

'Do you have any idea of what kind of style you would like? A certain era or cut? A tail? Asymmetrical?' Viv stood up and pointed at some of the dressmaker's dummies. Ava began to understand how their misunderstandings had developed. Each was a woman clearly accustomed to being in charge of the situation, but this was Viv's world and she had obviously dealt with much bigger divas than Lauren.

'I can show you the presentation I have made, if that would be useful,' said Lauren.

Ava's eyes widened.

'That would be lovely. Please do.'

Viv smiled impassively as, from the bowels of her enormous Mulberry handbag, Lauren produced not a presentation, but a classic wedding scrapbook. This was no recently put together item, but contained years worth of work. Lauren laid it on the coffee table between them and opened it carefully. It was as if she had suddenly opened a window into her imagination: there were cuttings (including some of Lily Allen's and Kate Moss's recent weddings), swatches of fabric, quotes from novels, plus her own doodles. There were even shots of ball gowns from various classic movies and a couple of the more romantic *Strictly* dresses from years gone by, including one of Alesha doing her final Waltz with Matthew and one of Jill Halfpenny's wonderful performances. Smiling to herself, Ava remembered the Waltz that Flavia and Vincent did.

Lauren turned to the first page carefully. There was a large photo of her namesake, Ms Bacall. It was an early image and her strong bone structure and proud gaze were not dissimilar to Lauren's. Nor were her long legs.

'I love her hair here,' said Lauren, 'but I don't want to look quite as manly as this. I'm tall but I need a dress that will give me curves – I want some curves.'

Ava had been envious of Lauren's long legs for so long that it hadn't occurred to her that she might be anything other than thrilled by her swimmer's frame. As she looked up at Lauren's face, concentrating hard, she saw a flash of the little girl she had played with thirty years ago: earnest, eager to please, wanting to impress her older sister.

Enthralled, Ava leant in, having to hold herself back from leafing through the pages herself, examining every single image or list. She was so used to being seen as the flakey, imaginative sister, living in a dream world, that she had taken Lauren's ambitious, successful side for granted for too long. Here was evidence that this was not all there was to Lauren, after all – she had been keeping her imagination secret for longer than she deserved.

'So, perhaps something bias cut?' ventured Viv.

Lauren looked a little blank.

'Like this one?' Viv walked over to one of the mannequins. 'This is obviously just cut in calico to give you an example of the shape, but in different silks, with different embellishments and lace, it can be very dramatic.'

'It's very 1930s-looking, isn't it?'

'And then there are various lengths of train,' continued Viv as she spun a couple of the dummies around.

'What are the different fabrics that can be used?'

Viv reached for huge books filled with examples of the various fabrics and began holding them up against the light to demonstrate how they would hang in full length before holding them to Lauren's face to see how the various colours looked against her skin. Ava tried to stay involved, adding the odd 'yes, exactly' or 'oh, that's perfect!' but she was largely ignored as the two other women slowly worked their way through potential ideas.

Ava's gaze slowly wandered around the rest of the room – there were areas of shelving filled with what were clearly not wedding dress fabrics: bright greens and blues, flashes of huge strips of diamante trim and peachy colours that seemed as if they wouldn't exactly suit the kind of wedding that Viv designed for. They looked more as if they were for show-girls, dancing on a stage. Ava paused on a bolt of deep red fabric and she imagined a skirt slit to the thigh, an elegant, toned leg kicking up from it. Suddenly a Tango was being danced across the back of her mind, complete with velvety rose. She noticed some fluffy, feathery trim on the adjacent shelf and saw it floating from the back of a ball gown, like something Ginger Rogers or Grace Kelly might wear.

Ava lost herself in wondering what else Viv might design, the number of magical dresses she must have created for women who never usually got the chance to wear them, and whether she herself would ever enjoy a day in such a dress.

Viv reached up onto another of the bookselves and pulled down a square coffee-table hardback of Hollywood goddesses. She was ostensibly showing Lauren examples of late-1930s, early-1940s dresses, but they had also stopped to pause and consider the accessories and hair on various screen icons.

'Hey, Sis, look, here's Gardner!'

Lauren was beckoning her over to the book.

'Oh wow, she's *so* amazing!' Moments later Ava was on her knees at Lauren's feet and together they pored over the pages. As they sat there Ava felt as if they were little girls again, just sisters dreaming about dresses. How did real life get so exhausting between now and then?

'When we would look at books like this when we were little I used to think once you were married that was it, you never had to worry about anything again,' said Ava.

'Ha! How long did it take before you realised it wasn't true?' asked Lauren.

'I think it was around the time Mel had Jake. I had been so jealous of her for a year or two, and then I realised that she was really no more or less happy than she had ever been.'

'Marriage is more a statement of intent than a promise of eternal happiness, isn't it?' ventured Viv.

'Exactly,' agreed Lauren.

Ava wondered what exactly Rob intended – and when he might consider stating his intentions. Then she wondered why it was his decision, or at least why she was leaving it up to him.

'I also think it's wonderful to pause and celebrate things. It's so rare to get everyone together for a massive party, to have just one magical day,' Lauren added. 'The idea of being your ultimate "you" for a day is *so* enticing! It's easy to imagine the reason why so many movie stars and models end up so bonkers is because they think that looking devastatingly gorgeous is the norm, but for a normal person like us it's so delicious to look the absolute best that you ever could for a few hours.

'I still want to look like me, though. It's creepy when you don't recognise the bride underneath three inches of make-up.'

'That's why I'm so glad we have met,' said Viv. 'Your dress shouldn't just be a matter of getting your body shape right, or fitting in with a theme, but it should reflect your attitude, your personality, your relationship.'

'That's a lot to ask of a dress,' observed Ava to no one in particular. 'I wonder if I'll ever have one like that?'

'Of course you will, Sis! And now let's discuss what we're going to put you in.'

'Well, nothing bias cut for me, please – not with these hips!' Ava's voice was still tinkling with laughter when she realised that she had wandered from the script of the day. 'It's your day, though – I'll wear whatever you want.'

'I do want you to fit into the 1930s theme, I'm not going to lie; I don't want you to be uncomfortable but I don't want you to make me uncomfortable either! I know you have the kind of figure that does well with a bit of structure ...'

'Compliments all round, thank you.'

'Let's hear what you would both like and then we can try and reach a happy medium.' Even with this amount of adrenaline coursing through her body, Ava understood that Viv truly was a pro.

'Well, you know what kind of thing I'd like.' Lauren leaned back as she said this to see what Ava would say next. 'I don't want to look as if I'm in fancy dress, which doesn't mean that I'm unwilling to wear something that I wouldn't normally wear. Ideally, I would achieve a similar effect to some of those *Strictly* contestants. You know what I mean, when Patsy Kensit or Zoe Ball or Kara Tointon steps out onto the dance floor for a Waltz and all of a sudden you realise they can be something other than you had expected. You see them in a different light when you least expect it: confident, magical, princessy, but not in a creepy way.'

'Oh yes, I know just what you mean!' interrupted Ava. 'Like last year – that purple dress Kara wore for the Waltz. She appeared onstage and I immediately texted Mel. "Deep purple, for a Waltz?" But then when Artem lifted it, and it became part of the dance and the lines of the fabric echoed the lines they were making, it was magical. It was like the dress was actually helping with the dance, the grace. Oh, I *loved* it!'

Ava opened her eyes, and saw Lauren grinning at her. She had perhaps become lost in her *Strictly* daydream.

Viv smiled and raised an eyebrow. She opened her mouth to speak, but Lauren beat her to it, saying crisply, 'I'm sure we'll all do our best, honey. But let's not forget whose wedding this is. Or whose budget.'

Ava blushed, prickly with heat. She felt her ridiculous flappy clothes sticking to her in the warmth of the room and realised it was short sighted of her to come ready for trying on clothes when this was just a preliminary meeting. There wasn't so much as a scrap of fabric ready for her to try on yet. She looked into the middle distance again in the vague hope that the ground would simply swallow her up. Viv led Lauren over to a worktop, where they filled in an intricate form with initial details of what the dress should be. She gave Lauren a handful of swatches of fabric to think about and arranged a time for their second meeting. Ava sat in the window, gently sweating as the crimson slowly drained from her cheeks. Yet again, she felt as if life was just something she observed, rather than partook in.

Viv turned to her, after looking at her watch. 'I'm afraid we're running out of time now, but Ava, how about we email each other? Lauren, we will of course cc you into everything and make sure nothing gets underway without your approval. Yes?'

'Fine,' said Lauren absentmindedly. She was holding a swatch of lace up to the window.

'I could take some measurements now and then I'll have something to work from – okay?' Viv reached for her tape measure.

'What do we do if my measurements change, though?' Ava asked quietly.

'Why are they going to change?' asked Lauren. The face of her little sister was no longer that of a child planning an exciting party but one of a woman who was losing patience.

'You know, if I diet or something like that.'

'Don't worry, I can take it in later.' Viv was looping the tape measure around Ava's waist under her T-shirt. The tape felt cold against her flesh.

'Are you going to diet for my wedding?'

'Well, no – not in an "I'm going on a diet for your wedding" kind of way, but I need to get fit. I want to get fitter.' Ava didn't like the level of focus on her all of a sudden. Now Viv was holding the tape around her bust. 'So, Viv,' said Ava casually, keen to move the conversation along, 'do you have lots of other work on at the moment? Any other big weddings, lots of sisters?' Her voice trailed away.

'This is the last bridal gown I'll be working on for a while, actually. I work on other projects during the autumn.'

'What do you do then?' asked Lauren.

'It's funny, after what Ava said earlier. I do the costumes for *Strictly*, actually.'

'*Strictly Come Dancing*?'

'Yes.'

'The dresses?'

'Yes.'

'Oh my GOD!'

'Well ...'

'I can't believe it – I'm going to have an actual *Strictly* dress!'

'Well, it's not exactly going to be an actual …'

'Exactly, Ave! It's going to be a bridesmaid's dress.' Lauren was once again shooting her a look that suggested she would rather have been at this fitting with a lame dog.

'Yes, yes, I understand. But still … No, never mind – I won't ask you about it, I just *won't*.'

'You're right – you won't!' insisted Lauren.

'Honestly, you can ask all you want but there's very little I could tell you,' said Viv.

'But those dresses, they're magical!'

'Thank you. It's wonderful to hear such a vote of confidence in our work.'

'Did you do that Cha Cha Cha one last year? Was that *you*?' Ava couldn't help herself.

'The gold and green?'

'Yes!'

'Yes, that was me – well, me and my team.'

'It was devastating, simply stunning, honestly! Some Monday mornings I imagine I'm wearing it, just to get myself out of bed. Seriously. Obviously I have to imagine myself with the body to match, but just the idea that there's someone out there, making dresses like that – and someone wearing them! Well, it's enough to make a drizzly Monday seem bearable.'

Viv was chuckling.

'What a vote of confidence. Thank you *so* much!'

'Oh, I mean it. Mum and I spent half an hour talking about that icicles dress from three years ago. Was that you, too?'

96

Ava remembered a particularly romantic dress worn by one of the contestants for a Waltz. Almost translucent, it had glistened as if made of ice.

'Guilty as charged.'

'Amazing! I want to shake your hand. Stunning, they are just stunning – and always right for the contestant. You must be so proud.'

'Yes, I love doing it – it's a great show …' Lauren continued to look murderous and Ava realised she needed to check herself. 'But for as long as you're here with Lauren I'm always going to be more interested in you two and the wedding. I work with so many people at such emotional times – it's important to remember that I'm here to sort out the dresses, not get involved in the emotions.'

'Yes, of course, I understand. But please forgive me for being fantastically excited.'

Lauren's face suggested that she was doubtful of this. She shook hands with Viv and thanked her profusely for all of her hard work so far before the sisters headed out to the car.

'I'm so glad my choice of dressmaker impressed you,' said Lauren as she steered the car out of Viv's street and onto the main road.

'You know I would have supported you, whatever you'd chosen,' Ava replied. She hoped it wasn't too obvious that she was still mentally flicking through each of her favourite *Strictly* dresses and wondering which ones had been Viv's creations.

'I suppose so. It's good to see you so enthusiastic, even if it's about something that is nothing to do with the wedding.'

'I have to take my kicks where I can get them,' said Ava. Her voice sounded crisper than she had intended, but she was tired. Tired of being enthusiastic about someone else's good fortune, tired of being one of life's spectators, tired of waiting for a little excitement of her own.

'Oh, come on! It's not as if you're never going to have a magical day to yourself.'

Ava shrugged, causing nonchalance to emerge as petulance.

'Don't look like that! It needn't be a wedding day, you know.'

Slowly, Ava turned to Lauren, who in turn became hugely committed to staring directly ahead at the road.

'What exactly do you mean by that? Because it didn't sound like a vote of confidence in my relationship.'

Now it was Lauren's turn for a shrug. 'Anyway, I'm going to write you a document tonight about the flowers; that would be the best idea. Keep things written down to avoid misunderstandings ...' she continued to focus straight ahead '... and to keep the emotional stuff separate from the business side of things.'

'No problem. You let me know what sort of thing you want and I'll let you know what I can do. Some of it may depend on what the church permits.'

'And I'll pay you.'

'We can talk about that later ...' Ava saw an image of herself as a Victorian servant girl, curtseying to her mistresses. '... Ma'am.'

Lauren continued to stare ahead; a brisk, businesslike cheeriness had come over her. The decision had been made that they were not going to fall out.

'So, are you really going to lose weight for my wedding?'

'I hope so.'

'Why?'

'It's not about losing weight, it's about getting fit and doing something with my body. The only reason I mentioned it was because—'

Lauren's car speakerphone rang. She jabbed at the screen in its little holder.

'Darling!' Her voice was like honey. 'We've had such a wonderful time – it's all going to be heavenly.'

Ava watched the houses go by as she listened to her sister chatting, accepting that the day she communicated with Rob in this way might never happen.

Chapter 6

Salsa *sans homme*

As she turned off the main road, Ava was glad that she had not had the chance to tell Lauren about the dance class, having convinced herself now that it was the worst decision she had ever made. Where once she had had an imaginary landscape in which a liberated, confident her twirled around a sprung dance floor while spectators watched, enraptured, now she simply had a mental slideshow of all her worst adult education experiences.

The first was the time she decided to take an aromatherapy course, only to be told off for asking too many difficult questions by the frail-looking teacher who professed to hold such faith in dreamcatchers. For a woman so enamoured by the healing powers of bergamot essence, Mrs Roberts wasn't a great advertisement for her therapies, and Ava eventually quit the course after a startling glimpse of her gnarled toenails in sensible leather sandals during one class. The second was the cooking class in Marylebone. She had accompanied Mel when someone from her office pulled out, which had ended up with her setting a tea towel alight instead of her Crêpes Suzette. A bullish French chef had given them a good talking to about respect and the roomful of city types had looked on pityingly in between selecting £700 coffee makers from the shop above the school. The third was the wine-tasting course she had bought for Mick, which he had attended once before announcing he wasn't into that kind of 'bourgeois fantasy of sophistication', then spending a couple of hundred pounds on a bespoke suit that slightly undermined his point.

Last, and worst of all, had been the driving lessons. Jeffery, her 21-year-old driving instructor, had not been the ideal candidate to teach Ava to drive – given that she was 30 when she started taking lessons. He had turned up late, wanted to discuss computer games during lessons and poured scorn on her nervousness while otherwise showing very little interest in her. Ava would struggle to suppress the desire to gag whenever she got into his tiny driving school branded Nissan – partly because of the thin layer of scurf liberally sprinkled across the dashboard, but also the bizarre but consistent choice of R&B 'beatz' that Jeffery liked to accompany her lessons.

Had she not paid for the course in advance she would have tried to switch instructors, but he had given her a good deal and she badly needed to learn to drive once she moved back to Wiltshire. She had been stuck with him. He had created an almost unique knot of tension in her stomach, though, and despite eventually passing her test on the third attempt Ava had avoided all forms of adult education ever since. There was simply no need to spend hard-earned money on recreating school's very worst moments.

How had she forgotten this was how it always panned out? Dance classes had seemed such a good idea this time last week, but now it was perfectly clear that they would provide nothing more than an elaborate form of social torture. What was she thinking of? The skittish excitement she had felt for the last few days curdled into dread – not just of the classes, the learning experience or the teacher, but the other students. Who else would commit themselves to this kind of madness?

As Monday wore on these questions swirled at increasingly dizzying speeds, so that by the time the shop was closing Ava was exhausted by the sheer volume of adrenaline hurtling through her. She dashed home, cast her clothes on the bathroom floor in haste and leapt into the shower. After a moment's paralysis in her bedroom, standing dripping in a towel, she chose a pair of running leggings and a loose T-shirt. She had no dance shoes so she put on a pair of flat plimsolls and threw a denim jacket over the top before heading out to the car.

Ava sat in the stationary car and realised she looked a state. Fine for the gym, but this wasn't the gym. Anyway, it was supposed to be fun, to add a little joy to her life. No point in doing this if she wasn't going to put her heart and soul into it. She slammed a hand on the steering wheel, then went back into the house. Upstairs, she rifled through her wardrobe until she found the dress she had imagined herself wearing in class.

A knee-length floral tea dress in thin, shimmery fabric, it had been a party stalwart a few years ago. It fitted her perfectly around the bust and waist, had a pretty sash that tied in a neat bow at the back and a full skirt, which she had been known to twirl on summer lawns at parties when she had been at her happiest. Its pretty pink and white pattern complimented her blonde hair, making her feel her ultimate self. Once a favourite, saved for 'best', it was now something everyone she knew had seen her in. Facebook was covered in photos of her wearing the dress and the seams were now starting to show the strain of a good time being had at so many parties.

The minute she had booked the classes Ava had pictured herself spinning under a nameless, faceless dance partner's extended arm – her ultimate self once again. Even considering not wearing it was a ridiculous moment of panic. She put the dress on, smoothed her hands down the sides of her body and gave herself a twirl in the full-length mirror. Next she pulled on the pale dance tights she had ordered online and placed a pair of strappy mid-height heels next to her handbag to take down to the car once she'd been to the bathroom.

Of course, the one day she had actually allowed for heavy rush-hour traffic the roads were totally clear and she arrived fifteen minutes early at the venue. She wasn't sure what the protocol would be inside the building – what was the dance class equivalent of attendees of Yoga or Pilates sessions' habit of simply unfurling their rubber mats and lying flat on them, staring at the ceiling or perhaps engaging in a little ostentatious stretching? Would it be like the gym, where it was perfectly acceptable to sit and ignore everyone, hunched over your phone? Or would there be socialising, chatting and polite introductions?

The answers to these questions were immaterial to Ava, however, who opted for waiting in the car until the very last minute. She turned the radio down and studied the redbrick former Working Men's Club. For the last few years she had driven past it almost every day and had never really known what went on in there. Perhaps she might have imagined old men drinking ale and playing bingo, had she bothered to give it much thought, but it had certainly never occurred to her that this was south-west Wiltshire's home of dance. The building had the same slightly creepy authoritarian demeanour as a lot of municipal Victorian buildings, and above the door was a small grey slab of concrete with the date of its completion engraved in it. It looked as if it was draughty inside, and it would probably be freezing in winter – there was almost definitely a broken window round the back, where a pigeon would occasionally flap in and terrify her.

A second car pulled up in the car park and a couple got out. They were at least twenty years older than Ava, but both looked to be in very good nick. Lithe and healthy-looking, she was smiling serenely. Her very blonde – possibly grey coloured – hair was tied back in a neat, practical bun. She was wearing an outfit that Ava's mother would describe as 'snazzy' – footless tights, leg warmers and what appeared to be a grey marl off-the-shoulder sweatshirt with some kind of logo on it. Though extremely slim, she looked well maintained rather than frail. This was a woman who had aloe vera juice at breakfast, not coffee.

104

With her was a man who looked as if he might be more comfortable on a golf course. He was wearing slacks, pumps and a pastel sweatshirt, with a lightweight pale blue blouson jacket over the top. As he flicked his key fob at the Rover they had arrived in, he didn't look back, but was clearly satisfied by the weighty clunk of the car locking. He was closely shaven but had almost long white hair, rippling back in dramatic waves from his face. There was something of the Melvyn Bragg about his swagger. Ava struggled to imagine him dancing, sure that he would prefer to be at home with a gin and tonic and a Jeremy Clarkson book, but she immediately revised her opinion when she saw him open the door to the club with a flourish, holding his arm out for his partner, who smiled graciously and headed in.

'After you,' Ava saw him say to her. There was a third word but she couldn't make it out while only lip-reading through the glass of the car window.

A moment later two much younger girls walked up to the building. In their early twenties, each had unfeasibly long legs in thick opaque tights and eye-popping short skirts. Their hair was long and scruffy. The way that one of them was fiddling with it suggested this was deliberately dishevelled in a sort of faux rock-star look. In fact, in both cases it seemed their hair was held up in a loose beehive with half a can of dry shampoo. Both were wearing ballet flats and carrying heels. In their other hand each held a lit cigarette, which they paused to finish outside the building. Absorbed in their conversation, they didn't notice Ava in her car although as one of them turned to stub out her cigarette Ava recognised her as the receptionist from Ruston's. She cringed inside, knowing this meant Sarah would probably hear about her new hobby within twenty-four hours.

She looked down at the dashboard to avoid the girls' gaze before they went in. It was still five to, still worth waiting outside instead of heading in. She glanced at her fingernails and briefly examined the cuticles before she heard the confident gravel crunch of footsteps alongside her car. It was a man, another one whom Ava would have been less surprised to see on a golf course. He was wearing tight, almost feminine jeans, which made his middle-aged bottom look very flat. Above it was a capacious chestnut-coloured leather jacket. As he walked, the man shifted his collar forward and adjusted it. The West Country's very own Fonz! His hair had the strange russet hue of a man who might not particularly welcome greyness. He seemed a cross between a travelling car salesman and a 1960s rock star fallen on hard times.

Ava checked the clock again, her pulse rate rising at the thought of how she would blend in between this parade of oldies and teenagers. Three minutes to go. A third car pulled up and two couples around her age got out. She immediately recognised the couple who got out of the front and passenger seats, as she remembered the husband buying several bunches of flowers for his wife about a year ago after she had prematurely given birth to twins. As she turned, it became obvious that the wife now looked fabulous. About Ava's age, she exuded the kind of healthy glow that Ava was sure raising twins was supposed to repel. How did they look so fresh? Was she raised on organic butter and fresh berries? Ava watched them follow their friends into the hall. As they reached the top of the steps, the man patted his wife on the backside and looked down at her smiling face, winking. *Perfection*, thought Ava as a little piece of her melted.

One minute left. Ava took a deep breath and brushed her hair back from her face. Time to do this. *Fake it till you make it*, she told herself. *Pretend you have a long and successful history of attending classes that improve not just your outlook on life but your health and confidence too.* When she looked across at the passenger seat to pick up her shoes, she realised that they weren't there. She remembered grabbing her handbag as she left the room but not picking up the shoes. They were still on her bed at home. She refused to let it dampen her resolve – this was no time to lose her nerve. Instead she swung her legs out of the car, did her level best to ignore her plimsolled feet, stood up jauntily and headed towards the doors.

She pulled the heavy wooden doors back and walked into the building. Behind the vast main doors was an echoing entrance hall with a couple of trestle tables covered in leaflets for other classes and trips. There was no obvious indication of where toilets might be – only some double fire doors which looked as if they headed into the main hall. Ava swung them back, feeling like a cowboy pushing the saloon bar doors in an unknown town. She almost wished she had a pistol and holster on her waist instead of a handbag.

107

The hall was in shade and felt chilly compared to the sunny spot Ava had had in the car. She looked around the room. There were several more trestle tables at the edge of the room. At one end was a raised wooden stage, with five or six steps running up to it on each side. A sort of mezzanine level, looking down over the hall, was at the other end. The floor was a beautiful parquet and around the edges of the room were wooden planks to head height. It was a design classic, just like many village halls, working men's clubs and school halls up and down the country.

The eldest of the women was at the front of the room, a foot up on one of the tables in an elegant hamstring stretch. Ava hoped she wasn't going to be expected to start with anything similar. The woman's husband was chatting to the other golf man nearby, while the two girls were sitting cross-legged on the floor, giggling and playing with their hair. The foursome her age now entered in sportswear from the back of the hall, presumably where the changing rooms were located. Everyone looked up as a screech of brakes and the sound of gravel spraying came in through the tall windows.

'That'll be Patrice,' said the older woman with a smile. She lifted her foot down from the table and stepped towards Ava. 'Hello, I'm Jenny. Jenny Miller. I've been dancing for forty years, so feel free to ask me any questions.'

'Thank you,' replied Ava. Jenny held out a hand. She had long, elegant fingers and neat, glossy but not painted fingernails. It was cool but not limp when Ava shook it. 'I'm Ava, Ava Dunne. I've been dancing for no years at all.'

Jenny smiled as if she could tell.

'So, who is Patrice?'

'Our instructor, darling.'

The fire doors swung again and Patrice entered. Ava half expected a blast of carnival trumpets to announce his arrival. There in the doorway was a short, sinewy man with dark hair and a Latin complexion. He was wearing tight, dark trousers and a cotton T-shirt with a deep 'V'. Ava could see the uppermost curls of a hairy chest poking out as Patrice moved from his hips to the front of the room. The foursome had reached him now, but the girls were whispering hurriedly, trying to finish their anecdote. There seemed a significant chance that he was about to launch into a dramatic Tango, a romantic ballad or to introduce a star of stage and screen as his wife and dance partner. With his swarthy presence, he owned the room. Ava began mentally composing texts to Mel, describing him to her as best as she possibly could.

Feet spread out, Patrice stood in front of his students and paused for a second, his broad hands raised to clap. Immediately the girls stopped their whispering and stood up. Ava's eyes widened with excitement, her nails digging into the palms of her hands as she anticipated his Latin American accent. A single clap boomed out across the hall and he had the class's full attention.

'Good evening, ladies and gentlemen, and boom! Welcome to our first class of the term.' His voice was the exact opposite of what Ava had been expecting. It was deep, yes, but completely English and really rather posh. He sounded more like a city trader than a dance instructor. She felt wrong-footed before she had taken even a single step and unsure of what to expect next if things were veering from the path of the cliché.

'Welcome to another twelve weeks of classes! We will be tackling four dances, two Ballroom, two Latin, then those of you who wish to continue will be tackling a further two.

'Some of you know me from last term. My name is Patrice. If you're Scottish you may call me Patrick, but otherwise you'll have to respect the fact I had a French mother. I am your instructor. I'm here to help you enjoy dance, to let it flourish in your hearts – and bodies. I am not here to criticise or intimidate, so any instruction I give you during classes is exactly that – instruction, not criticism.

'If you have any further questions, you can come to me after class – I always stay behind for ten to fifteen minutes to deal with queries, or my email address is available, if you would like it.'

He gave a further booming clap, then walked over to a bag on one of the tables and whipped out a piece of paper and pen.

'Now then, I appreciate that some of you know each other already but I would like us to go around the room and say our hellos. We don't seem to be a full class, but we can't wait any further. Jenny, why don't you start?'

Jenny stepped forward and looked around the room. She lifted her elegant hands to touch her clavicle and smiled at the rest of the group.

110

'Good evening. My name is Jenny Miller. I live in Coombe Bissett and I have been dancing for forty years.'

She extended her hand to the man she had walked in with, who now stepped forward as she placed her other hand in the small of his back. He turned to her and mouthed something. Again, Ava wondered what it was that he was calling her. She could tell from his fleshy lips that it wasn't 'Jenny' – they were too pursed.

'And my name's Barry: Barry Miller, of course, proud husband of Jenny here. Yes, I'm definitely her husband rather than her being my wife – know your place and all that!' He chuckled to himself, apparently endlessly amused by a joke that was surely not on its first outing. 'As you might gather – some time in the next ten minutes or so! – I have not been dancing for quite so long as Jenny here. Oh no! I've only had time for it since retirement a few years ago. Telecommunications, nice line of work.'

Barry was now warming to his theme and happy to be on a topic that was safer ground for him.

'There's no business telecommunications system that I can't help you with. Even today I have kept my contacts in the industry, so I'm always happy to give you advice. But my office days are all over now and I'm a man of leisure, which means Jenny has finally got her way and she's determined to make a dancer of me. Anything for a quiet life, I say …'

'That's wonderful, Barry. Thank you very much,' Patrice interrupted. He was now nodding at the other gentleman of

Barry's age. Barry stepped back alongside Jenny, looking as if he would rather be power-hosing a car. The man next to him moved his feet forward barely a couple of inches and cleared his throat nervously.

'Rocky. Rockingham Palmer. Always loved the ballroom stuff. Not so sure about the Latin business, but my travels have led me to make certain exceptions. Pleasure to meet you all. Live up on the Close.'

He stepped back quickly. As the introductions seemed to be moving around the room now, the two girls stepped forward together, holding hands and looking at each other for reassurance. The slightly blonder of the two had clearly been elected to do the talking.

'We're, ah, Dobby and Minx ...'

'I'm Minx,' interrupted her friend.

'... and we are here because we hate Zumba.'

The words 'are' and 'here' both rhymed with the last syllable of Zumba, as did Minx's follow-up 'yah'.

'We rilly love dance but Zumba was, like, soo hectic and we just want to, like, have the proper skills. Plus, at Zumba the girls are rilly into themselves.'

Everyone smiled understandingly. Ava suspected few really understood what they'd been saying, herself included, but there was no time to dwell on this because Patrice was now nodding towards her. She hadn't prepared anything, so she stepped forward as apprehensively as if she had been on the edge of a cliff.

'Hello, everyone! I'm Ava – Ava Dunne. I own the florist's in town and I've been a fan of dancing for as long as I can remember but this is the first time I've had the guts to give it a go myself since I was at university, footloose and fancy free. So, forgive me if I'm holding the class back before too long.'

'Thank you, Ava,' said Patrice, giving her a small bow. 'And no one holds the class back. We'll all be learning together.'

'Your shop is beautiful,' whispered Jenny as Ava stepped back. 'Really special.'

'Thank you,' said Ava, her pulse rate slightly lowering now that the spotlight was off her.

The rest of the group introduced themselves, including the couple glowing with health (the Hanburys, Katie and Jim) and their somewhat doughier friends (the Foxes, Betty and Jack). Just as Ava had relaxed into the mood of the introductions, Patrice gave another of his booming claps and announced it was time to start dancing.

'Salsa – it's not as hard as it looks. And Ava, you need to bring some heels next time. You're going to need a bit of wiggle!'

Ava smiled and nodded limply, now so nervous she felt sure her T-shirt was betraying her hammering heart with its rise and fall. She looked down at her plimsolled feet and blushed. Meanwhile, the Hanburys were striding confidently across the room, holding each other's hands. Ava didn't believe for a minute that this was also their first dance class.

Patrice lined them all up into a grid formation and brought Jenny to the front of the class.

'If you would be so kind, Mrs Miller, we could give the team a quick demonstration.'

Jenny stepped forward with a quiet smile as Barry's eyes bulged. Patrice took her hands and demonstrated the basic Salsa steps to the class. It seemed very fast, as did his subsequent explanation.

'So it's just one two three step, five six seven ... one two three step, five six seven. You see, one, five! One, five!'

Ava's eyes were darting from his feet to Jenny's and then back up to Patrice's face to try and listen harder to the explanation. She realised that it was going to be hard work becoming the fantasy dancer that she had imagined herself to be. At the thought of even beginning the dance, she prickled with nerves and shuddered to think of the *Strictly* celebrities on their first week. Standing not just in front of their peers but a live audience – and all of those viewers at home, too. But Patrice's commanding voice snapped her from her panic and her eyes darted back down to his feet.

'One two three step, five six seven! Let's have a go, team – let's learn to Salsa!' Patrice's lithe body seemed utterly relaxed, it moved in ripples rather than steps, and despite the obvious age gap between him and Jenny they looked as if they were born to dance together. What seemed like an incredibly English elegance as Jenny stepped around the room now had fire and passion as she moved.

The Hanburys were facing each other, hands gripped. Dobby and Minx were face to face but not touching, their arms merely held out in a faux dance hold. At the side of the room Rocky was standing in a rigid pose, his arms up,

114

but without a partner. For the first time, Ava was glad that she had turned up alone – no one would have to witness her hapless first attempt and suffer toe-stubbed consequences.

'Forward with the left, back! To the neutral position! Back with the right, front! The Salsa basic step! Is everybody ready?'

Barry turned to Ava with a broad smile.

'May I have the pleasure?'

'Well, I …'

'If my beloved is to be stolen by Mr Patrice, the very least I can do is not let you dance alone.'

He turned to her with the confidence of a man with a tremendous sense of what was gentlemanly.

'We simply can't have you learning to Salsa *sans homme* …'

'Erm, thank you,' muttered Ava, but before she had a chance to say anything else Barry seized her hands and was looming over her. The room began to do the steps, rocking forwards, then backwards, forwards, then backwards …

'Yes, class, *yes*! You are doing the Salsa! One, five! One, five!'

After an initial moment of hesitation, the class was indeed completing the steps. Following hesitation and furrowed brows (on all but the glowing Hanburys), the class slowly raised their eyes up from their feet to look at each other. Barry's pillowy hand slowly released its tight grip on Ava's and he gave her a broad smile.

'Well, look at us!'

'Not so bad after all,' she conceded.

'This is good work, team,' announced Patrice. 'If you can just do this 20,000 times, you will all be perfect! But now, we need music.'

He let go of Jenny and headed back towards his bag, from which he whipped out a set of Bang & Olufsen speakers and his iPod. After fiddling with the screen, he walked back to the head of the room.

'Remember – watch out for the hard beat! One two three step, five six seven.'

And with that the music started, the jangle of horns and thunder of drums. Suddenly the room seemed sunnier and Ava imagined herself fresh from the sea, her hair crispy with salt and the sun prickling her forearms. Barry seemed similarly invigorated and swung back towards her.

'One! Five! One! Five!' Patrice kept count as he seamlessly shimmied with Jenny, 'and the hard beat, and the hard beat!' He carried on shouting directions at the class as he and Jenny stepped towards Ava and Barry. Patrice gave a small nod towards Barry before letting go of one of Jenny's hands, all the while keeping up the steps. Jenny's free hand now took one of Barry's and then the other. Now the two of them started to move together, Barry's jowly face wobbling in delight at being presented with the top of the class. He gave Ava a quick wink over Jenny's shoulder and the two of them stepped away. Meanwhile, Patrice had stepped in to Ava and taken her hands. All of a sudden, she realised what it felt like to be dancing properly.

Safe in Patrice's broad, compact arms, his hot, dry hands holding hers firmly, keeping her hands raised in a perfect position, Ava felt the beat pushing her forward and back. The steps became automatic, instant, no longer a thought process but an instinct. Music flooded the room and she felt her skirt brush against her legs, then lift as air caught it. A broad grin swept across her face and Patrice smiled back, all the while repeating the steps so the class never lost their rhythm.

The music seemed to be getting louder and Ava could feel the blood flowing properly through her body for the first time since her angry run. Yes, she had found an extra surge of life, something far greater than mere survival!

As the track reached its crescendo, Patrice extended his arm and flipped Ava underneath it, leaving the dance to end on a spin. And that's when she saw him. The music must have hidden the noise of the wooden doors because as Ava snapped her head up with a flourish, giggling, she was almost face to face with him. One hand was running through his hair, his head dipped, his big brown eyes looked up. The man from the shop, who made her think of the Tango. Him …

Chapter 7

Friend Request

The rest of the class clapped and laughed, celebrating their first Salsa. Ava, meanwhile, was silent, bar the rise and fall of her breath. For a second or two she looked at him, and he at her. It was one of those moments where background noise seems terribly, terribly far away. And yet her breath seemed louder. Ava narrowed her eyes, gazing directly into his to see if there was a glimmer of recognition. He held her gaze for longer than a moment, then looked away. Nothing.

He ruffled his dark wavy hair awkwardly, apparently unaware the curls were springing back into place the minute his fingers passed them.

'Hi, I'm, erm, sorry I'm so late. I had – er, stuff – that, well, I couldn't make it any sooner. I got here as fast as I could.'

He looked directly at Patrice and the two men summed each other up.

'Really, it couldn't be avoided.'

It was all a bit too cool for school, not turning up on time for dance class and not even bothering to give an excuse for it. Patrice stepped away from Ava and towards the table with his bag and notes. Now it was just Ava and the man standing at the top of the hall in front of the others, who had now largely fallen silent.

'And your name is?' Patrice was holding the printed-out sheet of paper with details of the attendees on it.

'Monroe. Gabe, Gabriel. Whatever, I can't remember what I put on the form.'

Patrice didn't look up. He made a swift mark on the sheet of paper. Was that one eyebrow slightly raised?

'Gabe Monroe it is. Well, Mr Monroe ...'

'Gabe, honestly ...'

'I'm afraid those of us who turned up on time have been practising for a while now, and are already familiar with the basic steps.'

Patrice was unable to hide his irritation at being interrupted, though Ava suspected he might have been more forgiving had another nubile dance nymph turned up, whereas the arrival of a single man Gabe's age was going down like a Tango at a wake. He was now standing awkwardly, his weight on one leg like a recalcitrant schoolboy.

'Dobby, Minx, you seem to have picked things up rather well. Would one of you be so kind as to partner Gabe?'

Dobby stepped towards Gabe without hesitation, her head tilted coquettishly and an arm extended like a seventeenth-century courtesan. Minx bit her lip with excitement and grinned impishly.

'... and Rockingham, would you like to make sure Minx here is not dancing alone? Wonderful, thank you.'

119

Minx's face fell as Rockingham stepped towards her. Rocky stood there stiffly, his hands clasped in front of him as if listening to the vicar's wife hold forth at a village fête. Minx stretched to look over his shoulder, scowling enviously at Dobby, who was introducing herself to Gabe. The class regrouped, the practice continued.

But for the rest of the lesson things felt a little blurry for Ava. Patrice introduced them to a few more steps and some basic turns before they put them all together for the final fifteen minutes of the two hours. Jenny gracefully led her husband around the floor as he blustered and giggled, the girls made a good job of keeping their new partners going, while the couples at the back flitted between gossipy inattention and whoops and cheers when they completed a section without mistakes.

Ava concentrated on her steps and felt her body respond to the music, the beat and the effort blocking out those niggles and anxieties that she felt she had been carrying around for so long. She caught the odd glimpse of Gabe over her shoulder, but was never able to catch his eye again. Nevertheless she was aware of his position in the room the entire time, some internal tracking device unable to quite let go. Eventually she told herself she was silly ever to have assumed a man as flirtatious as him would remember a woman like her, now that he had the nubile Dobby to distract him. She focused on Patrice, whose attention was more than welcome and had the added bonus of helping her to pick up the steps all the faster.

As the class ended Ava was fizzing with energy – the adrenaline, the sheer physical exertion, plus the relief at having survived. She had achieved something, learned something new, and managed to do it without somehow embarrassing herself! Whatever happened now, she had forced a massive spoke into the ever-turning wheel of boredom and resignation in which she had been trapped. As she drove home along the country lanes she wound down the window of her car, felt the last of the late summer sun dappling on her forearms and sang along at the top of her lungs to the ridiculous random pop song that came on air. She wasn't singing to anyone in particular, yet she hoped someone would hear and absorb a little of her joy, even if it were the passing fields, slowly turning yellow ready for harvest.

She was still humming away when she turned her key in the door, slung her bag onto the chair in the hallway and headed for the kitchen. Opening the fridge door wide, she plucked at random ingredients. She was going to sling a salad together. Yes, she would be that person tonight – the kind of high-spirited woman who came home from an evening's dancing with attractive men to simply 'throw some ingredients together'.

'It's all I need – I feel so nourished after Salsa,' she imagined herself explaining to an inquisitive fictional interviewer.

This would be the year when autumn wouldn't slur into a mushy rush for Christmas, she decided as she bit into a forkful of leaves. The lamb's lettuce was slightly slimy; it might have been fresher, but Ava persevered. This would be the season of mists and mellow fruitfulness and all of the russet loveliness Lauren adored so much. Nothing would stop that now.

To Ava's great surprise, the rest of the week swam blissfully by. The shop had a steady stream of charming customers, almost all of them keen to enjoy the last of the summer's local blooms. Matt was as much of a darling as ever and Ava had a dreamy buzz as pleasant as the dull weight she had been carrying around for weeks before. As she felt lighter, her behaviour followed suit. Meanwhile the listings magazines and trailers for *Strictly* began popping up all over magazine stands and during programme breaks. She heard people chatting about it in the supermarket queue and found herself wondering again and again who the celebrities that year would be. A sense of momentum and anticipation was building: the evenings might be drawing in, but soon the darkness would be illuminated by a little *Strictly* sparkle. It provided a joyful distraction, as well as a jaunty little reminder of her dance class secrets.

Only the keen-eyed would have noticed the way that her eyes whipped up towards the shop door at the slightest tinkle from the bell. It was an instinctive movement, barely a blink. Perhaps she didn't even realise she was doing it herself but she continued to do so all week: because Gabe never came back.

Unaware of Gabe's existence, Rob picked up on Ava's lightness of mood and drank it up with relief. He popped into Dunne's one Friday lunchtime and was met by Ava's clear-eyed smile at the door.

'Hello, you,' he said, returning her smile.

'Hi! What are you doing in town?'

'I had to collect some shoes from the cobbler's and I thought I'd come and say hello.' He leaned in to kiss her. As he did so, Ava caught a waft of his aftershave. It was heavy, almost musky.

'I would have got them for you.'

'I know, but I had the ticket and a client left early, so it seemed silly not to pop in.' He handed her a chocolate bar – her favourite.

'Oh, thank you. What a treat!' Ava felt the little glow of affection radiate throughout her body.

'And listen, tomorrow night – let's do something fun. No work stuff, no family stuff, no wedding stuff ...' Ava flinched at the thought of the mounting wedding stresses, 'just us two.'

'I would love that, I really would.' She reached up to kiss him.

'I was thinking I could cook for us – it's the first night of your dancing show – and then on Sunday we could go for a nice walk and maybe a pub lunch?'

Strictly. He had noticed *Strictly* was starting. Maybe Lauren was right about the Summer *Strictly* Feeling after all: it was the beginning of autumn, not the end of summer.

'That sounds great,' said Ava. And she really meant it. She pictured herself curled up on the sofa, perhaps in her new jeans, with a fresh pedicure; Rob bringing her a glass of chilled white wine, the condensation still running down its side. It would be the kind of Sunday night that stressed married people with children envied as they picked the Wotsits from their hair and winced as they trod on tiny Lego figurines.

'It's a date!' Rob winked at her as he pulled the shop door to. Ava hummed to herself for the rest of the afternoon.

Ava didn't notice the text until she had been home for over half an hour. The Devil's medium, Mel often called them. And in this case she was most certainly right.

> Hon, I forgot I have golf with Will tomorrow. Won't be back till late probs. I'll collect you early Sun for that walk and lunch though? Xxx

The cowardice. Bailing on her twice in a month and not even bothering to call to say so. Suddenly the plans for Sunday seemed trite, pointless; it was just what every couple who didn't live together and had no proper plans did. Walk and lunch. Saturday night had seemed thoughtful, considerate, 'them'. Now she was being bumped for sport. Again. Furious, impotent rage coursed through her body. She put her phone on the cold, hard kitchen counter and poured herself the wine that Rob would not now be passing her tomorrow night.

Condensation appeared around the glass and then slowly dribbled down its stem while Ava flicked through the local paper to see if there was anything at all on TV. Finding nothing, she grabbed the glass and headed upstairs to find her laptop. She flipped it open, turned it on and lay on her stomach facing it, her legs bent at the knees. In the reflection on the screen she could see her calves and feet sticking up behind her head. Wincing, she realised she looked like a teenager who had been sent to her room. Then she frowned, wishing the cause of her ennui was as simple as a parent who just didn't understand her. She knew she was her own responsibility now. Adulthood, ugh!

She fired off an email to Mel to see if she was around and available to talk, then switched on her Skype just in case. While waiting, she checked out the latest celebrity gossip online, including an update on the romances of the cast of *Bishopstone Park* and the demise of an American starlet's size zero waistline. There was also a piece on who was doing well in this year's *Dancing with the Stars*, which she read with interest in between sips of wine. She tried to imagine David Arquette dancing and wondered if she had seen him doing so in any of his movies, then looked at some of the images of Kristin Cavallari. Recognising her from various celebrity magazines, she knew that she was already a reality TV star and wondered if *Dancing with the Stars* would turn her into a true showgirl.

As she scrolled down the page she saw that Ricki Lake was another of the contestants and remembered the studenty hours that she and Mel had spent watching her chat show. Curled up with hangovers and mountains of cheap takeaway, they had loved watching the show and turned it into a bit of a ritual. She looked at the promotional pictures of Ricki and, thinking about how they had all grown up, she made a mental note to remind Mel they should keep an eye out for her progress. They had long enjoyed comparing the two shows and keeping track of the dancers and judges who crossed between them, so she was sure that Mel would welcome a little gossipy heads up.

The jittery frustration of earlier was calcifying into a resigned sadness that she thought was behind her earlier in the week. Dance class seemed so long ago now, almost as if she had imagined it. Ava bit the corner of her lip and logged on to Facebook.

She used the site quite often and had a page site for Dunne's, as well as a personal page that she would look at from time to time. She had never really taken to it, though – unlike her friends with desk jobs, always eager for a distraction between meetings or while their boss's back was turned, Ava dealt with people face to face all day, rarely finding herself with time to kill. She knew that the minute Matt saw her messing around online she would not have a leg to stand on as far as keeping him off the laptop went, so she tended to avoid it altogether. On the few occasions a month when she did check in, the seemingly ceaseless parade of baby photographs, glamorous holidays and bizarre bursts of political commentary that usually met her tended to ensure she stayed away longer each time.

She scanned her own profile, wondering what others might make of it. Her photograph was now relatively old – an image that Rob had taken on a long Sunday walk they made on the South Coast. What had been intended as a romantic weekend in Dorset was blighted by grim weather and a guest house whose proprietor apparently did not see cleaning the bathroom following his previous guests' stay as an essential part of the job. Ava's heart had sunk when they entered the room and she winced when she spotted the limp, mildewed curtain hanging down into the tub, still nursing a stranger's clearly visible pubic hair. Consequently, the time she imagined they would spend consummating their first mini break was in fact spent agonising over whether to complain there and then.

'Could you really face using that bath?'

'Well yes, I'm not Mariah Carey! But that's not the point.'

'I know, it's ghastly! I'll say something.'

'But what if he throws us out?'

'I'm sure he won't.'

'He'll hate us all weekend if we complain now.'

'It's true, but we already hate him so what does it matter?'

'Fair point! And I suppose if this weather keeps up we'll want to spend as much time as we can here.'

'Okay, I'm going to go now! Don't unpack. Stay here.'

Minutes later the proprietor came in and scrubbed the bath in front of them, all the while muttering darkly about how he knew the room had been cleaned anyway and this must be a scam. So the bath was clean, the shower curtain certainly wasn't and the weekend was largely wretched. They had had some giggles watching breakfast TV together in bed with their surprisingly good breakfast, but it was hardly the crisp white linen and hotel-room frolics fantasy that Ava envisaged. Rob seemed awkward, unsure of what his next move should be, while Ava put on her new nightie, desperately trying to believe it wasn't a glaring case of too much given the moderate charms of the room.

The happiest that they were all weekend was walking along the blustery beaches near Corfe Castle, and it was during a brief glimpse of blue sky that Rob had taken the shot: Ava in his anorak, looking over her shoulder and grinning broadly. The wind had caught her hair perfectly, as if styled like her Hollywood namesake, and the light lit up the space around her as if she were glowing. She stared at the image and tried to imagine what others saw when they looked at it. Had they felt the same prickle of envy about their coastal mini break as she so often experienced about others' holiday snapshots? Had she convinced them as well as she had herself that the cliff-top second represented the reality of her relationship? She took another sip of wine and saw the small red notification button light up on the top left of the screen.

Before checking it, she filled in her status for the first time in weeks.

I have finally taken the plunge and started dance classes. Hot teacher, fab music, just down the road, what's not to love?

It felt unusual, announcing herself like that, but scanning her feed quickly revealed old school friends and distant cousins had no qualms about discussing their broken clutches or achievements at school sports day, so why shouldn't she?

She flicked up to the Notification and saw that it was a Friend Request from someone called Matilda Bennett. She had no idea who Matilda Bennett was. How did they know her? She squinted at the tiny avatar: a young girl with a huge mess of blonde hair, the image clearly taken on a laptop's internal camera after hours of faux-nonchalant posing. It was Minx. Ava smiled to herself at the way she had rebranded cutesy Matilda as the more knowing 'Minx'. Rarely had a nickname suited a girl less and it seemed bizarre that her noticeably more confident pal was named after a wizard's house elf. Ava opened Minx's profile page and marvelled at the number of friends and photographs she seemed to have there. As she did so, Mel's Skype name popped up, followed by her face.

'Hey, hey, hey!' she said in her familiar laconic tone. 'Here I am, live at the kitchen table …'

'Well, hello there and how are you? Bedtime seen to?'

'Hell, yeah! Rich did it tonight as he was out so late again last night.'

'Sheesh, he has been working hard lately.'

'I know. When does he get some cash for it, that's what I want to know.'

'Ack, start-ups aren't easy, though.'

They bantered back and forth for a while, each sipping slowly on a glass of something cool, comfortable with the gestures and habits of the other as they gazed at their screens. It was only when Ava tried to explain why she was so frustrated with Rob that Mel's tone hardened a little.

'Ava, honey, not cooking you dinner so you can watch *Strictly* in peace is hardly the greatest crime in the world! Rich crept home at almost three last night, stinking of booze.'

'Yeah, but he came home. He's yours. That's the problem with Rob, he's just so disinclined to actually be part of my day-to-day life.'

'Oh, come on! Are you giving me the "he won't commit" chat? What are we, 25? Do you really think any of us who are married are any happier than you? It's just a frickin' ceremony!' Ava watched Mel slam a hand down on the heavy wood of her kitchen table. She thought of Lauren and the wedding, how little she wanted that kind of fuss. Then she thought of the Hanburys and how entranced they seemed by each other.

'I know, of course I know that. It's not the wedding – just a conversation would do. But I have never had the feeling that he was truly, sincerely excited about the idea of being part of my life rather than merely my boyfriend. If he could just look me in the eye and tell me: "We're in the same boat now. We have chosen a boat together, we've hopped onboard and we're sailing in the same direction together." At the moment we're just two pedalos in the same lake, occasionally bumping against each other.'

'That would just be words, and you know what men are like about talking: they don't. They would do anything to avoid that kind of contact. You need to look at his actions. He's still coming to take you out on Sunday, isn't he?'

'Yes, but I don't want to be taken out, I want to already be there with him.'

'So you want to move in together? You want to let yourself in for a lifetime of picking up his socks after squash and not being able to have chats like this unless he's out?'

'Hi, Ava!' interrupted Rich from the other side of the kitchen before popping his head around.

Ava waved back before putting her head in her hands in exasperation.

'No, I'm not explaining myself very well here. I'm so sorry to whinge on like this, I know it just sounds like a chronic case of the grass always being greener.'

Mel raised an eyebrow.

'I must sound so princessy, but I know I'm not being entirely unreasonable. It's really hard to articulate. It's a feeling, not a specific accusation I'm making. Something has withered.'

'That's adulthood, sweetie. We're all withering daily. You want to know truly withered, try bringing up two toddlers with a man who has just started his own company. We barely see each other. I feel as if it's me running a small business with him, not Chloe. Family Inc.' Mel fiddled with the chunky silver bangles on her wrist, her expression increasingly strained.

'Hey, is Rich still there?'

'Ha, no! He's watching the footie. Listen, you need to get a grip and cut Rob some slack. I hate to sound all surrendered wife on you, but how about you try and do something for him? If nothing else it'll give you the moral high ground and something else to think about other than the bloody wedding!'

'That wedding ...' muttered Ava. 'As ever, you are entirely right, though! I'll get a grip. It's his birthday soon so I'll do something proper this year.'

Mel smiled.

'Babe, you know you're welcome here any time. Come up to London for dinner and *Strictly* – the kids would love to see you and Jake might even let us out on the town some time. Don't beat yourself up about this. You are right to demand to be loved.'

'Thank you, missus! You take care. Go next door and demand to be loved yourself.' At this, Mel roared with laughter and pulled the shoulder of her bright chunky cardigan down with a faux-burlesque wink. She said good-bye, and was gone.

You are right to demand to be loved.

Mel's words echoed back at Ava as she wiped a drop from her wine glass from the bed linen. The Skype screen had now vanished, leaving Minx's Facebook profile beneath. Ava looked at her photographs, recognising Dobby (Deborah) in several of them. She smiled at their innocent grins and noticed from the chat box that Minx was online. The Notification symbol flickered on again. A further Friend Request ... Dobby. Ava clicked 'Accept' and went to have a look at her page. But as she clicked she realised the request had not been from Dobby at all.

132

Gabriel Monroe is now your Friend.

For a second Ava stared at the screen. Was it too late? Could she un-click? No, it was done. Then the adrenaline hit her, and she leaped at the keyboard like a woman possessed. First, she looked at her status. Too much? No, yes, *no*! Well, it said Patrice was hot, so it stayed. Then, pictures. Frantically, she looked over the list of pictures she was tagged in, desperately untagging anything recent or unflattering, trying to hide family ones and leave the ones of Dunne's opening there for him to see so that he didn't think she had blocked him altogether.

How had he found her? *Why* had he found her? And what could she do now? It was one thing to let a teenager with several hundred friends onto her profile, but this ... this was a real nightmare. Apart from anything else she had just revealed that she was on her laptop on a Friday night. And she had said yes within seconds, as if she'd been sitting in wait. She bit her lip, wondering what on earth her next move might be.

A message popped up.

'So you're enjoying dance classes then?'

A pause. She imagined him at his laptop. Was he in a chair? A large, comfy leather chair that smelled faintly of the vetiver scent he always brought with him? Surely he wasn't at his desk on a Friday night. Or was he, like her, on a bed? Ava breathed out with her bottom lip pushed forward, fanning her dark blonde fringe up off her face.

'Yes. I guess you can say that. I love dance.'

133

There was no pause before his reply.

'I can tell. It was a treat to see you there.'

'Thanks. How did you, erm, find me?'

'Your shop. Your name. Dunne's is where I first saw you. And Ava, well, it's hardly forgettable.'

Her pulse was racing, her hands clammy with nerves. She could see the imprint of her fingertips on the letter keys. Did that always happen, or just now?

'I see.'

'Looking forward to seeing you next week.'

Ava scrolled frantically through his profile page, trying to discover anything at all about him, but it was like an empty shop. Nothing. He was tagged in a handful of pictures, best man at a wedding, sitting on a lounger in front of a Mediterranean setting, but none of the pictures had he put up himself and barely any of his information was filled in.

'Well, yes, and thanks for getting in touch.'

'I look forward to dancing with you.'

'Ha! You'll be sorry. I would probably hold you back.'

'I wouldn't be sorry, Ava. Ever. And you could never hold me back. Till next week … x'

Chapter 8

Born This Way

'Ta da ta da, ta da daaa! Ta da ta da, daaaaaaaaa! Wooo!'

To be fair, the *Strictly* theme tune was not sounding its best. Despite Ava having resigned herself to a solitary Saturday night on the sofa, indulging in some mild sulking and mulling things over, there was now someone on the other side of her front door singing the famous jaunty refrain again and again. Moments after the doorbell rang it began, startling Ava out of the reverie she was enjoying while hanging out the laundry in her tiny but sunny back yard.

When she heard the doorbell chime she instinctively shivered in dread in case it was Rob. She was now genuinely looking forward to her night in, having put on a pair of stained tracksuit bottoms the moment she got home from the shop. Elasticated trousers and a takeaway curry: those were her dates for the evening and she really didn't think she could cope with anything else after an exhausting day at the shop on barely any sleep. She and Matt had struggled to keep up with the volume of passing trade, and throughout it all she had had a grim light-headedness – the result of a night of half dreams fuelled by a glass too many of wine and a meal too few the night before.

During the night she had woken up several times, regretting not having had a proper meal. Each time she was tangled in her bedding, hair matted, halfway through confusing dreams where Rob and Gabe seemed interchangeable and yet irrelevant. Fragments of conversation floated through her half-sleep, all accompanied by an incessant frenetic Salsa beat. By morning she had been glad of a break from the cruel tricks of her own subconscious, but it turned out even her own imagination could not come up with anything more dastardly than the collection of 'Saturday children' who misbehaved in the shop while she had tried to serve everyone as quickly and charmingly as possible. At one point an excitable six-year-old boy had driven a Lego truck straight over her plimsolled foot, ramming a small piece of plastic into her ankle and causing her to kick up in pain and knock over a pail of delicate and expensive rare orchids. As the murky water oozed into her shoe for the second time in a month, Ava silently considered galoshes in the workplace.

Total absence of glamour aside, Ava simply wasn't in the mood for the kind of conversation she and Rob would end up having if he was at her doorstep with a bunch of flowers and a face that begged for forgiveness.

But he wasn't.

Ava realised the minute that the singing began that it was Lauren instead. At her feet was a beautifully packaged takeaway lasagne from the delicatessen in town and in her hands she had a bottle of red wine and a large folder. Ava opened the door, her head tilted on one side in resignation, and smiled.

'Ta da ta da, ta da daaa! Ta da ta da, daaaaaa!' repeated Lauren, kicking her foot to one side at the end of the refrain in an uncanny impression of Brucie himself.

'Hello,' said Ava. 'How may I help?'

'The *Strictly* summer feeling is here, and so am I! First night: tonight – the big reveal. I thought you might like some company. Well, I thought I might INFLICT some company on old misery-guts here!'

Ava laughed and raised her eyes heavenwards in mock desperation for help. It was impossible to say no to Lauren when she selected charm as her chosen method of inflicting a fun time on anyone. Ava gestured her head towards the kitchen and held the door open for Lauren, who wandered through the hallway. As she passed her, Lauren muttered, 'Looking good, Sis! That's an outfit that really screams "self-respect".'

'Oh, shut up! I barely got in from the shop.'

'You can't start on that slippery slope, Sis! You might be having an evening in, but you're watching the most glamorous show on the box so you can at least change into a decent pair of jeans. And I want to see a sparkle somewhere, please.'

It struck Ava how easy it was for Lauren to say that, with her effortlessly athletic figure and never-ending confidence. Her enviably long legs seemed to absorb any excess weight she ever put on, hiding the fluctuations that showed all too quickly on Ava's more hourglass frame. Lauren was in the same long boots that she had worn the previous Sunday, dark tight jeans tucked into them and a flowing, pale pink silk shirt. It was the sort of garment Ava would save for best, then end up spilling something on, or never getting full use of. For Lauren, it was perfectly appropriate for slopping around in with red wine and tomato sauce.

Ava headed upstairs and changed into a decent pair of jeans and some flat sandals with diamante detail across the straps. They would hardly make Flavia quake in her rhinestones but enough to show willing as far as Lauren was concerned.

'That's much better! Don't you feel more like a human being than a mass of cells now? On the sofa, please,' instructed Lauren, before bustling into the kitchen with the food and wine, where she shuffled around for a few minutes before emerging with the folder.

'I will give you wine now,' she announced as she stood, looking down at Ava. 'But if you spill it on these sketches I will murder you and hide your body in your own compost heap, then use it to make beautiful roses.'

'Understood.' Ava winced. She might have known there was a catch and she realised this was it, as she was presented with the sketchbook that Viv had made for Lauren's wedding dress.

She sat on the sofa like a nervous schoolgirl, and moments later Lauren returned with two large glasses of wine. As one of them was passed from sister to sister, Ava remembered it was only just over a day ago that she had imagined herself being in exactly this position at exactly this time – but with Rob instead of Lauren. For some reason, the wine had changed colour from white to red, but the emotion was the same: love. Ava pushed the thought to the back of her mind – this wasn't romantic but familial love. Rob had chosen not to be with her, but the fact that Lauren would be her sister forever was indeed a comfort.

'Cheers!' said Lauren with an infectious grin.

Hell, if this was second best it was still pretty damn good, thought Ava, as she clinked glasses with her sister.

As Ava opened the sketchbook, she couldn't help but gasp. There was no question this was the dress that Lauren should wear: it didn't just suit her, it was *perfect*. The delicately drawn images showed a waspish waist created by a wide, high waistband and a strapless bodice covered by a delicate lace bolero jacket shown both alone and worn with the dress. The skirt was long, thick panels of heavy silk to emphasise Lauren's long slim legs. This wasn't just an elegant dress, it was a magical one, but Ava couldn't help but notice that it was not a 1930s gown. It seemed more of a classic shape. Attached to the opposite pages on the folder were swatches of various fabrics. There were three in slightly different shades of silk: one ivory, one a dark cream and another almost a creamy brown, a small arrow pointing at the middle one where they were attached to the page. Next to them were two swatches of patterned lace and a further one of sheer lace, flecked with tiny sparkles of gold.

'Wow, Lauren! This is exquisite. I didn't expect anything less, but I didn't expect anything like this. Oh, I don't know what I expected, but these are amazing, just amazing!'

'I'm so glad you like it.' Lauren shifted the wide scrapbook across from Ava's lap to hers and started pointing at various details. The first wafts of lasagne began drifting in from the kitchen. 'This is the fabric I've chosen but Viv attached these two for comparison as it's so hard to tell between all the whites and creams with nothing to compare them to. That one's gross – so dark, like a cappuccino. This lace will cover the bodice and it will also make the bolero, and this one will be the veil. Can you believe it, I'm having a *veil*!'

'Oh, I *can* believe it, Sis! You're having the ultimate wedding and the ultimate wedding would not be complete without a veil.'

Lauren gigged and looked down at the sketches again. With one finger she briefly traced the edge of one of the illustrations as she gazed dreamily at it. In that moment Ava felt utterly at peace. She looked at Lauren smiling down at the scrapbook and remembered visiting her all those times in hospital, over twenty-five years ago. As she walked onto the children's ward with her father Lauren had been there at the end of the room, sitting up in bed and tracing the words in her storybook just as she was now. She had been very young, only 6 or 7 years old, and for a month or two she had been very ill indeed. Life for 11-year-old Ava had been a sudden whirlwind of urgent hospital visits, hushed parental discussions that were never quiet enough for her to avoid, and all the while an urgent, nagging sense of panic about what life would be like if her little sister didn't make it.

Ava somehow managed to forget that it had ever happened the vast majority of the time, but in this moment of pause she wondered how often Lauren remembered those months. The experience seemed to have given her an inner core of strength and courage, a fearlessness that so few have. She had seen some of the very worst that life has to offer, and she had survived; she had *chosen* to survive. The experience had clearly been formative and might go a long way towards explaining Lauren's bold lust for life, her determination to wring whatever victory, joy or just plain love that she could from it. But that frightened little girl was still in there somewhere, even if she was most of the time hidden by a terrifying career machine.

'*What*?' asked Lauren, sensing her older sister's gaze.

'Nothing, it's just lovely – and so different to what we talked about. You two really must have worked hard on it. I'm so glad Viv has done such a great job. I …' Ava considered confiding in Lauren. About Rob, perhaps about Gabe and the army of butterflies that had apparently taken up residence in her stomach over the last week or two – but where to begin? She knew from last night how needy and ridiculous it made her sound, but the moment had passed as Lauren was now pulling a second, thinner folder from the back of the first.

'I'm *so* glad you think so,' she replied. 'It's really going to be wonderful. And look, I've brought you a selection of images that we've worked on for your dress, too.'

'Oh, right – I thought that Viv and I were going to be in touch ourselves.'

'Yes, but you weren't, were you? You did nothing about it at all, so I told Viv what I wanted and we've drawn up some plans for you.'

Ava took a sip from her glass, which she was now gripping so tightly that there was a very real risk of it smashing in her hand.

'I know how much you love dance and the romance of the ballroom ...' began Lauren.

'Oh wow, that's *so* sweet! *So* thoughtful and generous of you at your own weddi—'

'... but that doesn't fit in with my English Country Wedding theme at all, so we have gone with something very Jane Austen: an empire line bridesmaid's dress.' Lauren grinned and lifted her shoulders. Hers was the sort of smile that over-made-up middle-aged women on department store cosmetics counters give you when they've suggested you need to start using anti-ageing cream for the first time.

Ava raised an eyebrow as enthusiastically as she could as she looked at the images of a dress that would suit someone with the figure of Keira Knightley to a tee. She imagined her large, unsupported bust wobbling above the high empire waistband as she thundered down the aisle behind a floating Lauren. Her waist, the only feature that she could always rely on, would be entirely hidden beneath the swathes of fabric around it, which would also double up as 'short leg emphasisers'. The fabric itself, a swatch of which was attached, seemed to be a choice between two prints that could easily have been named 'the spare room curtains that time Mum became obsessed by Laura Ashley in the

1980s' and 'ooh look, a tablecloth from the Hanburys' kitchen!' Ava might have been suspicious that this was all an elaborate practical joke if not for Lauren's patent enthusiasm for the designs.

She tried to mould the contours of her face into an expression that best said 'My goodness, what lovely suggestions!' Her logical side was firmly telling her that this wasn't her wedding, not her day; that she had to shut up about it and deal with the situation with a modicum of grace. Meanwhile, her emotional side was shrieking like a toddler – *Look at it! It looks as if it's been designed by someone who hated me, who wanted me to be miserable. When will I have a day, a dress that suits me instead of shames me? Why must I be made to look a fool for the happiness of others? Oh God, I'm going nowhere …*

As this internal battle raged on, her logical brain reminded her that there were only twelve minutes until *Strictly* began, that she had been longing to know which celebrities would be starring in it and soon she would. Her illogical brain responded by wailing about how excited she was, but how she wasn't sure she would even be able to see the gorgeous dresses without bursting into tears at the thought of her Regency Horror Frock.

Lauren, meanwhile, continued to babble on about key details of the wedding itself. They had chosen the hymns now – a selection of Christmas carols and traditional hymns so that 'everyone can really have a good singalong'. On each table would be an advent wreath and on each place setting a small festive plant for each guest to take away.

Then there were the matches with the happy couple's names on, the photographs of their time together decorating each table, the decision to have a Christmas tree in the venue, decorated in colours that would match the other elements of the table settings, and so on.

'We can discuss finer details another time,' said Lauren, glancing at her watch. 'The Winter Wonderland theme can't get too "Disney". It's a country wedding – it needs to be traditional. Traditional, but perfect.'

And with that she wandered off to the kitchen, where she removed the lasagne from the oven. Ava followed, having turned up the volume on the TV as high as she dared. Just as portions of oozing pasta hit the plates the familiar *Strictly* trumpet refrain began. Lauren filled their glasses, and after clinking again they looked at each other and whooped.

The sisters settled on the sofa. To an outsider their bodies might have looked relaxed, but they were primed like birds of prey, ready to pounce on their televisual feast.

'*Finally*!' said Ava with a grin and a sigh.

'I *knooow*! Goodbye, summer,' said Lauren, waving out of the window.

The credits ended and almost immediately the *Strictly* house band started up. Within moments the professional dancers came out onstage to the familiar sounds of Lady Gaga's 'Born This Way'.

'Oh, look at them!' shrieked Ava as Lauren gave an audible gasp. '*Grrr-rreat* look!'

'I wonder who made these outfits,' said Lauren, as the professionals strutted centre stage and began their dance.

The familiar – and unknown – faces paraded across the screen as the women sighed and whooped in equal measure.

'*Robin!*' squeaked Lauren.

'And *Artem*!'

'Do you remember how we just weren't sure about those two this time last year?'

'Yes, and now I love them both,' sighed Ava.

'Who's that?' asked Lauren, as a new face flashed up onto the screen.

'Must be a newcomer.'

'Ooh, exciting! I wonder what he's like.'

'I can get my laptop and see if there's anything on the site, if you'd like.'

'Nah, don't worry! I'm sure they'll tell us in a minute.'

As the professionals' dance ended, the presenters Bruce Forsyth and Tess Daly stepped forward to rapturous applause. The lights on set were twinkling and Ava could pick out individual faces smiling in the audience.

'Look at them grinning,' she said. 'Imagine if I got to go.'

'Yeah, amazing! But not so amazing as Tess's jumpsuit.'

In her canary yellow 70s-style jumpsuit, Tess certainly looked incredible.

'She looks great, as usual,' agreed Ava.

'Can you imagine what one of us would look like in an outfit like that?'

'Ha-ha. Maybe I should wear it to your wedding?' giggled Ava.

'Mum probably will,' replied Lauren, a twinkle in her eye.

'Oh it's so *goood* to be having these conversations again!' said Ava with a little yelp of glee.

And with that the celebrities were announced. To the chirpy carnival sounds of the house band, they started to appear from each side of the iconic staircase, nervously making their way down onto the stage. Some of the women looked unsure in their heels, while a couple of the men were clearly not used to wearing the bright, sparkly shirts required of them, but on the whole they were grinning and buzzing with excitement.

The sisters scrutinised each and every one of the contestants as they came down the stairs. Comments were flying between the two of them – 'Thank heavens! I was worried it was just a rumour', 'Ooh, I LOVE him!', 'She looks like she'll be good', 'I reckon he'll be interesting', and before long they moved on to speculation about who would be partnered with whom. Just as they mentioned it, Bruce introduced the idea himself, with a cheeky comment about matchmaking. The sisters gripped each other's arms and giggled.

'Matchmaking!' they said in unison.

And with that the show moved on to short video packages on each of the celebrities, followed by moments pairing them up with each other. Eventually they were introduced to the unfamiliar face, a new male dancer named Pasha Kovalev.

'I'm looking forward to seeing what we make of him,' said Lauren, with a fake judge's face on.

'I don't think much of your Craig!' chuckled Ava.

'Yeah, you're right – I'd rather be Bruno, I reckon,' agreed Lauren.

'Well, you're as stern as Craig,' countered her sister. Before long the two were in fits of laughter again.

The show continued with each of the couples being selected and the dancers and celebrities feigning mock shock or laughter at their couplings. One celebrity was even picked up and carried off, much to the delight of the studio audience.

'It's *so* exciting,' mused Lauren. 'This is just the beginning of their journeys. For some of them it goes on for months and months. Think how much will have changed by the final – I'll be married, and it still feels as if it's a thousand years away.'

'I wonder if anything will have changed for me …' Ava's stomach suddenly clenched with nervousness as she considered looking that far into her own future.

'Why would it? You don't want anything to, do you?'

There was a pause.

Ava began to answer but the celebrities were now onstage, all together with their partners, taking part in their first-ever group dance. Some looked utterly terrified, while others were clearly relishing the chance to show what they had already learned. Behind them the audience fizzed with excitement, clapping along to encourage them. As the dance finished the audience exploded into applause, some even whistling. Lauren herself let out a whoop.

'Oh, LOOK at them all!' she squealed. 'It's like catching up with family at Christmas!'

'I wonder which of the celebs we'll be seeing in a totally different light.'

'Mm, me too,' replied Ava. 'I'm such a rubbish judge of character, I never get people right on first impressions.'

An image of Gabe running a hand through his curls and looking up at her flashed up in her mind.

'Oh I'm pretty good, I reckon. I think I'll even put a bet on this year.'

'I would never dare – they'd be knocked out in the first week if I did that! Did I tell you that Mel and I are trying to get tickets?'

'Yes, but then I never heard the whole story. When will you know?'

'Any day now, apparently – she applied via the website last month and everything. I have everything crossed that we get some. It would be so much fun, and it's just a lovely Christmassy thing to do.'

'Yeah, the whole day would be fun – heading up to London, choosing an outfit, and then you might get to see them backstage or something.'

'I don't know about that, but it would just be *so* exciting to see it live. To see dancing done to that standard, in person, and to be able to applaud it right there and then.'

'I'm so jealous, but I won't possibly have a Saturday to spare between now and the big day.'

Ava didn't bother to let Lauren know that this wasn't actually an invitation.

The speculation and adulation flowed freely for the rest of the evening as the sisters polished off both the lasagne and the wine, then dived into a box of chocolates while they gossiped about celebs and dancing generally. Beyoncé at Glastonbury, the latest ballet at the ENO in London and a dance keep-fit video that Lauren was doing for the wedding ... They then switched to music television and had a laugh at some of the videos that they came across, marvelling at a few of the outfits and teasing each other with increasingly wild wedding outfit suggestions.

Over the course of the evening there was no topic not to be addressed, it seemed. Ava felt increasingly relieved that she hadn't told Lauren about the dance classes yet, so fast and furious were her opinions on absolutely everything. All of a sudden Rory had texted to say he was on his way to collect Lauren and there was a flurry of rushed goodbyes and promises to discuss flowers in the next week before Lauren was being driven away in her fiancé's car, waving manically from the passenger seat as she headed down the road.

Ava sighed as she closed the front door behind her, then looked around at the debris of an unexpectedly happy evening. She put glasses in the dishwasher and threw away the tiny silver foil wrappers from the chocolates, all the while singing the *Strictly* theme tune to herself in a jangly way. As she leant down to turn off the final lamp in the sitting room, she decided to have a quick check on her laptop to see if, after the first *Strictly* of the series, there was any word on tickets for a live show. She had, after all, promised to chase the situation up. Yes, she'd quickly do that before bed.

But somewhere quiet, very far towards the back of her mind, in one of its darkest recesses, Ava knew that this was not what she was really going to do. She would never dare acknowledge it to anyone, least of all herself, but somehow, once her laptop was open, it wasn't her email that she opened first because Facebook appeared on her web browser. And there it was. The one thing she had hoped to see but hadn't dared to imagine might be there: the tiny red square. There was a flip in the pit of her stomach, as if she had just been turned inside out.

A new message from Gabe:

I bet you're watching. I hope you enjoy it. Looking forward to seeing any tips you pick up in action on Monday night.

Her stomach flipped again. She looked around the room quickly, as if to check that she was not being watched by an invisible conscience. Her eyes rested on the framed portrait of herself and Rob on the bedside table. Taken at New Year's Eve, it showed them both smiling and waving at the camera. Hell, the photo was there but Rob wasn't! He had chosen to be elsewhere. So Ava quickly typed a brief, flirty reply to the message.

As her finger hovered over the 'send' button, she remembered Mel's words:

This is adulthood. You have a boyfriend. It's Rob. Just grow up and treat him how you would like to be treated.

It nearly stopped her, but somehow it didn't. Something else did. Although she knew she was an adult, she certainly didn't feel like one as she lay in front of her laptop, her own face reflecting back at her in the glass of the screen. What prevented her was seeing the time that the message had been sent: several hours ago. Gabe could be out now, pulling women in London by this hour. Or he might be curled up – or more – in bed with the woman he kept buying flowers for. Sending a reply now would be a clear indication that she had time to be online on both a Friday and a Saturday night. And it would never do for him to know that on two consecutive nights she was at her laptop instead of elsewhere, with her head thrown back in a passionate and beautifully lit tableau of desirability. She bit her lip and turned the laptop off. Enigmatic silence would have to do.

It was the right decision. Two days later Ava was sitting in her car outside the Working Men's Club, gladder than ever that she had elected not to send Gabe a reply that night. After a Sunday of unspoken but undeniable tension between herself and Rob, she had now driven herself half mad with wanting to know more about Gabe and yet she hoped that she would never, ever find another thing out. For now he was just about safe – simply the guy from dance class, a customer; someone she was polite to, but knew little of. He certainly wasn't someone she had shared many words with. And what could be wrong with that?

But it turns out that there is a lot that can be said without words. One could use clothes, for example. Perhaps it

151

was this that had led to Ava somehow – despite her busy day in the shop – finding time to pop out and buy herself a new dress. It was the sales, the very end of the sales at that; the final dregs of what summer had had to offer. Which of course meant that it felt like free clothes. And it would have been foolish for her not to take advantage of the beautiful silk dress that she had had her eye on for a couple of weeks for it was all but calling to her. It was expensive, even in the sale, but the most important thing was that she knew it made her look gorgeous.

Day after day she had walked past the small independent boutique just off the square, telling herself she'd have nowhere to wear it, but that Monday the early morning light had made it look particularly lovely as she walked past from her car. It wasn't in the window, but when she pressed her face up against the glass she could just about make out the fabric pressed between the other garments on the sale rail. Indeed, the morning light rendered it completely unforgettable.

So that Monday lunchtime she scurried back into the shop and tried it on for the third time. It still looked wonderful. Though hardly *Strictly*-esque, it was still gorgeous. Navy blue silk with small cream polka dots, it had a button-down front and full, flowing skirt. Its 1950s cut gave a slight vintage feel, but the way that it fitted her curves was just perfect. It moved when she moved, and it also allowed her to move comfortably. The buttons took a while to do up and presented quite a decision-making opportunity as far as how deep she wanted her cleavage to

152

appear, but if these were the greatest challenges the dress was presenting, she loved it all the more.

As she had entered the shop, Ava had tried to give the impression that she was a tremendously stressed business-woman, one on a tight deadline, but throughout the trans-action she felt as if she might as well have been wearing a billboard with 'THIS WOMAN HAS A CRUSH ON A MAN WHO IS NOT HER BOYFRIEND' written all over it. Nevertheless, she slipped on the dress a third time, confirmed that it was pretty much the best one she had ever tried and hurriedly gave her card to the woman at the till. On her return she had pushed the stiff cardboard bag underneath her desk and mysteriously left the shop bang on closing, somehow allowing herself time to shower and change into it before heading to the class.

Now sitting in the car – early again – she ran a hand through her hair and tied it back into a nice high ponytail that she imagined would be satisfyingly 'swishy' once she was dancing. As she lifted a hand past her face she caught a whiff of the scent she had also had a chance to apply at home: Caleche by Hermès. A classic. She continued to sit in the driver's seat and watched the Millers and the Hanburys head into the Working Men's Club – there was no sign of their friends.

Once the door closed behind them there was a moment's silence in the car park. Perfect early autumn calm briefly descended. Ava could almost hear her own nerves buzzing, the actual vibrations shuttling through her body. Only this time it wasn't just the dancing that was causing these flutters of anxiety: she wanted to look busy in case Gabe arrived to see her staring into space. She didn't want to make eye contact, to look as if she were waiting, or get herself into any situation she might not be able to trust herself in. And so she delved into her handbag and pulled out a lipstick. Cool from the darkness of her bag, it felt refreshing in the heat of the car. The case gave a satisfying little click as she opened it and she started to apply it in her rear-view mirror. Just as she had completed the first half of her top lip she heard the slam of a car door and the crunch of gravel underfoot. Whoever it was, she couldn't see yet, nor was she about to stop and look.

As the crunches drew nearer Ava saw from the very edge of her peripheral vision that it was him. At first she was thrilled that he would see her open mouthed, her lips making a perfect oval as she applied the plummy colour. But she was also irritated to have been caught out paying such attention to her appearance; she wanted him to think she had barely noticed him, let alone considered that he had noticed her. *You don't even know who this man is*, she reminded herself. *Stop applying make-up for another woman's man. Grow up!*

By now she could see that he had drawn level with her car. But instead of stopping and approaching her as she had expected he would, he walked straight on. Ava felt colour blossom in her cheeks as she wondered if he hadn't noticed her, or – worse – had spotted her and decided to pass the car. She clicked her lipstick shut, rubbed her lips together and then popped the neat Chanel tube back into her bag.

That was when she saw him: looking back at her as he pulled open the heavy wooden door to the hall. He smiled. Was it a smile or a wink? It was hard to tell – his extended arm pulling the door obscured much of his face, his sad eyes were wrinkled, but it wasn't quite clear whether this was simply an affable crinkly-eyed grin or something a little cheekier. Either way, the door was closing behind him by the time Ava realised what had happened and moments later she was pulling on the handle herself.

Inside the hall there was significantly less kerfuffle than last time – none of the awkward introductions or the shuffling across the room to get into positions that would suit Patrice. As Ava entered, there was a gentle bit of chat going on. People were calmer, catching up with each other and tentatively asking how their weeks had been.

'Hi there,' said Minx, as Ava bent down to put her handbag under one of the tables around the edge of the room.

'Oh hi, Facebook friend!' she replied. 'Lovely to see you on there.'

'Yeah, I thought it would be good to connect.'

'You have so much going on there – I barely use it!' said Ava, perhaps a little too loudly, but just loudly enough for Gabe to have heard. She turned so that she couldn't see his reaction, if any.

'I love it! But it's, like, rilly great getting out and doing stuff like this, too,' continued Minx.

'Well, exactly.'

'And I saw your flower shop, too – it's totally amazing. Like, sooooo beautiful!'

Ava blushed.

'Thank you, Minx! I'm very proud of it.'

'I can't even imagine how awesome it would be to work inside somewhere so lush.'

'Well, keep in touch – a bit of Saturday work might yet come up.'

Minx's face lit up, and Ava smiled back at her. *Yes, this was the reason she had come to dance classes: to meet an entirely different kind of person, to be taken out of herself.* Again she turned, to make sure she wouldn't catch Gabe's eye: she didn't yet trust herself.

Patrice arrived and immediately made his presence felt. He was every bit as attractive and commanding as Ava remembered, but also more at ease with the group. Almost at once they were down to the serious business of the Waltz.

Patrice carefully explained the basics of the steps, once again borrowing Jenny as his partner for the demonstration. The rise and fall of the dance, the elegant arm hold, the gentle music … they were all Ava needed to soothe her jangling nerves. She stood, concentrating hard as she watched the couple turn and smile at each other to finish with a flourish. She wasn't sure what happened next, but in the following minute or so Patrice had divided up the group and positioned them throughout the floor. Somehow she was now standing next to Gabe.

'It looks as if we're a couple,' he said, as he turned to her.

'I'm not sure I'm very good at this.'

'You'll be fine.' He took her hands in his. 'We'll just make it up together.'

Ava's heart was hammering, her hands felt like hot hams, and she didn't seem to have any control over what she was saying or doing. How was it possible to feel wide awake and at the same time as if she was sleepwalking? She looked up at Gabe. As he glanced down at her, a dark curl flopped over onto his forehead.

'I suppose we could just get it wrong together,' she whispered.

'I can't think of anything I would rather do.' He smiled at her. *Oh, those sad eyes!*

The music began and the room started to move. At first there were a few giggles from the girls, but soon the class swayed in unison, back and forth in time to the music. Instead of feeling more frantic on Gabe's touch, Ava slowly felt herself relax. He seemed to have remembered all of the steps and quietly moved with a steady confidence that she couldn't help but absorb. His hands were warm, but not clammy, and whenever Ava felt rising panic about the next move Gabe gently led her in the right direction. They weren't talking, but every now and then he mouthed the beat to her, encouraging her on as Patrice counted out the steps.

'Forward, side, close! Back, side, close! Front of the box! Back of the box!' Patrice walked past, clapping the beat. 'Very good, Gabe and Ava – *very* Hollywood!' Ava smiled at the compliment, as she felt the silk of her new dress brushing against her leg. Gabe moved his hand around her waist.

'You see, not so bad after all,' he told her gently.

Ava realised that she was now closer to Gabe than she had been to Rob at any point yesterday, a day largely wasted on watching the rain outside, flicking through the newspapers ... and sniping at each other. She and Gabe continued to move together.

'One, Two, Three; One, Two, Three ...' Patrice walked by again. 'Rise, and fall. Rise, and fall. As if you're on a swing ... Rise, and fall.'

They must have been dancing for some time now. Ava glanced at the clock the next time they turned. *Only seven minutes left. Should she mention Facebook? Acknowledge they were in touch beyond the dance class?* She decided not and carried on with the gentle swinging back and forth of the dance. The music continued to swirl throughout the room – they were all concentrating now, finally moving as a unit. Ava's body smoothly moved in time with Gabe's, carried along by the music and the new confidence she felt slowly seeping throughout her. She imagined what she must look like to a stranger watching the group, and for the first time in weeks she felt as if that stranger might be impressed. Her eyes flitted back up to the clock, and as she looked back at Gabe Patrice announced the next dance would be the class's last.

'... so, give me your very best – I want to see you *Strictly*-ready!' he called from the front of the room. Gabe suddenly grabbed Ava around the waist and pulled her towards him. He turned his head so that he was facing the back of the room, his mouth about a centimetre from her ear.

'Come on, let's show them what we're made of!' he whispered. She felt his lips on her hair. The music began and they danced their very best, laughing and smiling with each other, all of the awkward tension ebbing away. It was as if they had only ever danced with each other. As the music reached its crescendo, Ava was glowing. As it ended, Gabe dropped her into a ridiculous overly dramatic dip. Meanwhile, the rest of the class was oblivious as they applauded each others' efforts. For a second, his face was inches from hers, his hair almost touching hers.

'Meet me,' he whispered. 'Soon?'

But Ava had too many questions. When? Where? Most of all, who was he? Unsure of which question to ask first, she gazed into his eyes, her head tipped back, her mouth paused at 'Wh …?' – the shape of a kiss.

Chapter 9

A Good Saturday Night

As Ava closed the door on the shop that Saturday she leant forward and briefly rested her forehead on the cool glass. She shut her eyes for a moment and took a deep breath. It had been another hectic day – somehow the first falling leaves of autumn seemed to be making customers crave fresh flowers all the more. At one point mid-afternoon there had been a queue of people spilling outside and onto the pavement while she and Matt made up bouquets and wrestled with coloured raffia as fast as was possible in such a confined space. *Maybe*, she found herself wondering while up a ladder reaching for gladioli as a small child below stuck a calla lily stamen up her nostril, *it wouldn't be such a bad idea to get Minx in for some Saturday work, after all.* Suddenly an extra pair of hands was looking like a necessity, not an indulgence.

But Ava had no real complaints. She was of the opinion that the busier, the better – anything that kept her from thinking about Gabe was welcome. Gabe. About whom she still knew so little yet she wanted to know so much more, but was too scared to ask. All week long she had put equal efforts into running a business and trying not to think about Gabe. It was bordering on ridiculous, trying to hide her instincts from no one but her own internal judge. Every time the bell on the shop's door went, she looked up to see if it might be him. Whenever the phone went, she answered in a oddly 'seductive' voice – an attempt at the smoothness of long-stemmed roses that were in reality a little sleepy sounding. Meanwhile, her email and Facebook checks were reaching epic levels.

She decided she needed to focus on Rob, to do something for him, something for *them*. The first step would be to ask him what he wanted for his birthday when they met up, later that night. Whether it was golf lessons, a huge party or simply a weekend with the curtains closed and a box set, his wish would be her command. But first she was off to have a glass of wine with Viv, who had emailed her earlier in the week, mentioning that she would be in Salisbury that day and could show her the designs for her dress in person. Ava suspected she was trying to kill two birds with one stone – she was off to the theatre, after all – but she had also been ducking Lauren's calls and thought Viv's progress had perhaps been suffering on account of that.

Ava had leapt at the chance to see Viv – and without Lauren – and apologised in advance in case she was coming by in person because of 'over-Lauren-ness'. She was looking forward to seeing Viv. Her plan was to persuade her to tone down the more *Pride and Prejudice* elements of the dress, and maybe to wriggle a little *Strictly* gossip out of her. Had anyone arrived for fittings and turned out to be significantly bigger than expected? Did they have unexpectedly distressing personal hygiene? Had any flirting been spotted yet? There remained a nagging three weeks until the first proper show, and now that Ava had had a taste for it she was champing at the bit.

Ava lifted her head and looked back into the shop one last time. She was extremely proud of how her business seemed to have become so beloved by the town, how they had responded with such warmth to the care she had taken over it. After giving the door a little pat, she turned to cross the square. She had only taken a few steps before her thoughts returned, boomerang-like, to Gabe. By now she had quite a portfolio of 'thinking about Gabe' moods.

She would imagine them doing something entirely normal. Emptying the dishwasher together, maybe, but in a fun way – a better way than she did now. There would perhaps be some kind of Salsa beat on in the background and he would occasionally spin her around the kitchen. (*Whose* kitchen was not specified.)

She would replay the first couple of times that he had come into the shop, run through the conversations they had had, scanning for further implied information about him. Then she would finish off by thinking about that last dance they had had together.

She would try to remember his lips, having forgotten exactly what they looked like in the way that you can only do when something (or someone) is blindingly gorgeous. It was like attempting to picture the Sistine Chapel – just a blur of colour and a sore neck. She would try and recall a mental snapshot of what they looked like, and then imagine what they felt like. *On the back of her hand, on the back of her neck, her lips ...*

There were other fantasies, but this time she was thinking about how badly she had handled his suggestion of meeting at the end of Monday's class. She felt so flustered that an unusual defence mechanism had kicked in, preventing her from acknowledging that it had actually happened at all. After those two seconds in his arms – which had felt like an hour – she had closed off and joined in with the applause of the rest of the class. After that she had become incredibly matey with him, as if they were at a motorcycle maintenance class together. It was all she felt capable of doing; she simply didn't trust herself with anything else. By the time she had made it to her car she was almost braying like a horse with raucous 'innocuous' laughter. He had seemed to take the hint and backed off, but she wasn't sure. She wasn't at all sure what had happened. Throughout the week, there were even flashes of panic that he might have said something else entirely and now thought her quite mad. She wanted to meet him, but she couldn't possibly do it. How could she? Where would they go? What did he want? And with that she realised she had somehow made her mouth into that involuntary kiss shape again.

She pressed her lips together, flat against her teeth, and looked back at the shop as she crossed the square. *So pretty in the early autumn light*, she thought to herself, before immediately wondering if she had perhaps blown it with Gabe – but blown *what*? Her mind seemed to be playing an eternal game of ping-pong against itself. She reminded herself that she had a boyfriend she loved very much, who loved *her* very much, who made her feel safe. But somehow this week the idea of 'feeling safe' had started to bring to mind those moments in Gabe's arms: the perfect combination of freedom and reassurance, doing a delicate dance together. His steps gave the impression that he had been dancing his entire life, but it was never a chore. *Had the chance with him gone?* she wondered as the sun dipped beneath the buildings. *Was it ever there? And if it had been, would she ever get it back? Or would it just have to live on in her imagination, stored tightly away for rainy Sunday afternoons?*

As Ava turned off the square and into the tiny wine bar where she had arranged to meet Viv, it was only 6.30 but most of the tables were already taken. The bar was the front portion of a somewhat grand independent French restaurant where Rob had suggested they have dinner. The scene of some of their greatest dates, it was special to them both, and Ava had leapt at the chance of an intimate dinner instead of another evening squabbling over the remote control. It had made perfect sense when Viv had suggested a glass of wine there before her evening at the theatre.

Ava peered into the room, her eyes accustoming themselves to the darkness after the sunlight outside. The circular tables were all in traditional dark wood bistro style, as were the classic hooped-back chairs; both were old and worn in the best possible way. Every table had an old-fashioned wine bottle, a candle rammed into it and wax running down the sides. Ava loved it there – it made her feel like the romantic heroine of a 1970s Jilly Cooper novel enjoying an inappropriate liaison.

Her daydream vanished when she spotted Viv at a table towards the back of the room. Ava went straight over and there followed an awkward moment when she wasn't sure whether to shake Viv's hand or kiss her 'hello'. Viv immediately overcame the situation by standing up and leaning over to give her a warm hug.

'And how *are* you?' she asked, as they sat down. 'How are the plans going?'

'They seem to be going pretty well. Lauren seems alarmingly calm, although I'm still a little tense about our forthcoming flower arrangement chat.'

'She does seem relaxed, though – she seems terribly pragmatic.'

'Yes,' agreed Ava, as Viv poured her a glug of red wine. 'One thing you don't really have to put up with from Lauren is unexpected stress. She just steamrollers forward with what she wants and takes everyone else with her. But then you probably know that by now.'

'It's been a pleasure to work with you both on the dress. Honestly, it might seem like a stressful situation to you, but I'm used to starlets and brides.'

Ava gave a small internal sigh of relief.

'Anyway, you must be so busy now. Working on wedding dresses and the new series of *Strictly*. How are you fitting it all in?'

'Yours are the last two dresses I'm working on until the spring. But yes, we're working on the *Strictly* prototypes now. It's so exciting, it really is my favourite part of the series.'

'Why?'

'All those opportunities, all those fresh beginnings, so many chances ...' Viv lifted her eyes and gave a little shiver. She was clearly excited. 'You just don't know where the dresses are going. At the moment they simply represent a series of moods and emotions.'

'I suppose it's the opposite of the wedding dress. On your wedding day you want to look like you, but you in a wedding dress. No one wants to turn up at the altar looking like someone else entirely. But with these *Strictly* dresses the dancers must be relying on them to help turn them into someone else. Especially the celebs, you know, the ones known for something else altogether.'

'There's an element of that, more so at the beginning of the series. That's what's so magical about it, though – the contestants become better, their personalities start to emerge, and then they become the dances. So, by the end of the series, the dresses that I'm working on now are back to having the same kind of magic as a wedding dress: they help them be themselves, but at their very best.'

'I'd never thought of it like that. How wonderful!'

'Yes, and with the professional dancers the audience gets so used to seeing them that we need the dresses to help access different parts of their personality.'

'Yes, I see. They're all so gorgeous, though – really magical.'

'And Tess looked great, too!'

'Yes, but she would look good in anything, I suspect!'

Viv seemed such good company and Ava was so entranced by hearing about her work on the dresses that she completely forgot about the fleet of A-listers who would soon be wearing them. But before long they were talking about Ava's bridesmaid's dress. When Viv produced some updated drawings to show her, she immediately let out a sigh of relief. It turned out that Viv had already toned everything down somewhat, so that Ava was less likely to look like a corn-fed extra from an amateur dramatic production of *Jane Austen's Life Story*.

'I'm just rather conscious of being the older, unmarried sister. There's nothing wrong with that, but I know some of the parents might think otherwise. It's just, well, I'd rather look a little matronly than as if I were trying too hard. Attempting to appear younger than I am, winsome in costume, that sort of thing – it's everything I dread.'

'I understand. Really, I do. And you've seen some of the people I've worked with ...'

Ava cast her mind back over the years of anxious faces stepping onto that dance floor, looking their very best. She knew she was in safe hands and that Viv completely understood. She talked Ava through the changes she would be making, then arranged a time for her to come and try the dress on. Then they slipped back to chatting about their jobs, how they both found themselves working in creative industries with people at highly emotional stages of their lives. Wedding horror stories quickly followed, as did hoots of laughter. Ava was still slightly hoping that Viv would produce some earth-shattering nuggets of *Strictly* gossip, but nothing. All too soon, Viv caught sight of her watch.

'My goodness, the time! My poor husband ...'

'Oh no, your theatre tickets!'

'He'll be fine – I just lost track of time a bit. It's very rare to talk to a client who is interested in anything other than their own dress, you know.'

'Ooh, I hadn't thought of that,' said Ava.

'Oh, it's true,' continued Viv. But with that she was pressing a £10 note on the table and putting on her coat to leave. Ava did not have long to wait before Rob arrived. There was just time to order a bottle of water to go with the wine and enjoy the sensation of being alone, at leisure and in one of her favourite places. As he walked into the bar there was a moment before he spotted Ava, when she viewed him as a total stranger would do: a good-looking, muscular man, with the same colouring as her. His hair was dark blond, a colour Ava spent a fortune at Ruston's trying to replicate, and his eyes were a sludgy green, very similar to hers. He was tall, skinny, but not weak looking. Powerfully average. He looked flustered, though – a little different. Or was it just seeing him from this unusual perspective?

He saw her and waved, then came over to the bar table she was still sitting at. She stood up to say hi and he put his hands gently on her shoulders, leaning in, his lips pursed for a kiss.

'Is your hair longer?' she asked, after their peck.

'Yes, of course – it gets longer every day, Silly!'

'You know what I mean. Are you deliberately growing it out into a new style? Is it, you know, a thing? Or have you just not had time to get it cut lately?'

He ran a hand through it. Ava tried not to wince as an errant strand stuck out slightly to one side.

'Yeah,' he replied. 'I was just getting sick of looking so … so damn corporate.'

'Right-o.'

Ava's gaze drifted down to Rob's lower half. He was wearing new trainers, and weren't those skinny jeans? She thought of Gabe and the easy way he wore shirts and suit trousers; she had never seen him in a tie but he was certainly always dressed as an adult. There was nothing corporate about how he looked. Rob's new look was a little confusing, but this was not the time to address it.

They moved to a table in the restaurant and settled into looking at menus. Ava felt slightly overwhelmed by some of the fussier French dishes – a week of butterflies in her stomach had not done a great deal for her appetite. She decided on a steak, just as the waitress arrived.

'Are you ready to order?' she asked, as the two peered at each other over the top of their menus.

'I am,' said Ava, her head cocked at Rob.

'Yes, yes, me too.' He made a faux-courtly hand gesture towards her, inviting her to order. The waitress gave a small smile.

'I would love the steak, please,' said Ava.

'Oh, *I* was going to have the steak.'

Fast as a snake in the grass.

'We can both have it.'

'No, no! That makes no sense at all – it's just a waste.'

'Relax. If we both want it we'll both enjoy it.'

Rob ignored Ava, burrowing his face in the menu again, while she was left smiling meekly at the waitress.

'I'll have the Coq au Vin, please,' he said.

'No problem.' The waitress pursed her lips and scribbled in her notebook before moving on to side dishes and then leaving them. Ava looked at her almost longingly as she headed off to the kitchen to place their order.

Snap out of it, she told herself. And soon they were chatting amiably. Rob mentioned that he was planning to go to a gig in Bristol soon, with some friends from the squash club. Ava told him of her plans to head up and see Mel soon and how she was even hoping to go and see *Strictly*. Both agreed that it would be great if the two ended up being the same weekend and they could coordinate.

The food arrived and they both looked happy with their meals. Rob's eyes widened as he took his first mouthful, before he declared it to be as delicious as ever and offered some to Ava. She accepted before graciously cutting him a generous slice of steak.

To onlookers they must have looked like a blissfully happy couple but there was still a heaviness hanging over the meal. It was as if they were being polite for the benefit of an invisible relationship adjudicator who was judging them on 'having a good Saturday night'. And it was all perfectly civil. Ava even managed to make Rob laugh a couple of times with tales of customers and their bizarre antics in the shop. Then she took the leap and told him about her dance classes. She was braced for him to be surprised, suspicious even, or at least to give her a gentle ribbing, but it seemed as if he simply couldn't care less.

'Well, if you're enjoying it …' was as much as he could muster.

'Oh, I *love* it! I'm so glad I made the decision – it's a really fun group of people.'

'That's great news. I know you love your *Strictly*, I love my squash.'

And that was that. Ava had always known who Rob's 'squash mates' were, and what they were like. Not because she had snooped around or because she didn't trust them, but because she was interested. There was no anxiety, just a desire to be part of Rob's life. She was curious about people, she cared about Rob, and so of course she wanted a mental map of who the guys were and how they fitted together in his social circle. None of them would really become friends with her, she knew, and she had no real desire to get any closer to the wives or girlfriends. But she liked them, and was happy to know who they all were. In fact, just thinking of them reminded her of the birthday plans she was going to ask Rob about that night.

'How are all the lads?' she asked.

'Oh, they're great – had a right laugh down the pub with them last week.'

'So what do you chat about when you'e in the pub with them? Is it all squash talk, or is it, like, life stuff?'

'Dunno. What do you mean?'

171

'You know, like when I had my book club in London – it was only ever really an excuse to get together with a nice group of friends. We'd talk about the book for about half an hour before gossiping.'

'Well, we like talking about sport – that's like gossip for us.'

'Oh …'

'I suppose it's all sequins and fake tan at the dance class, isn't it? I'm going to come round in a couple of weeks and you'll be like polished mahogany.'

'Jeez, Rob, it's not like that!' Ava's voice startled even herself, coming out considerably louder that she had intended. She was shocked at how annoyed she was by his comment. 'It's just a dance class,' she muttered, hurt at the casual assumption he had made about her little gang. When she was in that room she didn't feel as if she was left out, or not good enough; she felt as if they were a little family, sharing something. And then there was Gabe. She looked down at her plate, slowly moving her knife and fork together.

'*What*?' Rob dipped his head to try and meet her eyes.

'Nothing, it's fine,' she said quietly. She knew she had to brush this slight aside or risk ruining the evening.

'Come on, *what*?'

'Honestly, it's *fine*. Nothing.'

She looked up and smiled but she could feel resentment forming a crust around her.

'Oh, come on! You can't think that dancing is anything more than for show, can you? It's hardly a sport.'

Ava thought of the sportsmen who had taken part in various series of *Strictly* over the years, how they had grown over the course of their time spent dancing; the hard work they had put in and the results they had achieved. Then there were the other stars, who had appeared on the show for a laugh and gone on to lose weight and feel fitter, to finally have some confidence in their bodies. She thought of the professional dancers themselves, the athleticism they displayed week after week, and how they could probably show the squash boys a thing or two when it came to fitness and discipline.

She thought of how she might explain this to Rob, convince him, but she couldn't quite care enough. Then she felt the tension between them tighten. Only this time it wasn't a sexy tension, more a sort of discord. Instead of those vibrations that shimmered invisibly between herself and Gabe, this was a calcifying sense of tension that might only be able to go one way.

As a result, Ava didn't manage to get round to bringing up her birthday suggestions. She didn't even feel like having a pudding. When the waitress asked if she would be having one and she declined, Rob threw his hands up in mild exasperation.

'Well, we'd better get the bill then,' he said, rolling his eyes at the waitress.

'Have a pudding if you'd like one. There's no rush – I'm just full, that's all.'

'No, no, no! There isn't any point in my sitting here eating if you're not, is there? The bill, please.'

Ava watched him glance at the waitress's tight black skirt as she left the table. Again she found herself too numb to protest. When the waitress returned with the bill, Rob dramatically threw the last of the red wine into his glass and plonked his card on the small white saucer. Ava reached for her wallet, but Rob held a hand out.

'No, no! This one's on me.' He winked at the waitress conspiratorially, betraying the fact that this act of sudden chivalry was perhaps more to impress her than Ava.

'Thank you, darling,' she replied, touching his hand.

The waitress seemed not to notice this territorial gesture. Nor did Rob. He stood up and shrugged, then lifted his jacket from the back of the chair and headed out via the bar. Ava got up to follow him, walking through the restaurant a couple of steps behind like a sullen geisha. After the earlier cordial mood she now felt as if she was wearing a huge sandwich board with 'Couple with Problems' scribbled on it. As she headed through the bar she accidentally slammed her handbag into a fellow drinker's arm. She immediately turned back to apologise and realised that it was Jenny Miller, sitting there with Barry.

'I'm *so* sorry' said Ava, as she looked back.

'*Ava!*' said Jenny. 'Not at all, don't you worry.'

'I didn't hurt you, did I?'

'No, I'm fine. How are you, dear?'

'I'm so glad you're okay. I'm fine, too. Isn't this a lovely evening?' Ava was genuinely pleased to see Jenny and happy to have the chance to chat.

'Yes, it is, dear. And it's a delight to see you.'

'You too! Are you well?'

'Oh yes, dear – we've had a lovely week. Have to find a way to fill up our Saturday evenings until the *Strictly* live shows start up again, though.'

'Ha! Well, yes, exactly – what do you think of the line-up?'

'It's really superb, isn't it? There are a few who I think show real promise. And I rather like the look of that new chap …'

'Pasha?'

'Yes, him! He danced beautifully in that final routine and I've been reading all about him on the site. A welcome addition.'

'Well, Jenny, if he has your seal of approval I'm sure he will go far!' replied Ava, as Jenny chuckled.

Rob, having collected his credit card, had turned and noticed that Ava was no longer following him. She looked up at him expectantly, hoping he would come over and say hello. Instead he lingered at the doorway, fiddling with his phone.

'I've been having dinner with my, er, Rob.'

'Oh.' Jenny glanced over at him. He did not look up. Barry smiled at them both with an expression that can only be achieved after years of knowing the best moment to duck out of a women's conversation. On the other hand, Jenny looked a little surprised. *Was it a surprise that Ava had a boyfriend or that Rob was Ava's boyfriend?* she wondered.

'It looks like he's ready to leave, dear,' she said.

'Yes, it does rather.'

'I'll see you Monday, though.'

'Of course, you have a lovely weekend ...'

On the drive home Ava made an attempt to explain who Jenny was but Rob seemed even less interested than he had been earlier and carried on scrolling through details on his phone. As she turned the key in the door there was an awkward pause. Where once there had been a rush to hang coats up before kissing in the hallway and then making their way upstairs without so much as stopping to turn on the downstairs light, now there was nothing. Ava put her hands together and said, 'Well, I feel like a little whisky now I'm out of the car. *You*?'

'Go on, then,' he replied.

Ava grabbed the bottle from the table in the sitting room and went to the kitchen for glasses. As she reached for the glasses she heard her phone buzzing in her bag. After 10 p.m. on a Saturday night was a strange time to be getting a message, so she reached for the phone.

Are you around? I really need to talk. Mel

Ava dialled as she poured two fingers of whisky into each glass. Rob had seized the brief pause and used it to hijack the TV. His feet were up and he had already managed to find a channel showing the latest from the Rugby World Cup. Ava didn't even know her TV had that channel as part of her cable package, but Rob was transfixed. She handed him a glass as Mel answered. Her voice was quivering.

'Ava?'

'Hey, what's going on?'

'It's Rich.'

'Is he okay?'

'He's having an affair.'

'*What?*'

'I *know*.'

Ava pulled a chair out from the kitchen table and sat down, fiddling with the lid of the whisky.

'Are you sure?' she asked gently.

'Of course I'm sure.'

'How did you find out?'

'The idiot left his phone on the kitchen counter and a text arrived – from a woman, saying she missed him.'

'That's hardly proof of an affair, Sweetie.'

And then it all came tumbling out. Since spotting the text Mel had been checking up on Rich frantically – his Twitter feed, his emails when she had the chance, calling his office with ever more bizarre reasons to get him out of meetings. Eventually she had become entirely convinced that he was having a full-blown affair and confronted him about it. His head had indeed been turned by someone and there had been what he described as 'an incident' at a sales conference, but he had promised it was a mistake – nothing more than a symptom of bringing up young children in a recession, of lack of communication combined with too much communication, of anything but true love on his part. He swore he still loved Mel.

'And do you still love him?' asked Ava.

'Yes. Of course.'

'Do you still fancy him?'

'Not right now, but yes. And he swears he does me.'

'Then you need to take the advice you gave me not so long ago: invest in yourself a little to get your confidence back up. Don't lie around whinging. Get a grip, get a manicure, get a haircut … Make sure you get up every day and remind yourself this is what you want. It's what you chose, and it's what you enjoy. You can make it work – it's just all part and parcel of adulthood, isn't it?'

'Yes, I know. And I know I've been a total nag recently.'

'Hold on! That's nothing to be ashamed of. You're trying to get two kids to school every day – you need to be a bit of a nag.'

'I suppose …'

'But you also need fun and you sound so low.'

'I do! I feel as if someone's punched me in the stomach. Honestly, I looked at my hand for ten minutes earlier and I barely recognise it as mine.'

'Do you want me to come up and see you, sooner rather than later? We need that girlie weekend!'

'Yes, please. Come up as soon as you can, anyway. Let's not worry about the fact we haven't got *Strictly* live show tickets. I'm longing to go – you know how much of a treat that would be – but it's seeing you I want more than anything else in the world. Can we just flop onto the sofa and watch it together, and have the big chats once we've had our fill of sequins and glitterballs?'

'Of course.'

'I don't want some kind of ghastly emergency summit. Just hanging out would be great, though.'

'I totally understand and I'm on the case. I'll email you as soon as I've spoken to Matt tomorrow.'

They hatched a plan that they would leave it a couple of weekends so the family could spend some time together, but then Ava would head to London in a week or two when Rich went up to visit his parents for a family do that Mel was ducking out of. They said goodbye to each other fondly, each reassuring the other that everything would be okay after all.

Ava hung up feeling shaken. Mel and Rich had been together for so long, over a decade. After her own parents' marriage, this was the one that Ava had been most convinced would last forever. And, better than that, she had been completely sure of the fact that they were happy, not just settling. It was hard for her to even comprehend the fact that their relationship could come loose in this way. She felt a surge of relief that she had Rob. *The grass wasn't always greener after all. Sometimes you should just treasure what you have*, she reminded herself. *Turning your gaze elsewhere could leave your happiness unattended.*

She went into the sitting room and sat down beside Rob.

'Hey, guess what, this guy's on *Strictly*! He's one of yours now …' He pointed at the screen, now showing one of the presenters: an ex-rugby player turned TV star. The man was giving commentary on one of the matches, while taking a bit of ribbing about his new role from colleagues.

'You're right,' said Ava, snuggling into the crook of his arm. 'He's one of my team now, a *Strictly* boy. He's weeks away from increased agility, national heart-throb status and a wardrobe of body-hugging Lycra. Just you wait and watch!'

At this, he chuckled to himself as if it was the craziest thing he'd ever heard, as if he was completely unaware of the previous years' stars and their achievements. Ava knew it was too late to try and persuade him. *Maybe this year he would just see it for himself*, she thought.

The programme ended and Rob flicked off the TV, then turned and kissed her. Ava kissed him back, suddenly reminded of all the reasons why she had fallen for him in the first place. Guilt flooded over her as she thought of the pain she had heard Mel in and the fact that she had even considered treating Rob in the same way. She held him tightly, stroked his face and passed a hand over his hair. He stopped kissing her and paused. They looked at each other a moment and then he took her by the hand and led her upstairs.

Later that night when Rob had gone back downstairs to fetch her a glass of water, Ava turned over in bed, smiling and calm. She saw her phone on the bedside table and reached for it. Flicking it on, she scrolled to Facebook, where she terminated her friendship status with Gabe.

There were some dance steps she didn't need to become accustomed to.

Chapter 10

The Twist of an Ankle

Breezy. That was Ava's new watchword, almost a superpower. And she planned to stick to it. If there was a way that she was going to get through the awkwardness of tonight's dance class, then breeziness is what it would take. Breezy, like the autumn – light, airy, blowing away the dead leaves to create fresh, crisp days. This was the sort of breeze she would emulate as she turned up. She loved this time of year anyway, and now she was about to bring some of that levity into her life.

Yes, she was a busy, happy woman, confident in her work and light on her feet. She would calmly, briskly float through the lives of others, leaving them refreshed but not shaken up. Yes, she could be this woman. She *would* be this woman.

And she made a good fist of being that woman all day on Monday. She put any thoughts of Gabe to the very back of her mind, locked them tightly in a box and covered it in heavy velvet. No looking back. She was now looking forward: a good boss, a good friend and a good girlfriend. All day long customers were grinned at, suppliers chatted with and corporate clients called and checked in on, some given extra flourishes with their order. Even Matt was indulged, lavished with tea and biscuits, and his request for time off cleared without query. She even offered to close up for him and left the shop with barely enough time to get to the Working Men's Club in time for class.

This week Ava was in more relaxed clothes than she had dared to wear before. No more silk dresses, no more favourite dresses, no more 'just popping home for a quick shower'. Tonight she was in the same pair of leggings she had been wearing all day at the shop and had simply replaced the baggy shirt she had had on earlier with a long grey marl off-the-shoulder sweatshirt. Her only concession to glamour was to make sure that she was wearing a pretty bra with straps that might be acceptable for public consumption, if glimpsed. But that was more out of politeness than anything else. The look was supposed to be 'casual *Flashdance* meets JLo on the school run', but she couldn't help but feel the whole ensemble had a slight whiff of 'I've taken a sickie on account of my dreadful hangover'. *If that was the case*, she breezily told herself, *then so be it*. She was a busy working woman who could not afford to keep skipping around town in flouncy dresses for the benefit of others. Her hair was tied up messily in a butterfly clip, no ponytail this week. On her feet were the Gabbarini dance shoes she had ordered online after getting a dreadful blister last week.

There was no waiting in the car. This time she screeched into the car park, locked up and galloped up the steps and straight into the hall. She plonked her handbag down and sat next to Rockingham, who, uncharacteristically, was holding forth in front of half the class. It turned out he was something of an authority on dance. He had never really piped up before in any of the previous lessons, but had suddenly found his voice and was standing by the door with Minx and Dobby, gesticulating and explaining like a latterday Peter Ustinov.

It turned out he had been to Spain with his late wife to watch some Tango championships. 'A glorious time,' he said, with a wistful gaze. 'Such a happy, happy trip.' He brought 1970s Spain to life as he told his ever-increasing audience about the various rules governing by the dance scene over there and some of the more magical outdoor dance spectacles he had seen. The way he spoke about his wife Grace was respectful, but dreamy. It was as if that forty-year chunk of his life before she died had been a blissful clerical error he couldn't believe he had got away with. Even the Hanburys were temporarily mesmerised, tightly holding hands as if to say, 'that will never happen to us'. But the goodwill that his story exuded was infectious and before long they were properly introduced and chatting to the group for the first time.

'I've been meaning to compliment you on your shop,' said Jessica Hanbury, finally looking Ava in the eye. 'It's absolutely gorgeous, so wonderful to have something like that bang in the centre of town.'

'Thank you,' she replied, blushing from the roots of her hair. 'That's really very kind. I do work hard on it, so it's great when people appreciate it.'

'If only it wasn't quite so nice,' replied her husband Nick. 'I'm forever having to send my PA in there to get bouquets for Jessie!' Ava would probably never know for sure, but in that split second she was sure that she saw the pale shadow of a frown as Jessica seemed to realise it wasn't Nick who had been selecting all of those peony bouquets. Either way, Ava would never tell. She was wise enough now to pretend she had never seen these things. Breezy.

A moment later Patrice arrived. Tonight he was wearing slightly higher shoes than normal. Cuban heels? Ava could not quite tell without tipping her head rather obviously. His hair had the sheen of a man who was comfortable with spending an hour or so with his own reflection, getting it 'just so'. And last week's more formal shirt had been replaced with another T-shirt with a daring 'V'. Again, the chest cleavage, the small sprouts of chest hair, the swagger.

We're well into autumn, what are you playing at? Ava found herself wondering. But as he gave that confident clap at the front of the class, she realised she loved him just the way he was. After all, who wants a dance instructor who looks as if he might be happier in a chemistry lab? At least he was fulfilling the role to his very best. He was living the spirit of *Strictly*, bringing it to Wiltshire for Ava and her new friends, and she appreciated him for that.

'Ladies and gentleman!' he said, legs astride, clapping in that commanding way of his. Ava smiled to herself as she turned to face him. 'Your attention, please! Nothing less than 100 per cent focus will do, because today is the Cha Cha Cha. We're flirty. Today we are all flirty, each and every one of us. Because the Cha Cha Cha is all about flirting! Are you up to it?'

The Hanburys smiled coyly at each other. Ava wanted to roll her eyes but chose to pretend she hadn't noticed. And where was Gabe? Oh, it didn't matter! *Breezy*, she told herself. *Breezy*. She tried to ignore the word 'flirty' now reverberating around the room.

'People, I would like you just for a moment to close your eyes and follow me. We're in a town square in 1950s Cuba. Yes, you're hot and thirsty and you've been trying all day to get the attention of the one you want. That's it – you've all got your eyes closed now. No peeking! You can feel the heat prickling your skin, taste the rum on your tongue, and you can smell the cigars and the gasolene in the street! You've given everything you've got to catch the eye of this one, you really have thrown everything you can at this chase ... so much so that you're now going to start a dance that requires five steps in four beats. Yes, people: the Cha Cha Cha! We're in Cuba. This is not a dance suited to the Wiltshire countryside – we are elsewhere! Don't forget, you *deserve* to be elsewhere!'

What only moments earlier had seemed like an excruciating corporate away-day trust exercise now started to feel like a free holiday. Patrice's descriptions really were transporting Ava to a world where she believed the Cha Cha Cha was a viable option.

'Keep those eyes closed, ladies and gentlemen! Keep yourselves in Cuba. You've fancied him or her for ages, so long. You've been yearning for him. You have caught glimpses, you have exchanged glances, shared moments, but you never truly got them! You keep seeing them flirt with other people, so now you're going to use dance to get their attention. Dance! The Cha Cha Cha!'

Ava was still standing there, her arms curled round herself as if she would somehow be protected in the event of everyone else opening their eyes and laughing at her. Steadily her heart rate was rising as she slipped further into the Cha Cha Cha fantasy. She tried to imagine the scene Patrice was describing: she saw a man in a Caribbean market square. He had dark, curly hair. She quickly replaced him with colouring more like Rob's Nordic pallor. Then, in a flash of defiance, she switched him back. *Why should this imaginary man not be allowed to have dark hair? He. Is. Imaginary. We're in Cuba, after all.* She smiled and hugged herself a little tighter, her heart now thundering away against her crossed arms. She wondered if the rest of the class would be able to hear it soon.

Suddenly, there was a bang in the hallway. She ignored it as she imagined her Cuban scene shaping up. In the Cuba of her mind she really was wearing a rather short skirt and her legs seemed impossibly long, as if she was staring at them through an amazingly flattering mirror. She took a deep breath, trying to calm her heart, which was now banging like a drum. It didn't help. That wasn't the smell of cigars around her: it was vetiver and leather. And no, they weren't in Cuba, they were here in the room. Just as she exhaled, she felt a warm, solid hand on her upper arm. For a moment, just a moment, she left her eyes closed and

186

waited until she could tell he had passed. Then she opened them. She flicked her head back with a flourish that seemed far more coquettish than she had intended and there he was, standing right behind her.

'Hi,' he mouthed, with a smile.

'Hi Gabe,' she replied, before turning back to face the front. Breezy.

'That was great, team,' continued Patrice. 'I feel as if we're all in Cuba now.'

He gave a crinkly-nosed grin and started to pace the room between where they were all standing. 'So, the Latin-style Cha Cha Cha! It's a dance primarily on beat *two*.' His hands gave another booming clap on the word 'two'. 'You are converting your timing. Don't worry too much about what that means for now, we'll see it clearer later. What you need to know for the moment is that this is one of the five Latin-style dances. The steps are compact, there is no rise and fall.'

Minx and Dobby caught each other's eyes and sniggered. Ava looked down at her shoes – she just couldn't let her mind drift in that direction. *Breezy*, she told herself once again.

'We are all about *strooooong* hip movements with this dance,' continued Patrice. 'The leg is straightening on the half beat. We are moving from the hip here. If you think you are not friends with your hips right now, now is the time to amend this – you need to be working together. May I suggest you close your eyes again, take a big, deep breath in and out again.'

Ava was convinced she felt his breath tickle her hair. *Breezy.*

'Find your hips,' continued Patrice. 'Say hello to them. Get ready. Are you ready?' A pause. 'Class, I think we are ready. I would like you to take the same partners as last time, please, and to take your positions. Don't worry – I'm going to explain to you what those positions are. Gentlemen, you need to face your partner and to place your right hand on her side, just below her left shoulder. Rockingham, that's glorious! You have more experience in this than I had given you credit for.'

'Thank you,' replied Rockingham. It seemed as if Class Legend status was incoming for Rocky since his earlier moment in the sun. Meanwhile, Dobby beamed at having briefly basked in the glow of Patrice's attention.

'Ladies,' continued Patrice. 'Your right hand should be on his left arm at the shoulder, and your partner should by now have your left hand. That's looking wonderful!'

Indeed it was. Ava was now facing Gabe, although even in her new heels his height meant that they were not quite at each other's eye level. She was staring directly at his lips. Those lips …

'Good week?' she asked quietly. He wrinkled his nose as if to say 'not really' and opened his mouth to speak. Too late! 'Less of the chat at the back, please, you two!' said Patrice almost immediately. They were left smiling at each other, the alliance re-formed. And so the lesson continued.

Ava made a good attempt at maintaining the breeziness, but it was hard. It was not like trying to be a fresh-faced but polite librarian, or even a slightly distracted butcher. This was the Cha Cha Cha – the whole dance was a massive tease. Even at their most basic level it was impossible not to feel the Cuban beat, the enforced flirtation coursing through their every movement. All of the feelings that Ava had cherished so very much on Saturday night seemed to be draining away like sand through a child's fingers. That gentle tenderness, the safety, the sense of a solid, shared connection that had made her wake up on Sunday morning glowing with contentment: where was it now? It was suddenly replaced, memories taunted by the energy and passion of the situation in hand. The ins, the outs, the laughter, hips against hips! Oh, it was impossible, as if they really were on some sort of Cuban mini break. The beat throbbed, their hands gripped and Gabe's eyes danced throughout. Every time he pulled her a little closer than perhaps she intended, both of them pretended it was the dance they were concentrating on: the steps, the hold, that straight leg on the beat. But, well, breeziness was somewhat more than a challenge.

Just as they were getting along so well, Ava felt a slight nagging at the back of her head. Why had she de-friended him so impulsively on Facebook – what was the good in that? It was so sudden, so definite, so difficult to undo. Now it would almost certainly be creating more tension. If ever there was the action of a guilty conscience this was it. *Has he logged on and noticed yet?* she found herself wondering. *And if not, why not? Why has he not tried to contact me again and realised we aren't friends?* Her heart thundered on, matched only by the beat from the considerably more powerful sound system that Patrice had brought with him this time. But despite all of these distractions, this was by a considerable margin the dance that she had found easiest to pick up. It was almost as if her feet knew what they wanted to do already. The lesson ended with laughter and applause for each other, followed by Patrice letting out a whoop and thanking them all for 'accompanying him to Cuba'.

'Never mind Cuba, some of you could be on *Strictly*!' said Jenny Miller with a warm smile.

'Thank you for such a great lesson,' said Ava, clapping back at Patrice. She was determined to regain that breezy stance and to get out of the hall as fast as possible before anything unpredictable happened. Now she leant over and gave Gabe a brief peck on the cheek.

'See you next week,' she said lightly. Eyebrows raised, grin fixed.

It was only as she pulled away that she realised this was the first time they had actually kissed. Somehow it had been easier for her to break that seal, to lean in and touch his face with her lips on her own terms than to keep imagining it. The simmering tension created by replaying the possibilities had exhausted her enough and she was glad to have brought a sudden end to it. On the other hand, Gabe seemed a little shell-shocked and was saying nothing, his mouth slightly gaping like a somnolent fish.

Ava grabbed her bag and scampered out of the hall into the car park, but as she stood there at her car door she rummaged around in her bag and realised that she couldn't find any keys at all. Sheepishly she went back into the building, which was now significantly emptier as others were getting into their own vehicles. She looked around the room – there they were, on the table, where they had clearly spun out of her bag when she had plonked it down before. She went into the room and reached for them. Patrice was still in there, just straightening the tables and turning out the lights, making sure everything was as it should be. She smiled at him, gave him a quick 'goodnight' and headed back out towards the exit.

As she passed the ladies', Jenny Miller was heading out of the room. She looked up and gave her a broad smile.

'How are you, my dear? It was such a delight to see you at the weekend. I hope the rest of your evening was good?'

'Hi Jenny,' replied Ava. 'Yes, it was a real treat to see you both. And I'm fine! I had a lovely weekend. I just wish I could dance as beautifully as you do – you make it look completely effortless. Apart from that I'm absolutely fine!'

Jenny held the door open for her. She was as willowy as ever and was today wearing an expensive-looking scarf festooned around her neck. A pair of long silver earrings dangled between it and her elegant ears. For a moment they stood smiling at each other at the top of the steps heading down from the Working Men's Club. Ava looked across the small car park to where she had been standing a minute ago. Now, in her place, was Gabe. He seemed to be waiting for her. She bit her bottom lip and made a move as if to head down the steps.

But at that moment Jenny put her hand out. Gently, but firmly, Ava was stopped. She looked up at Jenny, who had now moved her hand.

'Ava, darling, do you know what I might advise?' the older woman said, smiling.

Ava frowned, unnerved but still curious.

'No, what?'

'An affair.'

This was not the Cha Cha Cha advice that Ava had thought she was about to be given. It was not at all what she was expecting to hear. An affair? Her thoughts flashed back to Mel, sitting in her kitchen sobbing while Ava tried to console her. Then there was Rich, doing as he pleased in some non-specific hotel suite. But Jenny held Ava's gaze. Calm, but consistent nonetheless.

'Oh, it's a dreadful thing, feeling underappreciated,' she said. 'And sometimes an affair can help. Discretion is of course paramount, though.'

Ava stared at her shoes for a minute, then up towards Gabe.

'I'm just not sure what ...'

'Darling, I saw you on Saturday evening. And I've seen you here. I would not presume to say it's an either/or situation, but in my experience a partner doesn't need to find out about an affair. It can be most cathartic: it changes you, your aura.'

Ava noticed in Jenny something of the 1970s hippy that she hadn't seen before. All of the dancing had got in the way earlier, but suddenly it was as clear as day. She was no Greenwich Village cliché but there was a definite whiff of the mung bean about her. It had been that word: aura. How could having an affair change an aura? *Oh Jenny, you've lived near Glastonbury for too long*, she wanted to say. But she held back, lest she unleash a wealth of advice on macraméd organic aubergines and chi readings. Instead, she gave a small sniff of a laugh.

'Thank you, Jenny – I really do appreciate your advice but I'm sure I'll be fine.'

'Oh, you'll *always* be fine, darling. Of that I'm sure. But I've seen your spirit. You might have forgotten it a little, but I can see it: you can be better than fine. You can be marvellous, darling, marvellous!'

Jenny had taken Ava's hands in hers. Her hands were cool and dry. It was surprisingly calming, especially considering the exertions of the last hour and a half.

Ava looked back at Jenny, strangely touched by this demonstration of faith from someone who was barely more than a stranger. In the maelstrom of admin and emotion surrounding Lauren's wedding no one in her family seemed to have stopped to think that she might deserve or want anything more than what she had already in Rob. It was so curious that it was someone she hardly knew who was pointing this out to her.

In the car park others were slamming doors and driving off. Patrice appeared at the top of the steps, locking up the main doors behind them.

'Okay, ladies?'

'Yes thanks, Patrice,' replied Jenny. 'I was just giving Ava here some advice on her steps.' She gave Ava a quick wink.

Ava turned to them. 'Thank you both so much but I must dash now.' She held up her keys and dangled them in front of them, then bounced down the steps towards her car.

'Breezy does it,' she muttered to herself under her breath.

'How can I help?' she asked Gabe, who was now running a hand through those locks again.

'Well, and I appreciate I might be stepping out of line here ...'

He sounded hesitant, nervous, unsure of what he was going to say, and so Ava leapt on the silence like a predatory animal to seize the initiative.

'Ah, yes! A meeting. Yes, let's do it. Let's have a coffee some time – I'd love that. How often are you in town? Do you live nearby?' She was rattling through words, desperate not to let him say too much. He seemed wrong-footed by her sudden enthusiasm. Breeziness was more powerful than Ava had realised.

'Well, yes, I, er, live relatively nearby. And I'm in Salisbury at least three times a week at the moment. How does that, erm, sound?'

'Great. I can take time out whenever I want, really – afternoons are fine. Let's say Wednesday?'

She was now sitting in the driver's seat, her keys jangling in the ignition.

'Right then, okay – that sounds great.'

Jenny and Barry were pulling out of the car park. She was in the passenger seat, calm and still as ever. As they drove past Ava, she turned and gave her a slow-eyed wink.

She was so composed it was almost reptilian, but Ava trusted that it was meant with warmth.

'Perfect! Well, just call the Dunne's number if there are any problems. If not, let's meet there.'

But Gabe wasn't moving. In fact, he put one hand on the roof of the car and leaned in. The curls all flopped now and Ava got another sudden waft of his scent.

'One more thing ...' he said, his face now very close to hers.

'Yes?'

'I have some tickets.'

A pause.

'To London,' he continued. 'To go and see *Strictly*.'

Ava felt her pulse quicken. This seemed very unfair. Her mind was racing. How could he possibly have known how much she wanted to go this year? She felt sick with excitement and nerves. To see the show live would be a dream come true, but to see it without Mel, especially with her friend in the state she was ... And anyway, how could she possibly explain it to Rob? Thoughts were whizzing through her mind faster than she could possibly articulate. She had to buy herself some time.

'Right?' was all she could manage.

'And I wondered if you would like to go with me.'

'To London?'

'Yes.'

'To *Strictly*?'

'Yes. To one of the live shows.'

'With *you*?'

'Well, yes.'

'Hmm …' Ava looked straight ahead, her hands gripping the steering wheel, avoiding his gaze.

'No need to get overexcited …'

'No, that's a very kind offer. It's just that …' Her voice trailed off. How could she possibly say what she wanted to say? She imagined herself shrieking: *I have a boyfriend! I can't just skip off to London for the weekend with you, no matter how much I think that sounds like the absolute dream and exactly what Jenny was suggesting just then. Oh, my God! Now it all seems to make so much sense …*

'It's okay, it was a rather extreme suggestion anyway.' He looked down at his shoes.

'No, I'd love to. Really.' Ava looked up at him from the driving seat. She just wanted to lean forward and brush the hair from his face. 'It's just that I have so much on – I have the shop on Saturdays, I have a lot of family stuff going on. It's just …' Her voice faded out. She had entirely lost the thread of what she was saying, unable to articulate what she really wanted, or needed. She looked down at her lap, breeziness suddenly gone. Wherever she turned she felt trapped, with everyone else making the decisions for her.

'I'm sorry,' he said, with an attempt at a grin. 'I shouldn't have just blurted it out like that.' He was jangling his own car keys frantically now. Ava looked at him and saw that behind the clear skin and the glossy curls he looked tired. He was far from the suave stranger who had come into her shop a month ago. An icicle of conscience needled inside of

196

her: had she been seeing no more than she wanted to see in him? Had she upset him?

'You didn't blurt it out, and it was a really sweet offer. I wish I could say yes, but I just think … this time I can't. But thank you. Thank you *so* much. We can just chat about it more on Wednesday, no?'

'Yes. Yes, I would love that.' He leaned in and kissed her goodnight on the cheek. She closed her eyes and felt his curls brush against her face.

'Wednesday, then.'

But Wednesday never came. Despite the fact that Ava spent no less than forty minutes in front of the mirror that morning, doing her very best to look casual and yet alluring as possible. Then she spent the day in the shop trying particularly hard not to spill any mucky flower water, not to lift too much and or to get sweaty in the process. At lunchtime she only popped out for five minutes and got a small salad for the first time in ages – her stomach was simply too knotted to manage any more. Over the last couple of days she had slowly come to the realisation that this ridiculous crush on Gabe was just a reaction to the wedding, making her question too much. Now she needed to tread carefully and make sure she did not lose someone who might be a good friend.

She had planned to go to a different coffee shop to her usual place, one round behind the cathedral. That day she just didn't feel like seeing too many familiar faces. A calm cup of coffee in central Salisbury, that's what she needed and that's what they would have.

After rinsing out the plate she had eaten on in the tiny sink at the back of the shop, Ava rummaged around in her handbag for a lipstick. Weekday lipstick was not a 'regular feature' for her, and she suspected this was something Matt might notice, particularly as there was a bit of a lull in customers.

'So, have you got any big surfing plans coming up?' she asked, keen to sound as casual as possible.

'Oh yes, I have,' he replied with a grin. 'I want to go to the South of France – as soon as I can, really. We've been saving all summer.'

'For the trip?' asked Ava, now twirling the lipstick in her hand.

'Yeah, we've been properly squirrelling it away – the summer lasts so much longer on the coast down there, and Amy's wanted to go pretty much since we met. She says the food's amazing. And the lavender.'

'I went as a teenager,' said Ava, the lid now off her lipstick. 'I do remember it was very beautiful, but I don't think I even knew what surfing was back then. Or if I did, I must have thought they were only allowed to do it in California.'

'Yeah, I think my mum still believes that,' said Matt with a chuckle.

Ava seized her moment as Matt bent down to straighten some pots of lavender on the display at the front of the shop. She flipped open the lid of her compact and applied her lipstick neatly before pressing her lips together, then she snapped the lid back on the lipstick and closed her compact.

'When are you hoping to take the time off?' she asked nonchalantly when Matt turned around. True to form, he was oblivious to the fact that she'd done it, and soon they were talking dates.

'Look, if you've saved up, you should go as soon as you can and you should take a decent amount of time off,' she encouraged him.

Matt looked at her doubtfully.

'Seriously – I've got someone in mind to come in and help out on Saturdays and she could do some hours with me during the week if you went. You've never taken a proper holiday and you've really earned one this summer.'

'You're sure?' asked Matt.

'Of course! Listen, I'm the boss, aren't I? I'm going to call this girl, Minx, later and we'll sort something out – a quiet afternoon when she can come in and you can show her the ropes.'

'That would be awesome – and you look great today, by the way.'

Ava let out a girlish giggle, unsure whether Matt was just teasing her because of his thoughtfulness or if she really did look a little bit lovelier than usual.

The customer lull continued for a further half hour and Ava started to feel restless, hoping someone would come in and distract Matt. She wanted to be able to slip away shortly before three o'clock, implying she had some sort of corporate meeting that she had forgotten to mention.

Instead, the minute hand on the clock crawled round and Matt continued some lighthearted banter about Amy's driving lessons.

'I don't know what the instructor tells her,' he said, 'but every time I get in the car with her she is suddenly so tense. I mean, it's just a car. It really is just a car.'

'I hated learning to drive, though,' mumbled Ava, absent-mindedly pushing her cuticles away from her fingernails. 'You forget how terrifying it was so quickly. My first experience was a nightmare, a total nightmare.'

'But Amy says she likes her teacher.'

'Maybe that's the problem – wanting to please the teacher, wanting you to be proud of her.'

'I suppose …' Matt sounded doubtful. Ava watched the second hand on her watch creep a couple of millimetres across.

'What you should do is keep it breezy, don't let it become emotional.'

Ava suddenly realised that perhaps the advice she was giving was no longer for Amy, but for herself. She dug her fingernails into her palms – in and out, in and out, like a pulse.

'You're right, O wise one,' said Matt. 'I'm going to be like a charming robot next time I get in a car with her – like, seriously unemotional, but also dead charming. What was it you said?'

'Breezy, keep it breezy.'

'Breezy it is.'

Matt gave Ava a big nod, and as he did so they noticed a stout, middle-aged woman approaching the shop door.

200

'Good afternoon, Madam,' said Matt with a grin as she entered. But the woman did not grin back. She was wearing a stiff tweed skirt and a green anorak with small padded diamond shapes on it. Her hair was cropped short in a style that her hairdresser can only have heard described as 'no nonsense' when she chose it.

'Daffodils,' was all she said.

'*Daffodils?*' replied Matt. 'You're after daffodils?'

Ava glanced at her watch and realised it was now or never for a discreet getaway.

'Yes, daffodils,' the woman was telling Matt.

'Well, Madam, we don't tend to have them at this time of year,' he began, as Ava lifted her jacket from the hook at the back of the shop and reached for her handbag under the desk area. Matt's eyes widened in alarm as he saw her prepare to leave and so she turned to her laptop to check for emails before heading out, not wanting him to think she was leaving him in the lurch.

'They are very much a spring thing ...' Matt continued.

'I'd like some daffodils for my kitchen table ...' the woman repeated.

As Ava looked at her laptop screen Matt's voice, calmly trying to explain to the woman that she would never be able to find daffodils for her kitchen in September, seemed to fade into the background, suddenly irrelevant. Because there it was in her in-box: Gabriel Monroe. He had sent it to the public email address for the shop so it was written in a slightly more formal tone than those Facebook messages had been. Or was it the contents of the message itself that meant he was suddenly using this tone?

Dear Ava, I'm terribly sorry, but I'm not going to be able to make our appointment on Wednesday. Please accept my sincerest apologies and I look forward to seeing you as usual on Monday evening. I do hope the week is treating you well.
Best wishes, Gabriel

Ava frowned, then let her body sag, wondering what she could possibly do with all of the excess adrenaline now rushing through her body. She had her jacket on now and quickly realised that she couldn't stay within the confines of the shop with the woman still banging on about her daffodils. Not with Gabe's abrupt words ringing in her ears.

'Just popping out for stamps!' she spluttered before heading out of the shop, across the square and to the coffee shop, where she had been planning to meet him.

Once there, she ordered a cup of tea and sat for five minutes, trying to gather her thoughts. They wouldn't be gathered, though: they simply wouldn't. After ten minutes of staring at her tea as it went cold she returned to the shop without any stamps and tried to get on with the rest of the day as best she could.

Later that evening, as she went for one of her last dusk runs of the year, she wondered if she had done anything wrong. Had she offended him by saying that she did not want to go to London with him? Was it the Facebook thing? Maybe something else she hadn't even considered? It was all starting to feel like a bit of a mess. Her aura, as Jenny would put it, was not benefiting in the slightest.

Either way, they could have it out on Monday, she told herself in the shower as the water cascaded through her hair and down her back.

She sent a chirpy reply to his email, making sure that she included her mobile telephone number at the bottom. And then ... silence. He wasn't there on Monday, or the Monday afterwards; he just seemed to have vanished. Meanwhile, life plodded onwards: the shop, the wedding plans, the gentle progression of autumn ... Suddenly all of those chances, all those possibilities seemed to have vanished. Life felt as if it were closing up again. All those choices, all those chances had been so fleeting. She hadn't really seen them when she had them, and now they had vanished. Life, it seemed, could turn like the twist of an ankle.

Chapter 11

A Fresh Start

Rob was waiting in the car when the girls finally emerged from Viv's house, giggling and clutching magazines, hair products and notebooks. He didn't look up but carried on scrolling through whatever he was looking at on his phone. The radio was on rather too loud for a vehicle parked in a residential street, especially given that the windows were down. As she approached the car, the track playing was not one Ava recognised. Rob's spare hand was on the outside of the vehicle, his fingers tapping away on the car door to the beat of the music.

'So what's the deal with his hair?' asked Lauren as they walked towards him. 'It's, erm, rather different.'

'Yes. Yes, it is,' agreed Ava.

'It's, quite … Well, it's quite mid-life crisis-y, isn't it?' continued Lauren, tugging slightly at her sister's sleeve, trying to hold her back to finish the discussion before they reached the car.

'Well, it's just a bit longer. But I can see your point.'

'So what's going on?'

'Look, this isn't a conversation we can have now.'

'Okay.' Lauren held her hands up defensively and they both turned back to wave goodbye to Viv, who was visible at the window of her studio room.

Ava got into the front seat of the car, then leaned over to give Rob a big kiss on the cheek as she sat down, eager to prove to Lauren that there wasn't anything too serious to worry about. Lauren eased herself into the back seat, casting a quick glance around her, but saying nothing about the state of the car. She didn't need to. For all her attempted subtlety, it was written all over her face that the back seat of a small eight-year-old Polo just wasn't the same as gliding through the countryside in an Audi. Ava pretended not to notice and turned the dial down gently on the car stereo.

These minor details aside, the day had been an outstanding success. What's more, it had presented Ava with the first glimpse of proper wedding magic and a sense of romance that had certainly been lacking from the plans thus far. When the girls had arrived at Viv's, Ava had been the first to try on her dress and she was genuinely thrilled with the results. Gone were the dreaded matronly heaviness and the threat of mutton dressed as lamb to be replaced by smooth, classic lines. Seeing the dress in the admittedly gorgeous fabric that Lauren had chosen also made a huge difference. It was now a dress that was unmistakably one to be worn in the English countryside, but no longer did it have even a trace of the amateur dramatic costume that had been making Ava so anxious.

She didn't dare admit it in front of Lauren before she had tried her own dress on, but it actually made her look rather beautiful. Best of all, Lauren seemed to genuinely and openheartedly think so herself. She squealed with delight when Ava stepped out from behind the elegant grey silk screen in Viv's studio room, filled with trepidation at revealing her 'wedding look'. Nervous at the potential snowstorm of upset she could cause by saying the wrong thing, she had tiptoed out trying to recreate the effect of wearing heels. And after a moment or two of hand clasping, hugging and congratulating Viv, Lauren had reached into her huge shoulder bag and whipped out a Brian Atwood shoebox. As a thank-you present she had gone ahead and bought Ava the most devastatingly gorgeous pair of designer heels to go with the dress. And – ever the pragmatist – they were not just perfect for the wedding day itself, but deliciously elegant courts that Ava would be able to wear afterwards.

'They're gorgeous!' she exclaimed, holding them up at chest height like a glamorous Charlie Chaplin, holding his bread roll shoes and ready to dance. 'Thank you *so* much.'

'But do they *fit*? Try them on *now*! Go on …'

Viv stepped back and watched them, smiling, her hands pressed together. She seemed to be as thrilled as the sisters with the results of her handiwork. Ava would never be sure, but she did suspect that while she and Lauren were hugging each other and weeping with delight Viv had silently wiped away a little tear of her own.

Once they had composed themselves, Lauren tried on the calico for her dress. Not the final version – this was a replica of crisp calico cotton to show the style, the cut

206

and of course the fit of the dress. Even in the pale, unbleached fabric it was breathtaking. Lauren emerged beaming with excitement, her hands held wide to show it off.

'Ta daaa!'

'Wow, I don't know what to say. Just ... wow!' Ava looked her up and down, soaking up the image of what was clearly going to be a stunning dress, while Viv immediately approached her with a tin of pins and started tweaking and checking every seam and detail. Ava scarcely dared to imagine what the finished version would look like, once the delicate silk and lace were overlaying it. While Viv continued to pin and pull, making little marks on the hem with her dressmaker's chalk, Ava reached over with hair clips and Kirby grips, experimenting with different positions of 'up dos' against the dress's neckline.

Lauren carried on standing straight and asked Viv how work was going – 'The rest of work, though – your other glamorous life.'

'It's going really well, thank you. An exciting time for the show,' she replied.

'Yes, we saw the first glimpses of the dresses in competition last night,' said Ava, who had watched the first live show after work.

'Me too!' Lauren now seemed gripped by enough *Strictly* spirit to genuinely want to chat about the show despite standing there in her wedding calico.

'Oh, some of the dresses for the Waltzes were just dreamy! I don't know how you do it,' continued Ava.

'There's a lot to get through at this stage in the competition – by Christmas you've forgotten how many of them were there in the beginning!'

'Yes, we do the same,' said Lauren. 'You really start to care about one or two and you can remember their dresses from throughout the whole series, but you've forgotten some of them were even in it in the first place!'

'We did Cha Cha Cha in dancing class recently,' ventured Ava, barely daring to remember that particular lesson. 'I was just in gym clothes really, so it was fantastic to see them in the full outfits.'

'The beading!' said Lauren. 'It's amazing. Oh wow, it makes me want to scrap everything and have a *Strictly* themed wedding!'

Viv and Ava caught each other's eye, each as convinced as the other that there was no way on earth that Lauren would ever consider scrapping a single thing about this wedding.

'And the guys looked great too,' added Ava, determined to keep Lauren's mind off any last-minute changes.

'They do take longer to look totally comfortable in the outfits, though, don't they?' said Lauren.

'Yes,' said Viv, 'but that's often true of men in any kind of fancy outfits. Often they're the ones who don't put the effort in for a wedding, and the next thing you know it's the day itself and they can't believe they're not allowed to dress like that every day.'

'Ain't that the truth?' said Ava. 'You're as wise as you are brilliant. Honestly, look at her! It's going to be heavenly on the day.'

Viv and Ava turned to look at Lauren, who was beaming back at them, her head tipped coquettishly to one side.

'Thank you,' said Viv, looking up with a smile. 'Work-wise, it has been a great year for me so far – a really lovely mix of stuff. And of course I love *Strictly*.'

'I'm already looking forward to tonight's show,' agreed Ava. 'I'm allowed curry and *Strictly* so long as I don't "whinge on" during *Match of the Day*, apparently.'

'"Allowed?"' asked Lauren, her face crossed with something between curiosity and concern.

'Well, you know what I mean,' said Ava, with what was meant to be an airy wave. Her nerves betrayed her, though, and her hand flapped erratically out, fingertips catching on the shelving on one side of the room. 'Oh come on, you know what I mean. I can do whatever I want …' Her voice trailed off. She suddenly realised that she could never explain how hard it was to find something both she and Rob wanted to do. Not now, not with her little sister standing there in her wedding dress.

She couldn't go into the way that he kept changing his mind, the implication always being that the original flawed plan was somehow her fault. Neither could she mention the fact that he had swung from wanting a big birthday party and asking her to get a guest list together to then seeming keen on a mini break 'somewhere fruity', to now saying he just fancied a meal out and then going down to Bristol for that gig on his actual birthday. She didn't mind any of these plans, but the nagging sense that none of them was quite good enough for him was starting to wear her down. Where was the fun, the spontaneity, the sense that them, together, was enough for a good time? What had happened? And she could never, ever articulate to Lauren her anxiety that her residual guilt about her brief – now subsided – crush on Gabe was what Rob was picking up on. Whatever was going on, Ava knew she didn't want to spoil the celebratory mood. And so the women carried on chatting away about the show and the dresses. They moved effortlessly from *Strictly* on to discussion about other recent celebrity dresses.

'Well, I thought Charlene of Monaco looked amazing!' announced Lauren. 'But Ava doesn't agree.'

'I liked the dress – I mean, there was nothing wrong with it, was there?' mused Ava.

'I can see where you're both coming from,' said Viv. 'It was flawless but it wasn't just about an absence of flaws, was it? There was a lack of drama, no sense of costume to that dress.'

'But it was beautiful,' insisted Lauren. 'So elegant.'

'Not for me,' insisted Ava. 'You could never get me to love that look. I thought Kate Middleton got it just right, though.'

'The Duchess of Cambridge, *please*!' laughed Lauren. 'I agree, though.'

'Absolutely,' said Viv. 'Just the right amount of drama – she was marrying the future King, after all. But she still looked like her.'

'Exactly!' Ava agreed, clasping her hands and leaning forward. 'Like her, but the ultimate her …'

'And that's the dream for every dress,' mused Viv.

'Yeah, Kate Moss and Lily Allen kept their personal style too. What I would have given to see Gwyneth Paltrow's wedding dress, back in the day,' said Lauren, looking dreamy. 'It must have been knockout.'

Before long they were shuffling through old copies of *Hello!* and asking Viv questions about the amazing tailoring on pregnant celebrities' dresses during the Oscar season; also listing their favourite dancing movies, from *Singin' in the Rain* to the Tango scene in *Scent of a Woman*.

By the time they were ready to leave Viv's there was an air of celebration about the day, a sense of hope that all Lauren's planning and fretting, not to mention the ever-escalating cost, was not for nothing – it might actually end up being a day to remember, after all. And it was this hope that Ava decided to cling to and squeeze tight as the car pulled away.

'You two look rather happy,' said Rob, checking the rear-view mirror and then glancing at Ava.

'We *are*! I am so thrilled – so, *so* thrilled!' replied Ava with a little clap of her hands. 'Wasn't it great?' She turned her head to look at her sister in the back seat.

'Yeah, it really was wonderful. I'm properly excited now. Viv is such a pro – it's worked out so well with her, and the dresses are GREAT! Ava's going to look A-Ma-ZING!' She said the last word in a singsong voice as if to goad Rob with the promise of Ava's charms. He seemed oblivious, more intent on listening to the radio, now all but inaudible.

211

'I'm glad it has been such a success – I dread to think what would have happened if it hadn't been. And remind me why this appointment was so damn early?'

'Because Viv has to go down to London to make final tweaks on the *Strictly* dresses. It's all too exciting! It's on again tonight, remember,' said Ava, trying to prove there was some levity between them.

'The atmosphere there must be incredible at this time of year. I can't even imagine …' said Lauren.

'I'm sure I will be finding out all about it later,' said Rob, staring ahead.

'Indeed you will,' replied Ava with an attempt at a wink. She reached around and gave his shoulders a bit of a massage. *Why am I behaving as if I'm grateful to be allowed to watch my own TV?* she wondered. She thought of Gabe's offer, wondered idly who else he might be going with now, before turning to Lauren with a smile.

'Okay, Sis – I have to get back to the shop now, and Rob's off to play footie. What are you up to? Because we really do need to have this chat about the flowers, big time! I have to start planning, making orders, putting together designs, and I've been thinking of getting a Saturday girl in to help out, so if I'm going to do that I need to think about hours, train her up and make a plan for the day itself.'

'Well, Doll, it's funny that you should ask because I have my folder here right now.' Lauren waggled her eyebrows up and down and giggled. 'Ready to chat?'

Rob stared straight ahead, focusing on the road and apparently determined not to get involved with sisterly chat. He turned the radio back up, seemingly unaware of the basic equation that the louder the music, the louder the women would talk. The gesture was not only futile, but also slightly aggressive. Ava thought of the blank smile that Barry had given Jenny and Ava in that French restaurant: his resignation to the fact that there was a bit of women's chat going on was a skill, and one that Rob was rapidly losing or had never had. Ava chose to pay no attention.

Lauren snaked an arm around the front seat, depositing various images and designs on Ava's lap. As the two of them chatted away, she remained determined to stick to her Country Wedding theme and Ava gave a huge sigh of relief when she heard that she wasn't planning to have country garden style flowers in the middle of winter. She was equally pleased with Lauren's insistence that she didn't want things to look overwhelmingly Christmassy either.

'Urgh, you know what it's like,' said Lauren. 'I'm already half bored of Christmas and it's still two and a half months away.'

'I hear you, sister. It's a nightmare.'

'I thought you two bloody loved Christmas,' said Rob with a small smile. 'Another excuse to go shopping – what's not to like?'

When did he turn into this person? wondered Ava, wincing. She saw the shadow cross Lauren's face as he said it and knew she would be quizzed on the comment at a later date. In itself that would be awful, but worst of all would be the fact that she wouldn't have any answers. Lauren was right to look appalled, Ava reminded herself. In another situation she would never let any man of Lauren's or one of her friends' speak to them like that. She would question it without hesitation, so why did she continue to take it so tacitly from Rob? *It's just a phase*, she tried to tell herself. *It will pass. It must …*

She was jolted from her musings by an insistent tap on her shoulder from behind her.

'Anyway,' continued Lauren, 'I just think, by December people won't want to see another single berry. I want to see nothing in that church that could possibly be rendered in plastic and sold at a craft fair, or used to decorate a school. Only the kind of thing you might see in Fortnum & Mason, please.'

'Okay …' replied Ava.

'Let's put it this way. I want that church to be a Winter Wonderland. As if outside is inside, but none of the pain of that. What I want more than anything on earth is that the pillars down the central aisle are just covered in greenery. *Covered!*'

'Lo, I want to do this for you. Really, I do. But I have had a lot of trouble in the past doing things on stone pillars. So often it's nigh on impossible to actually fix anything on to the pillars without leaving any lasting damage. The churches are very strict. And even if they weren't, I wouldn't want to start messing around with them – it's just not right for an hour-long service.'

'But it's not just an hour-long service though, is it? It's a lifetime's worth of memories and photographs.'

'Well yes, but …'

'You've done it before, though – right? I mean, you found a way to sort it?'

'Well, yes, but in that instance what we had was—'

'Great, I knew you could do it! You and Matt really are an unstoppable team these days!'

'Seriously, Lauren – it might not be that simple. In fact, it could really turn out to be very complicated. It know this sounds weird, but flowers and ancient stone pillars are as fragile as each other – and a lot of people love them equally. Believe it or not, I can't just charge in and do this because *you* want it to happen.'

'I know, but if there's anyone in the whole wide world who I could trust to get this done, it would be you. I'm the luckiest sister in the world and I never, ever forget that!'

Lauren was now massaging both of Ava's shoulders instead of merely prodding them from the back seat. Ava turned to Rob with a smirk, looking for a glance of support, but Rob just rolled his eyes and carried on with his blank gaze at the road.

'Sisters …' he muttered with a shrug. To a degree he was right; these two had a bond stronger than most. Ever since Lauren's illness – which was of course for most of her life – Ava had had a real soft spot for wanting to do whatever she could to please her sister, even though she knew it was ridiculous. After all, Lauren was one of the most confident and competent adult women of her acquaintance.

Ava looked at the heap of lists and drawings in her lap that she had been presented with and wondered how on earth she would be able to turn that church into a Winter

Wonderland without wreaking havoc. The volume of work required looked as if it was going to be enormous. She made a mental note to get in touch with Minx on Monday and to make sure Matt's holiday did not coincide with the wedding. Suddenly her 'to do' list seemed to be growing like bindweed even as she sat there in the car. *The next couple of months will be all hands on deck*, she thought to herself.

A short while later Rob reached central Salisbury and dropped Ava off outside the shop before taking Lauren to her car and then heading off to football himself. Ava made sure to profusely thank him for helping out with lifts and being so patient. He sat there in the driver's seat and absorbed her thanks as if they were no more than he deserved.

Ava stepped into the shop and the place immediately felt like a sanctuary. Row upon row of flowers was bristling with freshness and potential. The smell was amazing and the handful of people in there all seemed to be enjoying themselves choosing something special for their loved ones. Best of all, the day seemed to bring a steady stream of customers of a similar disposition. For the first time in weeks there were none of the children who seemed intent on destroying at least half of her stock, and for this she was eternally grateful.

In the middle of the afternoon, as the sun was streaming through the shop front and casting a delicate hazy light onto all the flowers in there, a little girl entered and became entranced by the display. Her awe was so enchanting that Ava grew entranced by her in return. She was only about 9 years old, but already had a face wise enough to be slightly unnerving: close to beautiful but more interesting than that, it was the sort of face that might give you a withering glance, should you try and talk to her like a child.

The girl was dressed in a pink pinafore with a white cotton polo neck beneath it, thick navy blue tights and a pair of hot pink wellies. She had two long blonde plaits either side of her head and no fringe obscuring her pale blue eyes. The little boy who had entered the shop with her was clearly her younger brother, and an older woman seemed to be their grandmother. Both children were exceptionally well behaved and the grandmother seemed to be deep in thought, but it was the little girl who was completely absorbed by the wall of pails running against the side of the shop.

'We're here to get flowers for our mum!' announced the little boy when Ava approached the woman and asked how she could help.

'What a lovely treat for her,' replied Ava to the little boy, while his granny still seemed somewhat distracted.

'Yes, Granny says we can help choose.' He was holding her hand tight, eager to please.

'Young Toby here is correct,' said the older woman. 'We are getting flowers for his mother.'

Toby was now fiddling with a piece of coloured twine that he had found on the floor. He had dark curly hair and round, dark eyes that made him look almost cartoon-like in his impish innocence. Ava usually felt unnerved by children that age, always alert to what they might break next in the shop, but this time she trusted him. Perhaps because of how tightly he was clinging on to his grandmother, maybe he had a placid nature, Ava didn't know. Meanwhile the little girl was stroking the back of a curled calla lily, mesmerised.

'She's in hospital,' said the little girl, almost inaudibly. 'She is very ill.' She looked up at Ava, her eyes big watery pools.

'Oh,' said Ava, suddenly stunned by the intensity of the remark and the honesty of her face.

'Shush! Come on now, Ellie – the lady doesn't need to know that,' said the grandmother, briefly letting go of Toby's hand to stroke the top the little girl's head reassuringly.

'That's okay,' said Ava briskly. 'Don't you worry about me. Now then, what kind of flowers does your mummy like?' Ava bent down so that she was at eye level with the girl. 'How can we choose her the very best bunch possible?'

And Ellie took Ava up on her invitation. She asked to see and touch several of the flowers in the display, and for each and every query Ava either lifted her so that she could touch or see the flowers for herself, or plucked out and passed a stem for her to examine. Once the flowers themselves had been chosen, Ava let both children help to choose the coloured twine she would use to tie the bouquet and the paper to wrap it with. Then she talked them through what she was doing as she put the bouquet in order and tied it neatly with a twist, placing it in a clear plastic container of

218

water to keep it fresh. Throughout the entire process the siblings giggled and chatted with Ava as if they didn't have a care in the world.

Finally, the bouquet was complete and Ava presented it to Ellie for inspection.

'Will you look at that!' said the grandmother, reaching inside her handbag for her wallet. 'There will hardly be room for her in the ward now.'

All four of them giggled and Ava insisted that she wouldn't take more than £20 for the bouquet. The children thanked her for her help and Ellie leant up to kiss her.

'Please tell your mum I hope she gets better soon!' Ava said as they left the shop, the grandmother visibly choked by her kindness.

For the rest of the day the thought of those children preyed on her mind. For every romance she facilitated, every corporate space she made more bearable, there was also a sad story like this one. Ava hoped that the woman was not too ill, and that the flowers had brought her some comfort. She had so much faith in flowers and their ability to cheer any soul, even at their lowest ebb, she had to believe in a bleak hospital ward they would be of more comfort than anywhere else.

The knowledge that there were others out there with problems so much bigger than hers, and that small children like Ellie were dealing with them with so much bravery, made Ava feel both comforted and sad – and desperate not to let in too much self-pity about the mysterious vanishing of Gabe. She still looked up to the shop door with a mournful kind of hopefulness every now and again, holding out in case he made a return visit. Over time she came to think that she really wouldn't mind if he was buying flowers for some woman again – she just wanted to be able to say hi and apologise for any misunderstanding between them.

But slowly she came to accept that it was probably not going to happen. She had to move on, no matter how heavy her heart, and moments like this with Ellie did indeed help. That evening she shut up the shop determined not to waste a single moment of her life. After all, Ellie's mum was probably only her age. *You don't get many chances in this life*, she told herself.

When she arrived home that evening, armed with a huge bunch of roses from the shop 'just because', she saw that Rob had already let himself in and was installed in the kitchen with a beer.

'Hey you,' she said as she bent down to kiss him. 'Did you pick up any wine? I totally forgot.'

'I've got us some beers instead because of curry night,' he replied hopefully.

Ava said nothing, but bit her lip. She could not remember a time when she had drunk a beer with Rob. How had he never noticed that she did not like it? But she let it slide and they collapsed on the sofa for a bit of telly. She had been looking forward to indulging in a bit of *Strictly* with him, especially since his interest had been slightly piqued by this rugby player he seemed to have so much invested in. They ordered a curry and Ava laid everything out nicely in the kitchen to give a bit of occasion. *Heaven forbid they should become a couple for whom a highlight was a takeaway*, she told herself. And then, finally, as she heard the music tootling in from the other room, it was time for *Strictly*.

Except Rob did not watch. He didn't leave the room, or change the channel. Indeed, he probably thought that he *was* watching while the contestants appeared onstage, fresh from weeks of training with their elected partners. Ava was dying to see how they had all been getting along and Rob really seemed to think he was engaging in the excitement, too. But he wasn't.

Instead, after just ten minutes he whipped out his new iPad and tapped away incessantly on it throughout. At first Ava was mildly annoyed that he was not paying any attention. That she was reduced to the frequent 'Look, look at him!' or 'Look at that dress, my God, Viv has worked so hard, hasn't she?' irked her, but not excessively. After all, she had never expected him to be totally engrossed in it after all of his protestations. But then she started to wonder what he was doing. Every now and again she craned her neck in an attempt to see his screen, but each time she did so he would tilt the screen, just a fraction, to stop her from seeing it. Eventually she dropped the subtlety and just asked him, outright.

'What are you doing on that thing?'

'Nothing, just browsing.'

But as he said this she quickly turned to see he was on Facebook: Facebook *Chat*, to be precise. It was as if someone had suddenly opened a window wide in the room. She shivered. After all, if she could spend time online flirting with people she shouldn't be, why couldn't he? Until that very moment the thought never crossed her mind. She pushed it away, determined not to give it any further consideration, and tried to enjoy the rest of the evening. But the seeds had been sown: the seeds of curiosity and anxiety.

For the rest of the weekend Ava and Rob indulged themselves in the way only two people with no kids and good jobs can. They went for a roast in Ava's local pub, followed by a walk, and then spent some time talking about the wedding flowers and whether Rob would be able to help her, if it coincided with Matt's holiday. Ava tried not to be thrown when Rob decided to sleep at his own house on Sunday night. She chose to spend the evening with her laptop, researching how she might manage the wedding flowers instead of panicking about what Rob was up to.

On Monday morning Ava was the groggiest she had been for some time. Glad she had been the last in the shop on Saturday evening, she at least knew what would be waiting for her this time. As she turned her key in the lock she could see that the deliveries had been made: there they were, the lines and lines of flowers. *A fresh start, a new week, a thousand new gestures.* The sight of all of those flowers was reassuring to her – she knew where she stood with flowers and she could not think of a single situation where they might do more harm than good. They absorbed the meaning you gave them, without having meanings you could not read.

She gave the door a push and eased herself inside before turning to pick up the junk mail that had already gathered. But this time it wasn't just junk mail. On the top of the pile was a beautiful, stiff envelope addressed to her by hand: Miss Ava Dunne.

She scanned over the junk mail before throwing it in the bin and then sat down to open the envelope. Inside were some sheets of neatly folded paper that seemed to be printed-out emails and a handwritten letter. The paper on which the letter was written was thick, watermarked and ridged. Clearly expensive, it was the kind of product used solely by people trying to make a gesture or to get away with something. As she read through the letter, she felt her palms start to sweat to the point where she could see the imprint of her thumb and forefinger on the page once she'd finished reading it.

Dear Ava,

I am sorry to have missed you these last few weeks. I wish I could have attended dance class more often, but sadly it was not to be. I do hope to be back before Christmas but I cannot say for sure that I will be able to.

I hope you weren't offended by my invitation to see *Strictly Come Dancing* live. You are a wonderful dancer and your love of dance seems very sincere so please do take my seats – I will be unable to attend, so I have called BBC Audience Services and had the name changed to yours. They will go to waste if you are unable to make it to London. Please take a guest of your choice, whoever he or she may be. It would make me very happy indeed to know you had got some happiness out of the evening.

I hope you are well. You are in my thoughts a great deal. I miss you. I miss dancing with you.

Gabriel.

x

Chapter 12

Off to *Strictly*?

Her train pulled out of Salisbury station and almost immediately her mobile phone lost reception. Ava tipped her head back and closed her eyes, relieved that she had decided not to bother with driving. For the first time in weeks she was suspended in her own thoughts. However briefly, she was free – out of contact, alone, at peace. There was no busyness, no obligation, a moment's respite from the gloom that had passed over everything in the last month or so. She couldn't take calls, make calls or reply to emails, so she turned her head against the headrest and stared absentmindedly out of the window. In her lap she fiddled with the plastic packaging of the sandwich she had bought for the journey. The fields whizzed by and the reassuring chug of the train began to make her feel even more sleepy.

To keep herself alert, Ava flicked through the Saturday papers, catching up on celebrity speculation, must-have new season make-up colours and what she should be seeing at the cinema. She made sure that she paid particular attention to anything and everything to do with *Strictly*. There were paparazzi shots of the celebrities coming in and out of their rehearsals, and some gossip about who fancied whom, as well as shots of the best dances so far. Ava pored over the details, trying to remember everything to tell Mel, so that they could look out for any and all potential tension – of whatever sort – once they saw the dances live.

She chewed her sandwich slowly as she moved onto other, non-*Strictly* gossip, reading an interview with a star-let who was apparently experiencing a comeback before her twentieth birthday, and by the time she was finished she could barely keep her eyes open. She closed her eyes softly and drifted off into her own fuzzy thoughts. There was no reason for her to be as exhausted as she felt, so she ration-alised that it wasn't so much tiredness as relief washing over her. She had a little while to herself, not having to try quite so hard to look as if everything was fine, as if she was making it all work.

Ava had still not seen Gabe since he had left her the elegant handwritten note with the emailed seat bookings for *Strictly*, now stowed neatly away in her handbag, wait-ing for this evening. She had no way of contacting him other than email – she realised she did not even know where he lived as he had been late to that first dance class when everyone had introduced themselves. So she had replied to the Gmail account from where he had contacted her to cancel their coffee. It had been over a month since that email and she was still none the wiser as to why he cancelled on her. She doubted she would ever know. And so she had sent him a profuse thank-you note for the ticket and explained that if he really was 100 per cent sure that he would not be going she would love to use the seats to take her dear friend Mel, who had been having a hard time recently.

All she received in reply was a one-word answer, sent via a BlackBerry.

'Great. x'

She gave equal analysis to the 'great' and the 'x'. One word? Only one word – really, that was it? But then again, a kiss – a kiss from Gabe, what did it mean?

Once the initial heat of her analysis had cooled, she saw that it mattered very little what any of it meant. Whatever had been bubbling between them had now cooled off to such a degree that it was no longer an open flow of contact. Ava was left trying to make the best of an unpromising autumn. She had thrown herself at Rob, lavishing affection on him despite the continuation of his strange brand of makeover. He was now talking about making a short film – something to do with the reignited contact with an old university chum. His hair was ever more unruly and he had begun to mumble ominously about jacking in his job alto-gether and retraining as a plumber. He no longer wanted to eat out, but preferred to experiment with an increasing number of bizarre foods from the organic health food store in town. And at least once a week he would come up with a new and unusual plan for becoming 'less corporate', or furthering himself. From where Ava was sitting, it seemed he was only furthering himself from her.

He had turned down her offer of cooking a big Sunday lunch for him and his family to celebrate his birthday, curtly letting her know that 'I just don't like hanging out with my family the whole time like you do. I am not that man.' But she knew this to be untrue and couldn't fathom what was behind this sudden change of tack. Then he decided to make plans for his trip to Bristol: he would go to the gig, reconnect with even more old pals, revisit old university haunts in some kind of memorial pub crawl. It sounded ghastly, the kind of thing that Rob had spent the last few years actively avoiding, but Ava let him get on with it. When she mentioned these plans to Lauren she had once again been met with those words she had been trying not to let herself hear: mid-life crisis.

There was little she could do to stem the slow, steady lava flow of Rob's new image. It seemed to inch forward day by day, regardless of what might be in its path. She determined to try and keep a sunny nature and get on with her own life. *No sudden moves*, she would occasionally repeat to herself in moments of bewilderment and stress. She arranged for Minx to come into the shop and learn the ropes, which she immediately did, proving herself to be both charming, efficient and a real enthusiast for the flowers themselves. And she continued to go to dance class, despite being left dancing with Patrice each class now that Gabe had disappeared. Of course, classes were never the same again without him and she could tell that Jenny was aflame with curiosity when he stopped showing up, but Ava loved the dancing nonetheless. The class continued to work through several more of the classic dances and each week the sense of fun and friendship in the room only grew. Ava could tell that even if she wasn't losing any actual weight she was certainly getting fitter and healthier. The mayhem and emotion of dancing and the routine of running were a perfect combination, after all.

As the train pulled into Waterloo, Ava felt the creeping, familiar emotions that she always did on approaching London: a dizzying combination of excitement and unease. She had had some of the happiest and most exciting times of her life there, but also some of the darkest and loneliest. There was so much that the city had to offer, and so much she had given and taken to herself, but deep down she knew that she was not a Londoner. The crowds, the speed, the constant sense of urgency … She simply moved at a different pace and always felt overwhelmed when she arrived in town, the river of people flowing off the train immediately urging her forward, searching for her ticket as others whacked against her bag. *How had she done this every day for so long?* she wondered. Her daily commute was never dull compared to this chaos. She loved watching the colours of the fields slowly change, seeing which fields and flowers were emerging. This daily battle seemed like something she had done in a different lifetime, not just a few years ago.

She fought her way across the soggy concourse (was it busier than usual for a Saturday, or was this just her increasingly bumpkin ways?) and then caught the Tube up to Mel's stop in north-west London. She was looking forward to seeing her friend and her children so much, but as ever she had a slight prickle of anxiety about spending so much time in what was such a classic family home. It was just so … perfect.

While Ava loved the house and adored Mel's children, there wasn't a part of her that wasn't rendered slightly fretful by it all. Ava could turn up, be herself and indulge in playing with the kids for an hour, but sometimes it did feel like a living museum to what she did not possess in her own life. Had those chances passed for her now? Would she ever be able to recreate the same kind of family home that she had grown up in? She lugged her heavy bag down Mel's street, these thoughts flooding her mind as usual. But, as ever, by the time she pressed the doorbell, excitement and love had bubbled up and won out over any sadness. A moment later she heard Jake stampeding down the hallway and towards the front door.

'AYVAAAAAAAA!'

Marcie was not long behind him, and within seconds the children's sticky faces and hot little hands were pressed up against the glass of the elegant Victorian front door. Then Mel approached to open it, looming over the children, her smile visible even through the mottled glass. In seconds the friends were hugging each other tightly while the children squealed and hugged at her knees below. With that, Ava was once again enveloped in the bosom of the family.

'How are you?' asked Ava, looking into her friend's eyes with a slight frown as the children scampered below, keen to show her the Lego figures and drawings they had made for her.

'Oh, you know,' replied Mel, with a small wave.

Ava rested her hand on Mel's shoulder and looked at her properly. She could tell that she was tired and drawn, but given that she had two children under 6 it was not a new experience to see her exhausted. The change was about more than a lack of sleep, and sadder. Instead of her usual brightly coloured clothes making her look sunny and vibrant, today they made her look washed-out, exhausted, less than Ava knew her to be. Her hair was lank and her skin papery. Ava had seen the emergence of laughter lines on her face over the last few years, but these new lines were different. This was about not caring, rather defeated. Mel seemed to have sagged emotionally, and that was written on her face.

In addition, it turned out that Rich had now taken the opportunity to visit his family in Norfolk for a week. He had gone to 'really think about things'. It seemed a little strange to Ava that he needed so much time and space to think through the potential consequences of his recent behaviour, and that it needed to involve leaving Mel in sole charge of the children. But she had chosen to bite her lip when Mel explained this to her.

'Come on in,' said Mel. 'It's teatime.' She squeezed Ava's hand, as if it were her friend who needed the reassurance.

Mel led them down to the kitchen where the children had been making Rice Krispie cakes. They had certainly made the most of the kitchen: there was melted chocolate over almost every surface, sprinklings of crushed Rice Krispies all over the floor, and long-handled wooden spoons dangling at perilous angles from most surfaces. The sticky cakes themselves were in the fridge, the children explained as they danced before Ava, wild with excitement. Jake was in a pair of pyjamas with the shape of a skeleton on them, while Marcie wore full princess regalia. These were apparently outfits arranged especially for her arrival, not usual weekend wear. Mel dumped Ava's bag in the hallway and flicked the kettle on to make a cup of tea. Once everyone had a drink, the cakes were presented with great ceremony and there was a bit of chat.

But the initial novelty of teatime could not last, and once the sugary treats had been despatched the children scampered off to find new games, leaving Ava and Mel to clear up. They began wiping surfaces with a sense of tremendous purpose, and it was once their hands were busy that Ava felt brave enough to tentatively ask, 'But how are you … really?'

'Honestly, I would rather not talk about it at the moment.' Mel was pressing the cloth hard into the Corian, scrubbing at a particularly stubborn bit of dried-on chocolate.

'You can't keep all this in forever, though. You've been avoiding chats for a week. How are things? What's actually going on?'

'Ava, please.' Mel looked up from the worktop. 'Just because you are happy to chat about something – and I really am grateful that you are, I know it's not a barrel of laughs – it doesn't mean that that's what I want to do.'

232

'But you can't keep keeping everything in. Is there someone else you can talk to? Someone else you're discussing this with? Because if it's not me I need to know that it's somebody.'

'Please …'

'You can't keep everything buttoned down like this indefinitely.'

'I'm not going to!' Mel slapped her hand down on the countertop. The gesture was aggressive but the sound was muffled by the damp cloth in her hand.

'Okay, I'm sorry.'

'Look, it's not that there are any secrets going on here. I'm not keeping any important facts from you. It's just that this situation rattles around in my head all day, every day. I spend all week looking forward to my couple of days at work just because it means a bit of adult company, some people who know nothing about what's going on in my life. It's not because I'm hiding from you, or I'm ashamed of anything, or because I don't think you would understand. It's simply that I'm sick and tired of thinking about it. It dominates me, and I need to just be me. So, please – PLEASE – can we just enjoy the weekend for what it is? Like we used to before all of this kicked off. I just want to talk about dresses and gossip and dancing, and not my marriage. Never my marriage.'

'Okay, of course. And I'm sorry – I get it now.' Ava placed a hand on Mel's, still resting on the kitchen counter, gripping the soggy cloth. The women looked at each other, smiled that conspiratorial smile of theirs and then shared a hug. They held each other for a moment or two before Mel stepped back, put her hands on Ava's shoulders and said, 'Do you know what I think? I think Wine Time.' And with that she tossed the cloth in the direction of the sink, opened the fridge and got out a cold bottle of wine. She poured them each a glass and they plonked themselves down at the kitchen table. Healing banter about shared friends, errant celebrities and the latest quirks of the children started to flow, only occasionally interrupted by Jake or Marcie scuttling in to show them one of their latest creations.

Once that illicit glass of wine was finished the friends realised that time was pressing and they needed to sort out arrangements for the evening. Marcie immediately caught a whiff of their plans and followed them upstairs, where Ava rummaged in her bag and produced the outfit she was planning to wear before going into Mel's room to show her. Mel haphazardly got out a selection of items from her wardrobe, held them up against herself before asking the girls what they thought and then threw the items on the double bed. Jake remained oblivious and stayed in his bedroom with his Lego, while Marcie basked in the full attention of potent female company.

It was decided that Mel should wear an off-the-shoulder black-and-white striped dress. It was sexy, well cut and bold – not traditional Ballroom material – and at first Ava wasn't sure about the suggestion. But when she tried it on she understood immediately that this was what she should wear: it showed flashes of the old Mel, like a bird escaping from an aviary. That confidence, the punky attitude that had been flattened by an apparent overdose of domesticity, was once more allowed to show itself in this dress.

Ava knew this was a Westwood frock and that it had been bought at vast expense before her friend had children. She remembered that the entire process had taken almost an entire season: it was saved for, endlessly discussed and tried on at least three times in Selfridges. Ava had gone on one 'visit', Rich another, and then photos were taken and emailed to a select team of girly opinion-making friends. At the time Ava had not been able to understand what benefit such wild extravagance could possibly have. While she was in Salisbury, struggling to get Dunne's off the ground and piece back together a life she could be proud of, the fact that Mel was even considering such a purchase seemed to underline the fact that she had it all. But now, seeing her friend weak and in need of every boost she could get, Ava realised the dress had been worth every penny. It was a perfect example of a garment letting the wearer be themselves at their very best. She sat on the edge of Mel's bed, with Marcie nestled on her lap, and applauded when she tried it on.

Between them the friends got the children bathed, fed and into their pyjamas nice and early for the babysitter.

'I took them to the park for hours this morning,' explained Mel, as she popped Marcie's head through her pyjama top. 'Fingers crossed they'll be too tired to complain about anything by the time Dawn gets here. But we'll be long gone by then anyway so it shouldn't matter too much!'

They then took it in turns to have showers and started getting ready. Ava soon realised how tiring it was looking

235

after two little ones, while Mel treated herself to a long bath and emerged beaming with gratitude at having had the time to herself. She had always loved Mel's bathroom, which maintained a level of glamour and luxury Ava could only dream of, despite the two tiny toothbrushes in the family mug and the plastic basket of waterproof toys in one corner. Ava lay back in the bath, enjoying the sensation of wiggling her toes on the taps while listening to the happy laughter of the children. For the first time in weeks she had no idea where her mobile phone was and she didn't care.

Ava had selected a black sparkly top that she had bought for Christmas last year and was wearing it with a plush velvet skirt. She padded round Mel's spare room in the outfit with tights and bare feet, putting her make-up on, while Marcie sat back on the double bed, propped up with pillows almost as big as her, sucking her thumb and picking up every item of make-up that Ava put down on the bed: the sparkly eyeliner, the mascara in its green and pink packaging, the pots of eyeshadow with their clear lids and the metallic lipstick case with its satisfying clicking lid. They were largely silent, companionable, the love between the two as strong as between Ava and Mel, and was evident from the comfort they felt around each other. Once she was ready, Ava smacked her lips together in the mirror, scooped Marcie off the bed and wandered into Mel's room again.

They both gasped when they saw Mel fully done up for her night out. She had piled her hair up into a messy chignon and had perfectly applied dark smoky eye make-up on. Her lips were deep red and her sparkle was back. She looked, in a word, utterly gorgeous.

'Wow, Mummy, you're such a pretty lady!' said Marcie, wriggling out of Ava's arms and reaching out to touch the dress, then Mel's hair.

'Thank you, darling,' she said, smiling down at the little bundle of pinkness. She then looked up at Ava with a smile.

'You look fantastic,' said Ava.

'Thanks, hon,' she replied.

Marcie scrambled at Mel's legs until she picked her up for a proper hug while Ava looked on and smiled. Then, as Marcie let go of her mother and was deposited back down on the floor, she noticed a solitary tear silently make its way down Mel's cheek. She said nothing and avoided eye contact with Ava, who passed her a tissue from the bedside table without a word.

'Thanks,' she whispered, looking down.

The doorbell rang.

'Right, chipmunk,' said Mel, 'I think that's Dawn come to look after you.' And indeed it was. Dawn, the adolescent babysitter from down the road, was soon downstairs kissing the children and listening to their news. Though clearly pleased to see the kids, she was even more excited when she heard where Mel and Ava were off to. She immediately started to bombard them with questions about potential romances, celebrity partners for them to keep an eye out for and oohs and ahs about the dresses they'd soon be seeing up close. All three were so happy to be standing around bantering that it was only the doorbell announcing the taxi which reminded them that Dawn was supposed to be looking after the kids ... and that Ava and Mel had somewhere more exciting to be. A flurry of goodbye kisses and 'be good's followed and eventually they were in the back of a smart, spacious taxi, heading across West London to BBC TV Centre.

As the car pulled out of Mel's road the two friends fell momentarily silent, adjusting their outfits to avoid crinkling as much as possible and checking that all lipsticks and security details were present and correct. As she unfolded the paperwork Mel turned to look at Ava.

'Babe?'

'Yes.'

'I notice you haven't quite explained yet how on earth we ended up with these seats. Wasn't it me who was deputised with applying for tickets?'

Suddenly Ava was the one not so keen to talk about 'stuff'. Mel's earlier reluctance began to make perfect sense. She carefully folded up the email printouts and placed them neatly back in her handbag. It was ridiculous, but they had come to represent the last thread keeping a connection between herself and Gabe. They even had his name and email address on them from the original application in his name. Now she was almost dreading handing them over to security, despite knowing how silly that was. She looked into her lap and fiddled a little with the clasp of her evening bag. Where to begin with this one?

'Oh yes, it's funny,' said Ava, playing for time as best she could. 'A friend of mine from dance class got them for me. We were even talking about going together, actually.'

'I can't believe you'd even think about cheating on me too!' said Mel with a nudge and a giggle. 'What's her name then?'

Ava winced. There was a moment's pause.

Leaving her nose wrinkled she turned to face Mel, knowing that what she was about to say next could potentially throw a grenade into their friendship.

'It's not a she. It's, er, a man.'

'Oh, Ava!' Mel's tone had changed. 'Not *you*, too.'

'No, no, it's not like that!' Ava didn't know whether to be more upset that she had assumed Mel would react with such swift judgement, or that she actually had.

'"It's not like that!"' Mel let out a terse, bitter little laugh. 'That's what Rich said. I imagine that's what they always say.'

She turned away to look out of the window. The taxi turned onto Scrubs Lane and grim industrial buildings started to pass by once the traffic lights changed from red.

'Whoa, whoa, whoa! I swear, nothing has happened. Honestly, it really isn't like that. I haven't even heard from him for at least a month.'

But Ava's pleading tone was doing her no favours. She knew she sounded guilty, which in itself seemed incredibly unfair.

'So, it was a one-off thing?'

'No, there was *no* thing, no anything at all. Nothing happened.'

Ava felt as if she'd been walking across a wooden floor only to tread on a board riddled with dry rot. She felt herself plummeting through this conversation, unable to keep up or explain herself, to contextualise her feelings. Worst of all, a sour note had now been given to the evening and they were only just arriving at TV Centre. The taxi-driver's eyes flicked discreetly up from the rear-view mirror and then forward towards the gap where he was planning to pull over.

'Listen, I can explain everything.'

'You don't have to make excuses to me.'

Mel's jaw was tight, her face set. She was trying to pretend everything was okay, but Ava could tell it wasn't. They urgently needed to sort this out as fast as possible.

The taxi had now pulled over and was sitting on the side of the road by TV Centre. Instead of excitement at seeing the famous building looming towards them, the two women were engrossed in conversation and oblivious to their surroundings.

'No, Mel, they're not excuses,' continued Ava. 'I want you to know. I have longed to talk to you about this, but you've had enough on your plate. I just didn't want to muddy the waters, I suppose.'

'That makes it sound as if you think it's *my* responsibility ...'

The taxi-driver cleared his throat and brought up the total on the meter, not quite ready to interrupt. Meanwhile, all around them people were getting out of cars and heading for the audience entrance.

'No, no, of course I don't think that!' Ava was now pleading with her. 'Please, can we talk about this properly, once we're inside? Let's just leave it two minutes. Two minutes, that's all.'

'So, ladies …' The driver had finally plucked up courage to interrupt the conversation. 'That'll be £8.70, please.'

Both reached for their purses but Ava was fastest and managed to ram a £10 note into the driver's hand before Mel could beat her to it.

'Off to *Strictly*, is it then, ladies?' he asked, seemingly determined to inject a bit of jolliness into proceedings.

'Yes, we are,' said Ava, her voice shrill with the effort of trying to sound chirpy.

'We can't wait,' agreed Mel. And as she said this she extended a hand across the taxi seat and gripped Ava's before giving her a tentative, hopeful smile.

'We're going to have an *amazing* night!'

Chapter 13

The Famous Dancefloor

The women grinned at each other, then got out of the taxi. They headed towards the audience entrance and joined a queue of similarly excited-looking guests. Ava felt a sudden lurch of panic that the email wouldn't be enough, that it would all be a cruel joke and there would turn out to be some terrible misunderstanding at the entrance. For a few seconds she was completely convinced that the woman in the headset checking off names would laugh in her face and that they would have come this close to watching *Strictly Live* only to be sent home again, shamefaced, to relieve the babysitter.

The woman looked at the emails with a small frown, read through the text quietly, then looked back up at them and smiled.

'So, no Gabe Monroe, then?'

'Erm, no,' said Ava in a small voice, painfully aware this was the first time that Mel had heard his name. 'He can't make it and he said that he had changed the name, that it was all confirmed.'

There was a pause. Ava closed her eyes and pressed her lips together, desperate for this moment to be over. Then, without a flicker of concern from the woman, it was.

'Yep, that all seems to be in order.'

Ava smiled and exhaled.

'Oh, thank you!'

'No problem – thank *him*. Have a great show, ladies.'

'Wow, thank you *so* much!' replied Ava, before turning and smiling at Mel. Her face was softer than it had been in the car, but Ava could still read some curiosity and perhaps judgement in it.

'That's quite the "friend" you've got there,' she said. 'Sorting it all out for you and everything.'

'Like I said, it's a long story,' Ava told her as they approached the security check. 'Can we talk about this more in a minute, please?'

They stepped forward and sailed through the security checks, surrendering their phones when asked, and walked towards the queue of fellow guests waiting to be taken into the inner sanctum of TV Centre. As the line snaked around the side of the building and into the iconic forecourt, the atmosphere between the two of them was thick with potential: the potential for a magical evening never to be forgotten, or a humdinger of an argument that could change their friendship forever. They knew this conversation must be had, but they were awkward about the idea of doing it in front of a line of glamorous strangers.

Their fellow audience members had certainly made the effort, they realised, when they reached the end of the queue. Everyone from the elderly couple quietly holding hands as they waited to the mum and her over-excited teenage daughter were dressed up to the nines. On display were proud, stiff prom dresses, asymmetrical creations in bright, jewel-like colours and even a metallic jumpsuit. There were glittering tops, shimmering hems and pearlescent bolero jackets. Men were in dinner jackets and smart suits, and everyone had great hair. Ava was so glad she was in sequins and relieved that she'd made the effort with her shoes when she spotted the creations that others had worn. She also quietly realised that Mel looked fantastic among the guests, standing out in her stripes ... and she herself knew it.

Soon they were guided by a team of smiling runners down various corridors, through fire doors and past the back of the stage until they were installed in the comfort of the audience foyer. Once they were there the mood changed: there was nothing they could do now but relax and enjoy the evening, whatever disagreement might be simmering between them. They had no phones and so there was no way that anyone could disturb their night out. It was just the two of them, some wine and a room full of dance fans in party frocks. Electric. Soon the atmosphere in the room started to shift as people talked about the matter in hand: their favourites, the proposed dances and what they were excited about seeing. As others around them got into the celebratory Halloween spirit, so too did Ava and Mel, who finally relaxed enough to chat properly.

Perched together on a large, comfy brown leather sofa, with a glass of white wine each, the chat between the friends began to thaw out again until it reached a point of actual warmth. Ava gently explained the Gabe situation to Mel, who listened intently, her wine cupped in her hand. Eventually all of the details and nuances crept out, recounted in Ava's low voice so that their fellow guests in the audience foyer didn't catch wind of the personal nature of the conversation. When told from the beginning it made slightly more sense to Mel: Rob's growing lack of interest, his strange behaviour, the dance classes, how they had begun after Mel's hilarious description of their mutual acquaintance Emma being so transformed by them and how Ava too had gone on to take to the classes like the proverbial duck to water. Then, finally, she described Gabe, the frisson between them, the advances he had made, the fact that she may have misread them entirely – to her eternal shame – and then the way he had suddenly disappeared altogether after making his generous offer of the seats.

She may have been sympathetic, but Mel still had questions.

'Why haven't you just called him or something?' she asked, with the perplexed face of someone who had been out of the game for far too long to help.

'Well, for starters I don't have his number,' said Ava. 'But also, what would I say? What is there to say? Because when push comes to shove, I know very little about him off the dance floor, and, more importantly, nothing happened. In reality, it's none of my business where he is or what he does. It has been sending me a little crazy, I admit. It makes me feel like some kind of fantasist, slowly becoming unleashed from reality as the evenings draw in.'

'But if nothing went on between you, you could just play it breezy and be phoning for a chat.'

'Oh, believe me, I tried breezy and it got me nowhere. Just because nothing happened doesn't mean nothing was there. They are two very different things.'

'Eh?' Mel looked utterly perplexed by this last comment.

'Oh come on, don't tell me you've forgotten what it's like! There was just a vibe: total tension and chemistry. Except you can't talk about it, because the moment you mention it you risk making it evaporate. It was like when you watch a couple on the show – you can't exactly explain what it is about them that has changed, but you're sure there's something there.'

'Hmm … But *Strictly*'s a show, not your real life. And a lot of the time they're doing deliberately romantic dances, so of course you'd think that.'

'You know what I mean, though – there was something between us, and yet, nothing. But to mention it would be …' Ava's voice trailed off sadly. Even talking about it was making her doubt the fact that anything had happened at all. Only the fact that she was sitting there right now, at BBC TV centre, about to watch *Strictly Come Dancing* in the live studio audience was any kind of proof for her that there had been a connection between them.

'So you can't just call him and be normal in case you *evaporate* it?' continued Mel. 'You're clinging on to some kind of romantic condensation now?'

'I'm sorry, I don't mean to sound like a weird thrill seeker.'

'Well, I hate to break it to you but you do!'

Mel no longer sounded angry or judgemental. If anything, she seemed concerned for her friend. She was wiping the condensation that was trickling down the sides of her wine glass and thoughtfully dabbing at it with a white paper napkin. 'I can't speak for you, or how you feel, but it really does sound as if this is a situation fabricated by your imagination. I know what you're like, and you're a lot like Rich: you can make a mountain out of a molehill. You're not getting enough attention from Rob at the moment, so you've gone out and seized at the first thing that caught your eye – this dance class Gabe business. You have to admit it's all a bit of a cliché.'

'Look,' said Ava. She took a deep breath, determined not to say anything she regretted. Both the fun of the evening and the future of the friendship suddenly seemed to be at stake. 'My situation is not the same as yours. It just isn't. For starters, one is emotional and one is physical. Rich has actually done something. I haven't done *anything*. And you've been doing your very best to be a good wife and mother at home – honestly, I've seen you with those kids and that home, and you've been busting a gut while Rich has been gadding about. Whereas Rob seems to be in the midst of some kind of existential crisis that most definitely does not involve me.

'I'm not sure it actually involves anyone. He seems to have abdicated from adulthood altogether for the moment.

247

He's obsessed by not kowtowing to the man, and it's just snowballing now – his hair, his bands, his making a short film. I don't know what's happening to him and any attempt I make to talk to him about it is batted off with the implication that I'm just repressed, bourgeois, trying to be like everyone else. He's been a good boyfriend to me for years and now suddenly he can barely look me in the eye, let alone do anything else. And don't even get me started on the whole moving-in together or making any kind of progress as a couple conversation thing – he simply isn't interested.'

Ava paused, almost breathless at her own little speech. She had had no idea that such strength of emotion was just sitting there, waiting to be expressed. Now she exhaled deeply, blowing up her fringe from her bottom lip, then giggled stupidly, embarrassed by Mel's silent thoughtfulness.

'Well, it sounds to me as if you've already made up your mind about what you need to do: the Gabe situation is entirely separate.'

'Oh, I'm so glad you can see that about Gabe,' said Ava, sighing with relief. 'But then when I heard about you and Rich I was just so shaken. I realised what a wonderful life I have, how lucky I am, and how little I have actually been hurt. Because he isn't – Rob just isn't a bad guy. I've tried to tell myself that this is nothing more than a weird phase that will simmer down by the end of the year. It *must*, it simply must …'

'So you think there's something there worth saving?'

'I don't *know*! I'm in such a muddle. Of course I want there to be something there worth saving, but …' Ava looked at Mel plaintively, almost tugging at her sleeve in order to try and get some kind of answer or resolution out of her.

'Only you can ever know that. That's what's so intoxicating and exhausting about this whole business.'

Before the discussion could go any further, they were called onto the stage. A fleet of runners wearing headsets and carrying important-looking clipboards called them in groups, according to the notes on their original bookings. When Ava and Mel realised their group was being called, a smiling woman came and stood alongside them. She seemed to be bubbling with excitement about the evening, even more so than Ava and Mel were.

'Nearly there!' she said to Ava, 'on set! I can't believe I'm going to see those glitterballs for real!'

'Us too,' said Mel, smiling at her.

The woman clasped her hands with excitement. She was wearing a navy blue prom-style dress with layers of netting beneath it. Her dark hair was in perfect ringlets and she had a glorious burgundy nail polish. She looked like a sort of impish high-school girl, despite being the same age as the friends – if not slightly older.

'My name's Julia, by the way,' she said. 'And I'm a big fan.'

'We're Ava and Mel,' said Ava, pointing at each of them as she said their names. 'And we're huge fans too – and so lucky to be here for the Halloween show.'

'I know! I bet the set looks amazing,' said Julia, as a man came and stood alongside them. 'Oh, this is my husband Chris.'

'Lovely to meet you,' said Mel, and at that moment the queue started moving forward towards the set. For a few minutes they were led by the runners through the maze of corridors. Julia's heels were high and she was clearly giddy with excitement, but Chris held her hand several times to help steady her as they twisted left and right.

As they turned the final corner and caught their first glimpse of the set, the group gasped at seeing it for real. Not only were the glitterballs and the iconic chairs there in all their glory but the set looked spectacular in its Hallow-een splendour. Cobwebs and glittering dust were sprinkled everywhere.

The group seated themselves, with Julia's netted skirts spilling out over her own lap and on to those of Ava and Chris either side of her.

'Oh it's fine,' said Ava. 'Don't worry about it at all, it's a magnificent dress.'

'Thank you,' said Julia. 'It's the one I wore for my wedding, actually. The day I became Mrs P.'

She grinned at Chris.

'Wow, that's so romantic!' said Ava, as Mel craned her neck to look around and join in the conversation.

'I know,' said Julia. 'I honestly never thought I would have an excuse to wear it again. But to *Strictly* ... well, you *have* to look your very best, don't you?'

'My sister's getting married soon,' said Ava. 'So I know how much love goes into wedding dresses now. Good for you for getting a second use out of it. That's magical!'

Julia smiled and held Chris's hand. He looked slightly bewildered at being caught up in so much of this chat, but stroked Julia's hand gently, clearly happy to indulge her on a day of such excitement. The couple started to chat to each other quietly, as Mel and Ava watched the rest of the audience members file in.

As each group saw the famous dance floor for the first time exclamations and even little claps would break out from corners of the set, and friends and partners would clutch each other with excitement. Ava and Mel were no different, barely able to stop themselves from letting out little squeals of delight as they noticed more and more detail from around the stage. It was a combination of a dance palace and a horror story, and the atmosphere on set was electric. People were starting to chat to perfect strangers, pointing things out excitedly, noting how different certain angles looked compared with the TV. When some of the judges appeared momentarily there was a ripple of excitement, and not long after that the studio lights went down and the announcement was made that they were live on air.

'Well,' said Mel as the familiar theme music started up and they clapped along with the nation. 'I don't know what the deal is with this Gabe bloke, but he knows how to get a girl good seats, I'll give him that.'

Ava looked around, scarcely able to believe she was there. What a treat.

'He didn't choose the seats though, you know,' she whispered to Mel.

'You know what I mean, babe. No matter how things pan out for either of us, it was a lovely gesture and an amazing opportunity.'

'What a bizarre set of circumstances has led to us being here together so soon after we talked about it!'

'I know! We could never have known that the chance would come up so quickly, or in such an odd way.'

Mel's eyes were suddenly glossy – Ava couldn't tell if it was the lights or if they were damp with potential tears. Quickly it became apparent that it was the latter – one strong blink would mean she was crying again.

'*Don't*,' said Ava. 'We don't have to talk about it. That was my promise.'

Mel opened her mouth to begin but the music ended and they were spared any more discussion for now. Ava gave her hand a reassuring squeeze but it wasn't needed. Before long both were transported by the magic of the show.

It was a show-business whirl, seeing the dancers and celebrities up close a once-in-a-million opportunity. Though magical in comparison to the television experience, it also reminded them of hundreds of evenings spent watching, analysing and discussing. They were not just able to see the dancers and dances up close, but also to watch the reactions of the judges as they made their notes. And most of all, they thrived on the atmosphere created by the live audience, gasping along at every dramatic step, applauding each surprise and laughing at the humorous touches. It was completely mesmerising, and the friends gripped each other's arms as the dramas and complicated routines unfolded before their eyes. Hair, make-up, costume and even props were all in a Halloween theme, so that the entire night seemed to be a creepily gorgeous display of dance and magic.

For those few hours it felt as if they had been plucked wholesale from their real lives, their romantic dramas and the mundane obligations of adulthood. They didn't have to talk about their problems, think about or even acknowledge them. Instead their responsibility was to the beat, to the stage, to the dancers. It was an intoxicating experience.

At one point Ava looked to her right and then to her left. On her right was Julia, her eyes shining and her face flushed as she applauded a spectacular dance and then the judges' hilarious comments. *This woman is a total stranger*, she thought to herself, *but I know exactly how she feels tonight, exactly how much this means to her*. It had never occurred to Ava that the experience of a live show would mean such a connection with the rest of the audience. She had only ever considered the dancers and the judges, but now she was intoxicated by the way they were all sharing this high-spirited enthusiasm. Then she glanced to her left and saw Mel, giving the broadest grin she had seen out of her for quite some time. Suddenly she felt a rush of affection for Gabe – not for those stolen moments in the shop or at dance classes, but because he had been so kind as to give her the tickets and she had been able to treat Mel to an evening as special as this.

By the time they were finally led off set they were overwhelmed by how exciting it had all been. They stood chatting with the other audience guests for a little while, and after giving Julia and Chris huge hugs goodbye and promising to stay in touch with them via Twitter they called a taxi. Finally, they braved the cold like a couple of teenagers until their cab arrived. Moments later they were tumbling into the back of it.

'Oh man, I am starving!' said Ava as she shuffled about trying to free the bit of skirt that she was sitting on. 'Can we go home and have a festival of late-night cheese on toast, like the olden days?'

'Sure,' said Mel. It was impossible not to notice that she had a huge wobble in her voice. Immediately after she spoke, she turned her face to look out of the window, hoping to conceal what were clearly tears from Ava.

'Honey, are you okay? What happened?'

And before either of them knew it Mel was sobbing. Hysterical, wracking sobs that were making her shoulders shudder and her mascara streak down her face. Truly, this was ugly crying.

'What's wrong, what happened?' pressed Ava, unable to understand what had caused this sudden outburst. Mel had seemed so cheered all evening.

'I'm sorry, nothing has happened – it's nothing at all, I promise. And please don't think it's you. It's just that I was

254

so looking forward to today, I've been so down and it's been like a little lighthouse of joy in this grimness of the last few weeks. And then, even before the final dance was danced I was starting to feel dread.'

'Dread about *what*? Is there something I don't know?' Ava reached into her handbag and pulled out some tissues, which she handed over to Mel, pressing them into her hands.

'No, that's the awful thing!' Mel let out a kind of howl of tears at this point, almost panicking Ava by the depths of her misery. 'I was just dreading it all being over and life having to go back to normal on Monday. Except when I say normal, I mean this terrifying indefinite agony.'

'What do you mean? With Rich?'

'Yes, *exactly*! I can't imagine a time when I'll be able to start trusting him again. I am supposed to get up every morning and get stuff done and look sexy and seem perky, but I don't know when it will be over, when I'll know for sure that this dalliance of his is in the past. Some mornings I wake up and I think it would be easier if he said he was leaving me, then at least I'd know, there would be a definite. I could start planning; I'd get on with things and begin the process of getting over him. But this, this is like being constantly on trial. I don't know when it will end.'

'It *will* end, babe. Of course it will. You'll surprise yourself with how quickly this will all heal over. You two have a really strong relationship – and the kids! There's too much to play for here and you still share too much love between you.'

'That's what I have to believe. But what makes me so angry is that I feel as if I've been given a second chance, only I shouldn't have to have one! He was my husband: we were already on Chance One. And now I'm left with this exhausting sense that I'm on probation for something I never did in the first place.'

'That must be maddening, truly infuriating and so hard to move on from, but I'm sure he loves you and the children. However it works out it will be fine, everything will be fine.'

Ava found herself repeating those words, but she had no idea whether or not they were true. Everything she had thought she was sure about was becoming more and more wobbly each day, her certainties slowly peeling away.

'And do you know what?' said Mel, having been hit by a sudden tidal wave of rage. 'I don't even care about that stuff right now, I just want to make sure that you save yourself. If you're not 100 per cent sure about Rob, you absolutely have to get out while you still can. I mean it! I take back everything I said earlier and the other week. Just pack it in.'

Ava was frowning at her friend, not sure what the right thing to say was now. Her mouth opened and shut.

'You have to be so sure, babe,' continued Mel. 'You have to be so in love before you get involved with marriage and babies. If you're not sure now, you never will be. There can't be any indifference when you start all of that. You can't take chances about Rob. And I know what's making you anxious, it's the idea of having to start again at your age.'

Ava wasn't sure she was enjoying these truth bombs from her sobbing friend and glanced out of the window to see how much further they had to go.

'But at the moment the idea of being alone and being able to start again sounds like actual heaven,' added Mel. 'If it wasn't for the kids I would do that, I would just go for it. You could too, if you wanted.'

Ava realised she had to be the bigger person here. She couldn't take this personally, or at face value.

'Come on, love,' she said, rubbing her on the top of her back like a sick child. 'You're just saying stuff that you don't really mean now. Rich has had a wobble, he's been an utter idiot; people make mistakes, we both know that. But the important thing is he admitted it to you. He knows he's been a fool and he swears he still loves you. That counts, that *really* counts. Let's not get caught up on my circumstances, it's pointless us trying to compare things. As with everyone's life, it's about knowing which are the chances that count, not waiting for chances to find you.'

Proud of her sudden burst of wisdom, Ava thanked the taxi driver who was now turning into Mel's road. She told him what number to stop at, then paid him with a big tip and led the still-quivering Mel to her doorstep. There she got out another tissue from her bag and wiped underneath her friend's eyes for her.

'Have you paid Dawn already? Is there anything I need to tell her?'

Mel nodded emphatically.

'Yes, her money was on the kitchen counter. Maybe just check that she got it?'

'Great,' said Ava. 'I will go and let her know that we're back safely, and why don't you head on upstairs?'

'Okay, and thank you.'

They hugged on the doorstep then Ava let them in with the spare key she always carried, having been given one when Jake was a baby and she used to babysit. Ava went in and said good night to Dawn, saw her off down the road and then went in to the kitchen, kicked off her shoes and found the bottle of wine they'd had a glass of earlier. By the time Mel came downstairs with her make-up off and the children having been kissed goodnight, Ava was at the hob making them two rounds of cheese on toast.

Mel was now swathed in expensive-looking tracksuit bottoms and some sort of cashmere shawl. She pulled out a chair from the kitchen table and sat at it cross-legged, like a child. As Ava turned to pass her a glass of wine, she looked around the kitchen and thought how often she had dismissed her friend as having absolutely everything while she herself was still struggling. She took a glance at Mel, now so vulnerable, and realised everyone was struggling.

They sat there with their wine and their cheese on toast and chatted for two further hours. Everything that Mel had been trying to keep a lid on earlier was finally unburdened now that the excitement of the day had died down. She had, to put it simply, been trying too hard to be perfect, to be all things to all people and not allowing herself to just

258

'be'. They talked about how she had to invest a little more in herself, do something like dance classes or join a book group, anything that wasn't simply for the benefit of the kids or her home. Ava's diagnosis was that she had to rediscover her 'Mel-ness'.

There was a pause and then Mel apologised for the things she had said earlier.

'I didn't meant to be so judgemental,' she explained. 'And I certainly didn't mean to start telling you what decisions to make. I guess I got a bit carried away.'

'It's fine,' said Ava. 'I get equally frustrated because … well, there isn't really anything to judge – I almost wish something had happened. At the moment I've had all of the angst but none of the fun. And now Gabe has vanished, I have no way of working out if that spark was actually him or just stuff I had imposed on him because of Rob being an idiot.'

'It's so tricky,' agreed Mel.

'Yes, but either way, we'll always have each other – and cheese on toast. And French toast, all of the toasts – they'll be ours forever.'

'Absolutely, I'll drink to that!' said Mel, raising her glass. 'And thank you *so* much for coming up. Please thank Mystery Gabe if you ever hear from him again, but I'm sure you will.'

'Of course I will – if I do. Either way, it's been a weekend to remember.'

They headed upstairs one after the other, and it was as if the last twenty-odd years had never happened. After

259

brushing their teeth, they hugged each other goodnight and went to bed. When Ava got into her room she looked at her phone for the first time since she had arrived in London: nothing from Rob, nothing from Gabe. She didn't know if it was heartache, despair or a sense of relief that washed over her as she climbed in between the crisp sheets.

Early the next morning the children were up and about, excited to have time with their Ava. Marcie lavished affection on her and even Jake enjoyed being taken to the park with some fresh company to show off. Mel made the grown-ups a huge cooked breakfast and they eked every last ounce of Sunday fun out of the day before Ava headed back to Waterloo and home on the train.

As Ava's train passed through the outskirts of London and ever closer to Salisbury darkness began to surround her carriage. Now the reality of another week began to creep up on her. The magic of last night – the glamour, the excitement, the sense that anything, absolutely anything might be possible – was already starting to fade. She cast her mind back to one of the contestants talking to the camera. 'I can't believe I have another chance,' she had said, grinning from ear to ear, completely invigorated by the revelation that she had had a bit of faith shown in her by the audience.

Those words kept nagging away at her, as if she had been saying them directly to Ava. *Did she too have another chance?*

The train rattled on and as she closed her eyes in the darkness she imagined it was hurtling on towards the edge of a precipice. As it pulled into Salisbury she felt her nerves gathering, the storm looming. She collected her car from the car park and dumped her overnight back in the passenger seat before heading home. On the way back she stopped for a bottle of wine from the local off-licence. She didn't really feel like it, as she was exhausted from such a full-on day of playing with Jake and Marcie and still a little queasy from eating so late the previous night, not to mention the wine. But she knew she had to be fully equipped for what was to come: she must be ready.

As she pulled into her little road she saw Rob's car already parked outside her house, as planned. He had always said that when he got back from his weekend in Bristol he would sleep over at her house as usual, so he could get to work easily in the morning.

She hovered at the doorstep, took a deep breath, turned her key in the lock and let herself in.

'Hi there!' she called out, loudly enough that he would either hear her over the noise of the TV or upstairs from the bedroom.

'Hi,' he replied, quietly. She turned her head from the coat rack where she was hanging up her coat and scarf to see that he was just sitting there in the kitchen. He was at the kitchen table, a glass of water by his hand. The TV wasn't switched on, there was no laptop out, no iPad in his hand, nothing. He was quite simply sitting there in the semi-darkness.

She put her handbag on the hall table, pulled on a cardigan and sat down at the table facing him.

'Hi.'

'Hi.'

And then she said it, those few words that can only mean one thing.

'We need to talk.'

Chapter 14

Dancing to Different Beats

'You've done *what*?' Lauren was clearly not best pleased by Ava's news. She was in her car, talking into her hands-free kit and bellowing like Bono at Wembley. 'WHY?'

In truth, Ava had hoped for a little more sympathy when she called her sister to tell her what had happened the night before. She pretty much had it all planned out in her head. First, she would tell her about the grim conversation, then move on to the reasons, and afterwards Lauren would offer sympathy for the upsetting way that things had panned out. *Perhaps she'd come round with lasagne again*, Ava thought hopefully as she drove to the shop, having decided to call Lauren as soon as she got a quiet moment.

In her head she replayed the way that things had unfolded when she got back from London and how she would explain them to her sister: the heavy Sunday night blues that had descended over her as she'd approached the house and how it had seemed that Rob had been sitting there for hours. He really did look as if he knew this conversation was coming, but he wasn't the kind of guy who would say it himself.

When she had sat down at the kitchen table he had had such an air of total resignation. He seemed to be waiting to get it over, yet unprepared to do any of the heavy lifting himself. Ava had talked quietly and calmly, giving him the reasoning that she had unexpectedly found herself planning all the way home on the train from London. At first, he had taken it in the spirit that was intended: equally calmly and reasonably. Ava had told him that she felt they weren't going anywhere, that their relationship had run out of steam, and that it wasn't fair for her to expect him to change things about himself, if what they wanted were different things.

She pointed out that he had seemed increasingly distracted, not that invested in their relationship, and that he appeared to be seeking to make a few changes of his own in life. Taking a deep breath, she then reassured him that she thought he really should go off and do all those things for himself and be the very best he could be but clarified that she couldn't hang around to see how it worked out for him. It wasn't fair for her to have to sit around and wait to see what kind of boyfriend she ended up with in a year's time. She said that she was sure he would understand this.

Rob didn't dispute that things were changing for him and for the first time he actually opened up to say that he was now seriously considering giving up his job, going travelling, doing some courses and all sorts. But then his tone changed and he did seem more than a little affronted that he should be expected to go through this alone.

'This evening I was going to talk to you about how I think you should be a bit more supportive,' he told her with no sense of irony.

'Oh, I see,' said Ava. 'The thing is, I'm really not sure what it is I'm being supportive of any more.'

She pulled her cardigan closer to her, yanking the sleeves right down over her hands as if this would somehow protect her from the sadness and frustration of this conversation.

'What do you mean? It's *me* you're supporting.'

'But I'm still not sure exactly what that entails. It's not as if you have some great passion that I could really get behind. If you really wanted to give all this up tomorrow because you had realised you wanted to be a pro surfer more than anything else, then great! I could get behind that. Or if you dreamt of opening the very best cheese shop in the country, even if you wanted to go into politics – those are all things I could get behind. But the problem here is you don't seem to know who you are any more, which leaves me kind of dangling. Don't think I don't support this exploration, but please don't expect me to sit at home like the good wifey while you do it! After all, it's not as if you're offering me any guarantees that you will actually be interested in sharing a life when you return from this strange life-odyssey.'

'How can I?' said Rob, with a shrug that reeked of petulance.

'Exactly, you can't! So you can't ask me to stay.' Ava looked down and let out a deep breath. Then, pushing her hair back from her face, she said: 'Rob, we don't get

265

many chances in life, we have to make every single one of them count, every day, so I can't waste a year waiting for you to make a decision between making short films or plumbing, or whatever it is to be. And you can't afford not to go and do whatever it is you need to do to be settled. You have been a wonderful boyfriend to me, but it can't go on.'

'But I love you.' Rob put a hand out across the table to touch hers. 'I want to make you happy.'

'What do you think makes me happy?' Ava asked, sadly.

'Your shop, your family, *Strictly* and dancing stuff?'

'And those are all things that you actively seek to avoid in my life.'

Rob had looked forlorn and then resentful. Suddenly, as if a shadow had passed over his face, his expression turned to one of anger.

'You just don't think I'm as good as Rory – that's it. All this wedding nonsense has gone to your head! You're jealous of Lauren and now you've decided you want an upgrade.'

'That's nonsense, it's just nonsense. This isn't about practical things. If I've learned anything this weekend, it's that material wealth won't help you sort your marriage out. Ever. Come on, that just isn't fair!'

'But I love you.'

'I love you too, but …'

'I know, we're dancing to different beats!' Rob laughed and gave a shrug. And in that moment she understood exactly why she had loved him for so long. They stood up and hugged. Rob still spent the night at her house, curled around her, but in the morning they both knew this was the end. Now the task in hand was to move on with as much respect for each other as possible – and without causing too much of a fuss around Lauren's wedding.

A few short hours in, that first task actually seemed to be going very well, but the second … well, Lauren was clearly not pleased.

'Why would you do such a stupid thing?' she asked, spitting down the phone. Ava winced and held the receiver slightly away from her ear. She had grabbed the five minutes that the shop was empty to call Lauren and seek a bit of sympathy from her. With Matt gone to buy adhesive tape – their roll having mysteriously vanished – she thought she would have enough time for a nice little chat. But a nice little chat it was not.

'Well, because we weren't in love any more and we needed to do other things with our lives, apart,' Ava tentatively explained.

'You guys could have made it work, though. You could have tried harder,' said Lauren, clearly exasperated. 'It's so late for you to be starting again.'

Those were the exact words that had taunted Ava over and over for the last few months. Every dark, sleepless night, every time she had checked her email not knowing what she was hoping to find, every time she considered walking down the aisle at Lauren's wedding as a single woman. Almost 40, was it too late for her to be starting out again?

But that threat no longer held any weight with her. Not after the weekend. *Strictly*, her chats with Mel, her newfound confidence from dance classes had combined to make her realise that there would always be more chances. There might not be many, but they'd always be there. 'It's too late, you've made your choice, you've just got to stick with it now' was an idea that now bored her, having rattled around in her head for so many months. So, when she was finally confronted with someone saying this out loud to her, she leapt back at Lauren like a coiled spring.

'*No*! I'm sorry, Sis, but it's not too late. We don't have finite chances, we just don't! We get to make some chances ourselves and I'm going to do that.'

'Good grief, what's happened to you? Have you swallowed a copy of *Eat Pray Love*?'

Lauren's acidic observations were now starting to grate.

'Lauren, please! I'm sad about this, really I am. But I'm also hopeful. I don't want to make you sad, or to ruin your wedding or anything like that, but I would like you to be kind.'

'Okay, okay! I'll be kind, but I do need to see you on Friday morning with Matt, at the church. We're going to talk to the vicar about what we can and can't do with regards to getting ivy on the pillars.'

'This Friday?' asked Ava.

'Yes, *this* Friday – it's the only time the priest can make it. That church is so beautiful, it's pretty much booked up, night and day. Why else do you think we had to have the wedding on a Sunday, doofus?'

'Okay, I'll do my best,' said Ava, flicking to her diary.

'Sis, it's not really a "do my best" situation. You *have* to make it. The priest doesn't have any other appointments until way too late.'

'Okay, *okay …*'

'And I'm sorry to hear about Rob, really I am. I just wish …'

'Yes?'

'… I just wish it could have waited until after my wedding.'

You couldn't fault Lauren's honesty, of that you could be sure.

'*Right …*'

Ava pressed her nails into the palms of her hands, trying desperately not to lose patience.

'I know how that sounds,' Lauren's tone softened slightly. 'I'm not as bad as all that, but I had so hoped I would be magical and romantic for everyone. Yes, it will mess up the seating plan, but I had also hoped Rob would enjoy the day and be, you know …'

'No, I *don't* know. What are you talking about?'

'Inspired,' said Lauren.

'*What*, you thought your wedding would help me get married?' Apparently Lauren's all-encompassing self-confidence had allowed her to think exactly this. If her spirit could be bottled and sold, it would make her a fortune. *Not that she wasn't clearly someone already well on their way to making a fortune*, Ava mused.

'Yeah, you know what guys are like. They so often need to have someone else check it out first. I thought if Rob saw Rory have a good day then ...'

'Sis, I really need you to understand something.'

'*What*? I have to get out of the car in a minute ...'

'If I wanted to get married that much, I would have done it! I have a lovely life, great friends, a wonderful job, I love my family. What I want is romance, to feel treasured, to know that someone really loves me, not that they've settled for me out of a fear of being left alone. And more than that, I CANNOT allow myself to settle for anyone either!'

By this point Ava was pacing the shop, trying to let out some of the pent-up frustration that she felt from trying to express herself properly to her sister. With that final sentence she had banged her fist on the bouquet preparation area, causing a pair of pinking shears to leap up. She shocked even herself with the noise, and as she turned she saw that Matt was now back in the shop, kneeling in the doorway and bent double to tie his shoelace. He was doing a good job of discreetly trying to look as if he had not just heard Ava's impassioned rant.

Ava was met with silences all around her. Matt continued to busy himself with his shoelace and Lauren was clearly stunned at her end of the phone.

'Right ...' she eventually said. 'Well, might I suggest evening primrose oil and an early night. And I'll see you and Matt on Friday.'

'Okay, fine! But please, show a little respect – your

wedding isn't the only event of national importance going on right now.'

Ava slammed down her mobile and let out a yelp of frustration.

Matt stood up, looking tentatively at his boss to see if it was safe to ask if she was okay.

In the end he opted for the more delicate 'Cup of tea?' route.

'Yes, please, Matt! Yes, please,' Ava replied without hesitation. 'And what are you doing on Friday? We must get Minx in to cover the shop for a couple of hours because according to Princess Lauren we need to head up to the church in Wilton to talk about the flowers for her wedding. I'm afraid I'll need your help with ladders and the like. Are you okay with that – and on the day?'

'Yeah, sure,' he said. *Was that guy actually fluster-able?* Ava wondered what it would take for him to be upset or panicked.

'It should be fun,' he continued. 'Exciting to be involved and all that – a bit of romance in the family is never a bad thing, no?'

Ava said nothing but busied herself by shuffling a few invoices around to avoid his gaze. She was convinced just a momentary glimpse of eye contact would result in him giving her a cheeky wink that would indicate exactly what Lauren had thought – that Rob would somehow be 'inspired' by attending the wedding.

A moment later the kettle had boiled and Matt busied himself with making the two mugs for them, all the while whistling along to a tune that Ava vaguely recognised from the TV. Once the brews were done, he stepped over to the worktop area where Ava was sitting. In order to find a flat space to put it after her invoice shuffling, he had to set aside a packet of rather old-fashioned Christmas cards that had been delivered earlier in the day. They were charity cards that she had ordered in a sunny haze back in August, decorated with a large angel on them. Very traditional, they were for clients and suppliers. Matt glanced at the angel image, then back at Ava.

'Pretty angel, isn't it? Oh, that reminds me – your pal came in again earlier. When you'd popped to the bank.'

'What pal?' Ava had no idea what he was talking about. She picked up her tea distractedly.

'Gabriel,' he said, tapping his index finger on the Christmas cards.

Ava felt as if someone was very slowly shifting the floor beneath her. Her stomach lurched.

'Gabriel?' she asked quietly.

'Yeah, you remember,' said Matt, now on a stool and reaching for some roses. 'The dark-haired guy, smells good, nice and polite. He always comes in and lets you do what you want, doesn't mind paying. Lovely guy, lovely!' Matt was blowing a bit of dust from the shop's brickwork from a perfectly pale rose.

'Yes, I know the one,' said Ava. Her mouth was suddenly very dry. She reached for her tea, took a huge sip before realising the liquid was way too hot, and then gave an odd, swallowing gasp.

'What did he want?' she asked as casually as she could.

'The usual.'

'The usual?'

'Yeah, he's in about once a week, I reckon. Usually when you're out the last couple of weeks, I suppose.'

Ava started to feel slightly short of breath. *Gabe had been coming into the shop?*

'So he just buys flowers?' she asked.

'What else would he do?'

'He has never asked after me?'

'Well, yeah, usually he does. But then so do most customers. Everyone loves you. No one ever buys a bouquet for a second time and doesn't ask me to send you their best. I can't tell you every time, or you'd get big headed, Avie.'

She was standing in the middle of the shop, her brow knotted, running a finger around the edge of her mug of tea. Then, suddenly, the penny dropped.

'Oh, Boss!' said Matt, with a giggle.

'*What*?'

'It's like THAT, is it?'

'No, no, don't be silly …'

'It's okay, I won't tell Rob. It's safe.'

'Well, it's funny you should say that, but Rob and I aren't together any more.'

'Oh man, I'm really sorry about that!' To be fair, Matt did *look* sorry, but then an impish grin returned to his face.

'Then that means you're free for Mister Flowers.'

273

'Don't be silly!' Ava giggled and blushed like a schoolgirl who had just had her pigtails pulled. Then the blush turned to the heat of shame at what it must look like to Matt.

'I suppose you want to know what he said this time, then?' said Matt, with a smirk.

'Go on then,' she told him.

'He specifically said that he had been hoping to catch you and he told me he hoped you were well. He chatted quite a lot, asked how long the shop had been around, if it had always been yours, that kind of thing. Now I come to think about it, I reckon he was playing for time, hoping you'd be back.'

Matt giggled and nudged her in the ribs as she thought about that queue in the bank and the crazy woman who had upturned her handbag in the line, making a huge fuss and demanding everyone stand back to help her find every single penny that had rolled out of her wallet – 'so that the bank doesn't claim it as theirs'.

'Then he spent a fortune on a bunch of lilies and left.'

'So, he left no note or anything? No contact details?'

'No. He said he'd be back soon and I thought that if he was that pally with you then he could, you know, call.'

'Okay, thank you, Matt.'

Ava's mind was racing. *Were these casual visits a result of him just 'popping by'? Who was it he was buying flowers for? Why didn't he email or something?*

'He's a nice guy, though,' mumbled Matt, as he got back on the steps to reach some elegant foliage.

But Ava didn't answer. She took another sip of tea and wondered what to do next, if anything.

As it turned out, life was kind to Ava, presenting her with a week to leave her with little time to ponder either her sadness over Rob, or whether or not to try and contact Gabe. The pressure of trying to keep up with normal business affairs, not to mention getting the huge orders and designs for the wedding, was more than enough to occupy her. Every time her mind drifted towards the shallow waters of self-pity or lovelorn indulgence, the phone would go with either customers, or Mel or Lauren wanting updates on absolutely everything.

Lauren remained a little prickly about the fact that Ava's break-up might cause a slight romance-deficit at the wedding, and their mum was similarly horrified. Ava did not hear from Jackie until the Wednesday and was mildly put out that it had taken her that long to call and give her condolences. When she finally rang, Ava almost immediately began to wish that she hadn't.

'I only want what's best for you, darling.'

'But you don't know what's best for me, Mum.'

'I do think settling down would be good for you. Look at how happy Lauren is!'

'Yes, but Mum, Lauren is in love.'

'Stability is underrated in this modern world.'

'I really rate stability very highly, Mum – that's why I've worked so hard on my business. What's important to me is feeling cherished, not feeling that I have just settled.'

'Oh darling, still such a dreamer! But how much longer can you afford to be?'

And so she continued. It was just at this point when Ava really started to wish one member of her family would take such a flying leap that she ended up in hospital.

In the end, the one person who was injured was Matt. Ever the enthusiast, the chatterbox, the one most eager to help, he had leapt at the chance to assist with the wedding flowers and turned up bright and breezy on the Friday morning. After a cordial chat with Lauren, Ava and the vicar, he had shot up the ladder and was happily looking for points where he could affix flowers to create the desired Winter Wonderland. As the girls stood below, chatting and pointing, Ava with her big box of cuttings and examples, Matt shuffled around, delicately exploring the stone of the pillar, then dragging the ladder to another area and doing the same there.

In the end, all it took was a sneeze. He had been complaining about his girlfriend Amy having a filthy cold all week and, given the chunkiness of his sweater, it looked as if he was its next victim. After plonking the ladder on the flagstone floor of the church, he shimmied up it again before letting out a huge sneeze. The force of it caused his head to jam forward and bang the stone pillar in front of him, which in turn stunned and caused him to topple off the ladder.

'*Matt!*' cried the sisters in unison as he fell. They ran to where he lay, staring up at the wooden beams of the church ceiling.

'Matt, are you okay?' asked Ava. 'Did you hit your head?'

'My leg ...' he said blearily before closing his eyes. Ava looked down and saw that his foot was bent back in a position no leg should comfortably be able to accommodate.

'Lauren, we need to call 999. He might be concussed, and we can't lift him with his foot like that.'

Half an hour later they were in the ambulance on their way to Salisbury General. Matt was lapsing in and out of consciousness, his ankle swollen to grotesque proportions. When they arrived at Casualty, Ava asked Lauren to leave them and explained that she would be back soon to sort out the flowers. Lauren's previous pushiness was now replaced with warm hugs for everyone and she promised to come back with food if they hadn't been seen in a couple of hours.

Once Matt was taken through to X-Ray Ava wandered off in search of a cup of tea. She had never really spent any time there before and found the map plans particularly confusing in her flustered state. As she walked slowly down a seemingly endless, gleaming corridor, she spotted two small children darting out of a room. They were each holding teddy bears and dancing about in the corridor ahead. As Ava walked towards them, she realised that she recognised the profile of the little girl. At that moment the child turned and saw her.

'Look, Toby! It's the lady from the flower shop!' she said, tugging at her brother's T-shirt.

'Hello there,' said Ava, smiling now as she approached them. 'It's Ellie, isn't it?'

'Yes!' said the little girl, now running towards her. And as she reached her Ava noticed an adult frame come out of the room, quietly closing the door behind him.

It was then that she realised, when everything clicked into place: the flowers, the sick mother, the strange disappearances.

It was Gabe.

Looking up, he saw her and smiled.

'Hi there,' he said warmly. 'What are you doing here?'

Ava noticed his body stiffen as he saw her. He reached down to take Toby and Ellie by the hand. *How dare he!* she thought. *His wife in hospital, two children to look after, and there he is gadding around at dance classes, inviting women on trips to London. Who does that?* She felt her world folding in – all those chances, the confidence with which she had left Rob, so cocksure there were plenty more Gabes in the sea. It never even occurred to her that there might be malice or lies intended in his actions.

'Hi,' said Ava quietly, still too dumbstruck by this realisation.

'Is everything okay,' he asked, 'what with you being here? I don't mean to pry, but are you hurt?'

'No, no, it's not me! It's Matt from the shop. His foot …'

'Oh, I see. We're off to the café if you'd like to join us. It's lovely to see you.' He dipped his head to try and catch her gaze but she was still staring down, stunned.

'Okay.' She felt numb. There was nowhere else she could go. She'd been heading off to get a cup of tea anyway. She might as well join them for the children's sake, if nothing else.

'How is the shop?' asked Gabe as they proceeded down the corridor.

'Oh I love the flowers shop!' said Ellie, reaching for Ava's hand. 'Can we go there again?'

'Of course,' said Gabe with a smile. He then turned to smile at Ava, with a look that seemed to say 'Kids, eh?' She smiled limply back, then turned to Ellie to say, 'Yes, come by any time you like.'

Toby was tagging behind them now, driving his plastic truck along the edge of the corridor. It struck Ava that a bright blue, shiny, laminated corridor would be a perfect play area for a little boy like him. And they both seemed so comfortable, as if they spent far too long in the place. She remembered those months visiting Lauren when she was small – it just wasn't right for a child that young to know their way round a hospital so well. Ava felt a huge surge of sadness swell in her. Too much had happened, too soon – Lauren, the wedding, Rob, the children, Mel … All of those emotions were rushing at her as they turned into the café. Gabe pulled out a seat and helped Ellie onto it, then pulled out a second for Ava.

It was only then that she noticed what Toby was doing: scrabbling at Gabe's leg, holding out a Kit Kat to him, saying, 'Can I have this one? Can I, please? Please, Uncle Gabe? *Please*, Uncle Gabe?'

Chapter 15

Salsa Time

'*Uncle* Gabe?' Ava asked Toby. She put her hand out gently and moved a curl behind his ear. 'Uncle …?'

'Yeah, Gabey the baby,' said Ellie, with a giggle. 'That's what we call him because he's just a big baby!'

Toby laughed with her before scrambling onto a chair and turning back to him, waving the chocolate. 'Please, Uncle Gabe, *please*?'

'Of course you can have it, big man. I promised, didn't I?' said Gabe.

Then he turned back to Ava, asking, 'So what can I get you? Would you like to stay here with these two, given that they are so taken with you, and then I'll go and get us some treats.'

'Sure,' said Ava. There was a ringing in her ears as confusion and potential piled in on one another in what felt like her now very crowded brain. 'I would love a cup of Earl Grey.'

As she said it, she looked down at the sleeve she was fiddling awkwardly with and realised she was wearing a really quite hideous shirt. It was comically unattractive. She had got dressed that morning ready to clamber ladders in a dusty church. *It's a Friday in autumn*, she had told herself. *What can possibly happen to you that might in any way require you to look hot?* Consequently she was sitting there in front of Gabe in a tatty shirt so huge and grey that it almost resembled a fisherman's smock. It was a far cry from the silky, waist-cinching dresses that she had danced in with Gabe, all of those weeks ago. In that moment it felt as if it had happened a hundred years ago, maybe even to someone else. She ran her fingers through her hair and quickly wiped under her eyes, belatedly checking for any smudged mascara left over from her tears in the ambulance.

'No problem,' said Gabe. 'An Earl Grey coming up.'

He put a hand on her shoulder reassuringly. It was the first time she had felt his touch for a very long time. Something inside of her melted, as if a part of her that had been tense for a very long time was now relaxing. Suddenly she felt extremely tired. Gabe headed towards the counters, leaving her with the two small children. They carried on chatting amiably, including her in details of recent purchases and parties they had coming up. After a minute or so, Toby rummaged in his brightly coloured rucksack and pulled out a small toy truck. He tentatively began driving it up and down the stripes of the laminated table top. Ellie stared, almost reproachfully.

'Uncle Gabe doesn't like me playing with this one so much,' said Toby.

281

'Why not, sweetheart?' asked Ava in the same chatty tone that they had all been using earlier.

'Because of the accident,' said Ellie without hesitation.

'What accident?' asked Ava.

'The one that hurt Mummy and Daddy,' she answered quietly.

'Are they okay?'

'Daddy is still asleep.'

'So, Uncle Gabe is different from Daddy?'

'Yes, of course,' said the little girl.

Ava looked into her clear, honest eyes. Was this why she seemed so wise, so old before her years? Was it just that she had seen too much for her tender years? But Ava felt she couldn't ask any more about anything. Prodding a nine-year-old for details on the potential single status of what now turned out to be her uncle simply wasn't done, no matter how much this revelation had set off a whirlwind of butterflies in Ava's stomach.

'I see,' said Ava. 'That's sad.'

Toby, in a world of his own now, continued to drive the truck. Up and down the table, around the salt, round the pepper and back to the edge. As he went, he made revving noises, leading it carefully around its course.

'Yes, it is,' Ellie continued quietly. 'I wish he would wake up, like Mummy did.'

Ava nodded towards her and smiled. Reaching out a hand, she stroked the little girl's pale blonde hair. She really didn't know what else to do. 'I'm sure you have lots of people who love you and all think the same thing,' she replied, at a loss for anything more comforting to say. The confidence she felt around Marcie and Jake had suddenly evaporated; she didn't know what else she could offer, what might hurt Ellie more and what might provide a crumb of comfort. Luckily she was saved by the return of Gabe.

He produced the treats from the café tray with a flourish and presented them to each of the little ones in the style of a silver-service waiter, giving bows and speaking in ridiculous faux-formal language. Then he leant over behind Ava's neck and placed the cardboard cup of Earl Grey down in front of her.

'Madam …' he said, with a wink.

'Why, thank you, sir,' she replied. At this point Toby presented her with his juice carton, asking her to put the straw in for him. She remembered doing this for Jake recently, under happier circumstances.

'I wasn't sure what the lady wanted in terms of sugar and milk, so I brought a little of everything,' continued Gabe, producing a fistful of sachets and tiny cartons. Ava picked out some milk and a brown sugar.

'Thank you … Uncle Gabe?' She hoped her inquisitive tone would be all that she needed to get confirmation out of him. Luckily there was a gleeful 'Uncle Gabey Baby!' from Ellie.

'Yes, these are my niece and nephew.' He looked puzzled, as if he didn't understand what she was asking. Then he ruffled the children's hair. 'We're here for visiting time. Their parents were in a nasty traffic accident a couple of months ago.'

'Well yes, I've been piecing this together. I'm so sorry to hear that, really sorry.' Ava stirred her tea with one of the little wooden sticks he had brought with the milk and sugar. She did her best not to make too much eye contact with him in case the children felt left out and tried to join in this decidedly adult conversation. 'I had no idea. There is so much I didn't realise ...'

'I'm beginning to realise, but yes, my duties here are avuncular only. Daddy is still ...' he began to say.

Ava mouthed 'coma', to which Gabe nodded sadly.

'So, how is Mum?'

'It's been a tough old road, but she's rallying. What we're all working towards is that she might be home for Christmas. It's ambitious, but not unreasonable. It was a nasty accident. She was out for the count for a week or two as well. Farm machinery, flooded road, grim. It has been difficult, but I think we might be over the worst now, dare I say it.'

'So have you had to step in with our two small friends here? Must have been somewhat time consuming ...'

'Yes, exactly! But that's been the best of it, to be honest. It has been a total pleasure in a very dark period.' The colour drained from his face and he looked at her with those wide brown eyes. Ava locked his gaze. 'It has been horrific. To see my sister like that ...' He ruffled a hand through his hair and swallowed, trying hard to compose himself. Blinking slowly, he gave a big exhale. 'We thought we would lose ... and as for him ... It all happened just after I applied to do the classes. I had no idea.'

284

'I see. So, even back in August – the flowers?' Ava was cringing at the selfishness of asking about the flowers, but while the gates of conversation were open she couldn't resist; she had to check.

'Yes, they were for her, always for her. And thank you for them, they made such a difference.'

'I can't believe you didn't say anything. People are so often such wrecks when they come in. The things they sometimes tell me, it defies belief. But really?'

'Absolutely. She had a bunch there when she came to – she said she could smell them.'

'Wow, that's so great to hear! I'm thrilled that something like that could be any help at all. It's so special to be able to do anything for people at moments of such intense emotion. That seems so long ago, though, so long for these two.' She nodded towards the children, who were now contentedly munching on chocolate bars.

'Oh, you *have* helped me,' he told her with a smile, 'more than you can ever know.' He glanced at her over the top of his coffee cup, his gaze holding hers. His other hand rested on Ellie's head. Ava felt a bit of herself melting further.

'I just wish there were more hours in the day,' he continued. 'I had … well, I had quite a lot of stuff of my own going on. Work, sport, you know – life. I loved those dance classes. But I don't know …'

'Do you think you'll ever go back?'

'I don't think so. It's half term now and then next week I'll be doing all the hours I can just to catch up. I'm taking it in turns with my parents to get these two to bed every night, so probably not. I long to, I had a real ball there, but it's a question of priorities at the moment.'

'I understand.' She wanted to burst into tears. 'That's a real shame.'

'It really is. I wish I could have taken the whole course – I liked the crowd there, too.'

'I have become very fond of everyone I met there,' she said, scarcely able to believe she had dared to say this.

'So did I,' he told her. He was fiddling with her empty sugar sachet. She looked at his strong, tanned forearms, then his hands. She remembered his hands taking hers in that hall. It seemed impossible that they would ever dance together again. An inch from his arms, Toby's head was now resting on the table, driving his little truck doggedly back and forth. Ellie glanced from her brother back up to her uncle's face. He was staring at Ava, his eyes softened.

They stayed in that position for a moment. Ava didn't know what might possibly happen next, she just wanted to stay there. Then she remembered why she was there.

'My goodness, it must have been forty-five minutes by now! I must go back – that's how long they said Matt would be in X-Ray. I've got to get back and see how he's doing. I'm so sorry to rush off like this.'

'Okay, no problem,' he replied. 'Please send him my very best. He seems like a lovely guy and he's certainly a great florist, almost as good as you.'

He stood up and gave her a hug. She buried her face in the shoulder of his soft navy sweater. Suddenly the stress of the day hit her and her whole body, pressed tightly against his as it was, gave a shudder. She immediately took a deep breath. This was neither the time nor the place to burst into hysterical tears. Matt needed her, those children did not need to see another adult in distress, and of course it was deeply, *deeply* unsexy. Ava bit her lip and looked downwards. Gabe lifted her chin slightly with his thumb.

'Hey you, it's going to be okay,' he said. 'It's *all* going to be okay. Trust me, I'm an expert on how things go round here.'

'Thank you,' she replied. And they had another hug, this time including the children, who were now at her knees.

Then she walked down the blue shiny corridor again, smiling to herself as she heard the children calling out her name and wishing her goodbye. She wondered if she would ever see them again.

In the weeks that followed the landscape of Ava's life seemed almost entirely different. Matt needed to have more than two weeks off work but returned as soon as he was permitted. His leg was still in plaster but they set him up with a chair by the workstation, and, all things considered, he coped admirably. Ava urged him to take as long as he needed, but he said he was bored at home and missed the company. Before his return Minx had ended up working every spare hour that she had outside of college, doing her best to help Ava out as much as she could. She rose to the challenge and started to really fit in with the team, as well as proving to have a good eye and a steady hand with the flowers.

Ava made the most of her work crisis by immersing herself in it. She worked all week, staying late at the shop to make sure everything that Matt usually got done had been taken care of. Weekends she spent running, planning designs for the wedding flowers and catching up with friends with whom she had lost touch during the dying days of her relationship with Rob. There was another tear-jerking visit to Viv's house, where the sisters tried on their finished dresses and lavished praise on her magnificent handiwork. And then there was the final Sunday lunch with the whole family – their last one with Lauren as a single woman. It was also the first lunch that Ava had turned up to alone for several years. She didn't mind nearly as much as her mother, though. After all, it was what she had chosen. It was very much *not* what Jackie would have chosen, however.

During this strange, not-quite-lonely time Ava had two other great consolations: dance class and *Strictly*. Of course *Strictly* was a weekly treat. As she and Lauren had predicted when they'd watched the very first show together, the contestants experienced highs, lows, laughter and tears – and had done it all in a series of Viv's spectacular creations. Each week the show seemed to get better and better, and she and Mel were transfixed all the more, having seen the show live.

As for dance class, Gabe never showed up again, not that she had expected him to after their chance meeting in the hospital, but the class nonetheless turned out to be some-thing of a balm for the soul. Every week she knew there would at the very least be a little pocket of time when she had the safety of losing herself in the beat, the music, the camaraderie. It came to represent a plain of safely and yet joy in her social week.

She wrote the class schedule up in her diary and began to look forward to the different dances and the different moods they would recreate each week. One week they were due to try the Foxtrot and she would anticipate a serious 'Ballroom' frame of mind, only to find the class helpless with giggles about how it was the one dance that Rockingham simply could not get to grips with. Another week she found herself looking forward to the Jive, imagining this would be a joyful return to her dancing days at university. But while she enjoyed the class, she drove home feeling melancholy and introspective, dwelling on the past and how things had turned out. How it was possible to feel blue after jiving was beyond her, but as she made herself supper that night she wished it had been Waltz Week instead.

One thing remained true, though: whether it was Latin or Ballroom that they were doing, slowly but surely her classmates started to become real friends. The Hanburys, who had once seemed so irritating, so smug with their organic, ethically sourced and brushed-steel lifestyle, suddenly revealed themselves to be just as cheery and neurotic as any of Ava's other friends. It turned out they even knew the strange, haughty woman who sometimes came into Dunne's to order romantic flowers to be delivered to herself.

'Her husband has two mistresses in London,' Katie Hanbury once confided when they were chatting in the car park. 'He's there all week and she just lets him get on with it.'

'Nooooo!' replied Ava conspiratorially. 'What goes on in other people's lives makes you wonder why anyone worries about anything. Every now and again I hear gossip that just blows my mind and it's almost always about someone I was previously either slightly scared of, or even slightly envious of.'

'Oh, I know exactly what you mean,' agreed Katie. 'Thank God someone has the courage to admit it, though. And the thing is with this woman, she's actually very lovely. She only seems cold the first couple of times you meet her and then you realise she is simply shy.'

'How does he even have time for *two* mistresses?' queried Ava. 'That just sounds like faff!'

Katie screamed with laughter and good-humouredly shoved Ava's shoulder.

'Well, what I heard was that it's one for the city and one is an old school friend that he sort of reignited with. It's ghastly! But I think she knows if she can stay with him for a year or so longer she will get more money in the settlement. He's one of those traders who had a pre-nup, so he made her sign all sorts.'

'Ugh! Stories like that seem hilarious at first and then they just make me depressed. Hearing that actually makes me so relieved I'm single.'

'You're single?' asked Katie.

'Yes, relatively recently – I broke up with my boyfriend a while ago. It just wasn't – well, you know. It just wasn't going anywhere any more. And at my age …'

'Oh, don't give me that, you're looking great,' said Katie.

And so it continued, with the friendships further strengthened by a dinner party at the Millers' gorgeous house in the countryside. There were other guests beyond the dance class group, all fabulous, eccentric and easy to chat to. Ava was seated next to a charming man who had written a book about tulips, and Jenny proved a stunning cook, despite her slight frame and granola-influenced tastes. Rockingham was also there, garrulous as ever, telling tales of life in the fast lane while making sure that everyone else never had less than a full glass. And Jenny made a particular point of moving her chair to come and sit next to Ava during pudding.

'Now, Ava, darling, Katie Hanbury tells me you are single. Are you quite all right? I had no idea or I would have suggested a glass of wine some time sooner,' she said, spooning cream onto Ava's wheat-free chocolate torte.

'Yes, thank you, Jenny – I'm fine, actually. It's sad, of course, but it was all my own doing. And I've been so busy these last few weeks I have barely had a chance to think about it.'

'Heartache is ghastly, though …'

'I promise, I'm not heartbroken. I wish I had more time to think, if anything.'

'But you *have* been thinking about other things?' asked Jenny, her face a picture of elegance and innocence.

'Well … oh, you mean …?'

Jenny smiled at her discreetly.

'I have at least found out where he went, and why he never turned up for classes any more.' Ava explained about the car crash, the children, and how she had seen him in the hospital with them.

'And what does this mean for the two of you then?' asked the ever-impish Jenny.

'I don't know, Jenny. I just don't know. It was wonderful to see him, and those kids are a dream, but he has a lot on and so do I. You can't force these things, can you? I do think that if he wanted to see more of me he could have got in touch before now.'

'I'm sure there's a simpler explanation than that,' said Jenny. 'When you're ready, perhaps you should get in touch with him. I don't like to hear you being so defeatist.'

'It's not been a great few months, Jenny, but I'm sure I'll perk up soon.'

'I'm sure you will too, darling. Where's the Cha Cha Cha in you? Let's see a bit more of that!'

Ava laughed her off, but as her head hit the pillow later that night Jenny's words floated back into her mind.

As happened every year, Ava looked up one morning and Christmas was rushing at her like a runaway train. The shops, the advertisements, the magazines full of ideas for 'Festive Season Looks', suddenly they were there, taunting her as if she was remiss for not having it all tied up already. She had no real plans for Christmas, and realised she had no work Christmas party to go to, either. There were no office mates either, except for Matt and now Minx, who she offered to take out for a nice pub dinner in a few weeks' time. She flicked disconsolately through the Sunday supplements wondering who these other women were with their go-getting lives. Did they all have the right serum for post-party freshness, office-to-party heels and a secret Santa for everyone they worked with? It seemed an impossible and magical world she would never be part of.

She suddenly remembered the dance class was having a Christmas party. Instead of actually learning on the date of the final class, a vote among them had decided they would all go for a slap-up meal in a pub serving tasty tapas, which also happened to have a room above it for hire. Friends and family were welcome to come along too, either for the meal or the dancing (or both), and it was generally acknowledged among the group that they were looking forward to showing off their newfound dancing skills. The plan had been put together with a suspicious absence of angst or argument. Ava had been looking forward to the evening a lot and chastised herself for momentarily forgetting it.

When Ava asked Lauren if she fancied coming with her, she was met with a face that said 'Are you mad? How could I possibly have time for something like that?' so she backed off pretty quickly and didn't dare ask again. Then, a day later, Lauren called in a conciliatory tone and said she was thrilled that Ava was going to such a fun party, that she was really sorry she wouldn't be able to make it herself and that she could have a plus one for the wedding if she wanted, but that she was to feel no pressure as she was sure she wouldn't need it.

For the first time Ava felt the absence of Rob, who had now been gone long enough for her to start to forget the very worst aspects of their relationship. As his favourite sportsman made a slow and steady climb through the rounds of *Strictly*, she always thought fondly of him and wondered if he was still following his progress in any way. Occasionally she thought about texting him, but they had agreed to have no contact for three months, if possible, and maybe have a drink together in the New Year when she could see how things had gone with his extensive life laundry. Nostalgia was starting to rose tint her memories of their time together, and one particularly tedious evening she found herself wondering if she should perhaps call to see if he wanted to come to the wedding after all.

So it was that on the night of the Christmas party Ava approached the pub alone. It was still a couple of days before December, but the whole of Salisbury was bedecked in flashing festive lights, trees and tinsel. This pub was no different. Ava had a momentary panic that she hadn't made enough effort, especially when she remembered that in the early days of knowing these people she was buying silk dresses just for classes. There was no silk dress tonight: instead, she was wearing the same outfit she had worn to *Strictly*, as a sort of superstitious tribute: her black sparkly top and velvet skirt with high, metallic shoes. She could see her friends chatting inside as she approached. They were all seated around a large oval table, already pouring wine and chatting excitedly. She felt a lump in her throat at the very thought that she might no longer be seeing them all every week; it felt like more of an ending than Rob did – the classes had been such a constant through a time of tumultuous change.

Before long she was seated with the rest of her pals and the chatter was once more in full swing. Rocky was telling tales of Tango in the Balkans – 'I was a terribly young man, but so lucky to have seen these things at the age I did.' Minx and Dobby were sitting alongside him, listening respectfully as their eyes widened at his tales. Minx looked up and waved as she saw her, mouthing 'Hi!'

As she had come into the room the Hanburys were sprawled over each other and squealed when Ava came to say hello. The minute she sat down next to them they began chatting about who they could set her up with, drawing in comments from anyone who would listen, including some people that Ava had never even met before. Apparently there were hundreds of people available, she'd be a great catch and she could pretty much take her pick, it seemed.

With that the wine and conversation were soon flowing like no tomorrow. Anything could have been going on outside of the room and they would all have been oblivious. But then, just as they were giggling over Patrice's anecdotes from the time when he worked with some of the *Strictly* contestants from years gone by, in walked Gabe.

'Hello, darling boy,' said Jenny, standing up and walking over to greet him. 'Come and sit down here.'

He walked towards Jenny and gave her a big hug, then turned to the table and said hi to everyone. The group was thrilled to see him and stood up or sat forward in their seats, wishing him well, saying how much they'd missed him and asking if he was coming back. When Ava stood up to kiss him hello, she asked quietly after his sister.

'It's looking good for that Christmas return,' he whispered. 'Nothing definite, but maybe in a week or so ...'

'I'm thrilled,' she said, giving his hand a squeeze.

He joined in companionably with the rest of the table for the meal and after five minutes there was no sense that he had missed out on any of the gossip by not being in class for so long.

Once the festive tapas had been enjoyed, the gang headed upstairs and began to dance. There was a selection of family and friends there: some were people who had taken previous courses with Patrice, others pals who were curious about taking a future one, and some were just partners looking to party, but everyone was in high spirits and up for attempting a bit of Salsa – and attempt it, they did.

At first, a few of the students tried some of the other dances they'd learned – Patrice spun round the room with Jenny in a stunning Cha Cha Cha, while Ava had let Rockingham treat her to a Jive routine both remembered from an old movie. Half-made up, half-remembered and 100 per cent hilarious, they entertained the rest of the group for five minutes before the real fun began – Salsa time!

Patrice went to change the music and invited all of the guests to join in, and then most of the students grabbed partners or friends and took to the dance floor themselves. After a few seconds of awkwardness the dance floor was full once again.

After some initial delicate moments of avoiding eye contact with other potential partners, eventually Ava and Gabe found each other. And so began the dancing: the twirling, the embracing, the tapping and the hips. Oh, the hips! Ava could not believe that he had stopped attending classes halfway through the course. When it came to Salsa he was easily as good as anyone else in the room, and she was sure that he hadn't forgotten his ballroom skills either. She started to feel her temperature rise: the heat of the room, the candles, the wine ... Her velvet skirt was heavier than she realised once she started moving in it, too. Soon her head was starting to swim, as if there was barely enough air in there. She was enjoying every second of her time on the dance floor, but suddenly felt as if perhaps she might not be able to keep up if she continued to dance at this pace. At the end of one dance she pulled back and told Gabe that she wanted to go outside for a breath of fresh air.

'I'll come with you,' he offered.

'Oh, there's no need. I'll be fine.' She was already out of the room and a couple of steps down the stairs, convinced she might pass out if she stayed in there a moment longer. It was as if months of longing and sadness had been unlocked on the dance floor and she simply couldn't keep them in any more.

'Ava ...' He caught her hand. His fingertips, now familiar again, grazed hers. 'Wait.'

They clattered down the pub stairs and outside. Ava was feeling extremely hot now and leant against the brick wall, facing the pretty pub garden, now empty and frozen over.

'Look, it's freezing,' he said, taking off his jacket and offering it to her.

'I was too hot, though,' she protested.

'Okay, but please, take it.'

'Thank you,' she replied. He draped it around her shoulders as she stepped away from the wall.

She leant back again and took a deep breath. He did the same, leaning next to her on the wall. Taking her hand, he turned to face her.

'It's been so lovely to see you again,' he said. 'I wish I'd seen more of you these last few months.'

'Yes, but I'm glad your sister's turned a corner now.'

'I know! What an experience, though – it fills you with a lot of "live each day as your last" kind of thoughts.'

'I can imagine,' she smiled, before adding, 'Lately, I've been doing a bit of that myself.'

'So I heard,' he nodded. 'I had no idea, or I would have called you sooner.'

'What do you mean?'

'I thought you had a boyfriend – you wouldn't have a drink with me, you wouldn't come to *Strictly*. I once saw you in the square outside your shop and Matt confirmed it when I casually asked if your partner was a co-owner.'

'But we broke up, ages ago. Partly because ...'

'I know that now.'

'How? I trusted Matt ...'

'No, he's very discreet. It was Jenny.'

'Oh, I see.'

'Yes, I see now, too. I see more clearly now than I have for months.'

And with that he leant in and kissed her.

Chapter 16

May I Have this Dance?

In the week that followed, it felt as if life had suddenly been transformed from black and white to full colour. All those wasted months, wondering if she was a fool to have wished life could hold a little more to it, all those missed connections and misunderstandings. They seemed trivial now she had been given this extra chance.

And that was how she saw it: there was nothing definite between herself and Gabe. 'After all, a kiss in a pub garden is hardly a proposal of marriage,' she told Mel later that week over the phone.

'But it is proof there's still more of life out there to be grabbed,' her friend insisted.

'Exactly – that there are still chances to be taken, risks that are worth it, after all,' said Ava. That was the only seal of approval she needed, and she swiftly turned the topic back to Mel and the kids, and how things were going with Rich. As it turned out, he had put in some sterling work to prove how sorry he was and was trying hard to regain Mel's trust. There were no extravagant gestures – no strange, profligate gifts, no mid-life crisis wardrobes, no unnerving

300

public displays of affection – he had simply started to hang out with his family a bit more, to listen to Mel when they chatted and to enjoy her company again.

'That must sound so dull to you, in the first exciting flush of a romance,' said Mel, sheepishly.

'No, not at all! Nothing to do with you being happier is dull to me,' Ava told her. 'If anything, it's … well, it's romantic, isn't it?'

'Well, in a domestic kind of a way.'

'That's what I mean,' said Ava. 'Romance finds its way to people via different routes, but it's still romance. It gives me hope that we can all carry on falling in love again.'

'Blimey, Ava! To think only a few months ago we were taking the Mickey out of Emma for becoming a changed woman after dance classes! You're a changed woman.'

'I'm still me,' she insisted. 'I'm just me, after having taken a chance for the first time in too long.'

Ava really had no idea how this chance would pan out, but for once in her life she was fine with it. She enjoyed chatting with Gabe a few times, but was painfully aware that with The Wedding of the Century coming up and his sister Julia still in hospital, the chances of that second date looked pretty slim in the near future. She held her nerve, though, and about ten days later she received a call while on her way home from work.

'Hey you! How are things?'

'They're good! Hectic, but very good.' Ava adjusted the hands-free kit in her car. She had only recently bought it and still felt as if she were a contestant from a business game show, barking orders to a mysterious unseen servant in a moving vehicle.

'How is the family? And how are you coping?' she continued.

'That's why I was calling – it's good news at last. Julia is coming home tomorrow.'

'That's fantastic! I'm thrilled for you. How is she coping? And her husband?'

'She still gets tired quickly, she'll need a lot of help and support – emotionally, as well – but the fact that the doctors are letting her home in time for Christmas is …' He seemed choked. 'Well, it's exactly what everyone needs. And her husband is conscious now too, so we all have our fingers crossed that he'll be home with her soon.'

'Oh Gabe, that's wonderful news! But I can imagine of course she will need lots of support. Please let me know if there is anything I can do to help.'

'It's not help I need now, it's company – so what are you doing Saturday night?' he asked, his voice alive with excitement.

'Oh, I …'

'Come on now, don't tell me I can't take you for dinner just because it's the *Strictly Come Dancing* final?'

Ava laughed. 'You know how much I love that show! But no, that's not the reason: it's the wedding on Sunday. And because of how many weddings are on the Saturday, I can't do the flowers until that afternoon and into the evening. It's going to be hours of painstakingly pinning winter orchids

302

and rural foliage onto those stone pillars, and after what happened with Matt I'm really not up for rushing the job.'

'Oh, I see. I'm so sorry, so silly for me to have forgotten. Never mind, another time. After the wedding then.'

For the first time Ava felt a prickle of panic that he seemed so casual about this. She tried to push it to one side and concentrated on the business to hand for the rest of the week.

Saturday was as busy as ever and she heard several customers bantering with each other about the outcome of the *Strictly* contest that night. She was jealous that they would get to see all the excitement live as it went out across the country, especially after having witnessed the excitement of a live show close up. As the day grew quieter, she closed the shop with Minx's help and gave Matt a quick call to check he was okay. Despite her protestations that he should have no more to do with the wedding, Matt was determined to help out and had been delivering ivy garlands and small advent centrepieces (the only Christmassy concession Lauren permitted) to the country house where the reception was to be held. With his foot still in plaster he couldn't drive, but he had assembled them at home in front of a few DVDs, then persuaded his beloved Amy (who had now passed her test) to drop him off at the venue with everything.

It's looking awesome. You've done your sis proud. M
x

came his text.

303

> It's you who should be proud! I'm eternally grateful
> and can't wait to give you all the gossip next week.
> Axx

was her reply.

After texting, she loaded everything she needed into the back of the Dunne's mini-van, now parked at the front of the shop, and headed off. The church and its location had seemed so adorable when she had visited in the past – but that had been in broad daylight. Now, as she drove down the small path, she realised how isolated the building actually was. She arrived at the large wooden front doors and let herself in with the key that Lauren had delivered that afternoon on her way to have her wedding manicure done. Inside, she found the light switch and waited for the crackle of electricity to spread throughout the church. Then, still swathed in her winter coat and the hat, scarf and gloves she had been wearing for the drive, she lifted the pre-done arrangements for the front of the church out from the back of the van. Each time she left the church she was struck by how dark it was outside. There was no light at all, bar that coming from inside the church, and it was only around seven o'clock. The still, velvety darkness was too much for her, so she lifted everything she needed to decorate the pillars and placed it in the church as fast as she could. Then she went back into the building and closed the door firmly.

It was completely silent in there. The old heavy stone seem to absorb any sound she made, so for at least half an hour she sat in silence, putting together the garlands and laying them on the floor ready to be pinned up. Then, just as she was ready to get up on the ladder, she heard the crunch of car tyres on the gravel outside.

Ava froze. She waited, listening to check if it were Lauren, or other family voices she might recognise. Nothing. A car door slammed, and then sturdy footsteps made their way towards the closed and locked door. Whoever it was gave the handle a bit of a shake and then knocked.

Ava remained totally still, trying to work out who it might be. She felt in the pocket of her fleece for her mobile phone and then realised the reason why it had been so very quiet in that church was because she had no signal. The door rattled again and then, 'Ava?'

She sighed with relief and ran her hands through her hair. 'Gabe?'

'Yes. Can I come in?'

She ran down the aisle towards him and pressed her hands on the door to talk to him through the gap. 'Hold on, I just have to find the right key.'

There was a moment of awkward fumbling before she had unlocked the door and he was inside the church and standing there, in the doorway, with a large canvas bag. He still had the bag in his hand when he seized her by the small of her back, scooped her up towards him and gave her a big kiss on the lips.

'Hello, you,' he said, smiling down at her, his hair flopping forward onto her face.

'What are you doing here?' she whispered.

'You couldn't come out to dinner so I thought dinner should come to you.' He held out the canvas bag. 'And you were going to miss *Strictly*, so I thought you deserved a quick dance yourself!' He let go of the bag and held her in a ballroom hold before turning her around a few steps, right there at the back of the church. How did he even know the American Smooth? She was sure he hadn't attended that class, but felt herself gliding across the flag-stones in his arms and giggled helplessly.

'That's nuts!' she said, half-heartedly trying to conceal the fact that she was completely thrilled.

'I wondered if you might need some help, too. Oh, and I missed you,' he added.

Then he opened the bag to produce a mini picnic of pork pies, cherry tomatoes, a couple of pieces of cheese and some delicious ginger beer.

'I thought you might need sustenance ...' he explained as he went about putting his treats on the back pew and then came to help her with the remaining flower arrangements. He held the ladder, cut the wires and helped her with positioning until the church was truly transformed into the Winter Wonderland that Ava knew Lauren had dreamed of for so long.

Once it was done, they stood together at the back of the church to admire their handiwork.

Gabe took her hand and continued to hold it. 'This is magnificent! You have a real talent. I hope your sister is as proud of you as I am,' he told her.

'Thank you,' she whispered, glowing with pride, and stood on tiptoes to kiss his cheek.

'But do you know what? I reckon there's still another hour of *Strictly* left to play. We can live the dancers' dream tonight after all, you know.'

'Do you really think so?'

'Absolutely!' he said with a grin. They loaded up Ava's equipment into the back of the van and he put the remnants of their picnic in his car. After this, they stood awkwardly, shivering outside their respective vehicles: a decision had to be made.

'I have to be at Lauren's very early in the morning ...' Ava began.

'Of course.'

'And my house is closest ...'

'Yes, yes, I think it probably is,' he replied.

'So ...'

'Yes ...?'

'What would you think about coming back to mine? I have to get up very early, though ...'

'I don't think we should worry about tomorrow just yet,' he smiled. Then he kissed her, and followed her home.

Less than twenty-four hours later Ava was back in the church. And so too was Gabe, because after they had driven back to Ava's house, whooped and yelled with glee at the excitement and drama of the *Strictly* final, she had told him about Lauren's offer of a plus one for the day. Caught up in

307

the moment, she realised that she had to invite him. They had driven home to hers and snuggled up on the sofa together. At first it had been tentative, the idea of being so relaxed and intimate with each other suddenly so alien, but slowly the magic of the show proved infectious. As the finalists dazzled with their Latin sequences, the pair marvelled at how fast their feet were moving.

'I can't believe she has only been dancing as long as I have!' exclaimed Ava at one point, instinctively grabbing Gabe's arm for emphasis.

The dresses were exquisite – vibrant and romantic in equal measure. And for once Ava wasn't entirely consumed with jealousy, knowing she had a bespoke dress of her own upstairs, ready for tomorrow. Perhaps this would be the one in which she would look like her ultimate self, she thought, as the winning couple twirled beneath the confetti cascading down on them. And it was at that moment when Ava realised she couldn't just say goodbye to Gabe now: she wanted him at her side the next day, too.

'I'll understand if you have other things to do with your family,' she said softly, after blurting out the invitation.

'No way! They're thrilled to be spending some time with each other at last, all under the same roof. I would love to come.'

And he did. She couldn't quite believe it until she saw him with her own eyes as she walked down the aisle behind Lauren.

When Lauren arrived, looking exquisite in Viv's creation, her eyes immediately lit up. Her hair was piled high and her make-up, which included a flash of dark lipstick showing beneath her veil, perfect for the wintry weather. The dress itself, with its gold-flecks fabric, looked just as magical as every other princess who had got married that year, but, Lauren being Lauren, she was not going to miss out on giving her opinion on everything. When she reached the church on her father's arm she briefly pushed the veil aside to get a glimpse of the decorations before turning to wink at Ava. With a tiny squeal, she whispered, 'My Winter Wonderland!' before heading for the altar.

Moments later they were processing down the aisle to the sound of the organ, and there was Gabe, sitting on the end of the same back pew where they had picnicked so recently. He winked at Ava, who blushed and continued down the aisle, feeling every bit as gorgeous as she had hoped in her dress. Those weeks of dancing had paid off after all, as she felt strong and slim beneath the soft, shimmering silk. Not a trace of the Jane Austen matriarch about her. Instead the dress flattered her newly honed slimness without making her look as if she was competing with her sister. She did indeed feel the very best she had ever looked.

Sitting at the back, Gabe was one of the first out of the church, and it seemed he agreed. A blushing Ava made sure to introduce him to Lauren and Rory before they were swamped by too many wellwishers.

Once they were at the reception venue, Lauren grabbed Ava's arm and dragged her off to the ladies'.

'Look,' she told her, hands on hips, her tiara glinting almost menacingly. 'Today is all about me, let's keep that nice and clear. But wow, what a comeback! Well done, *you*! And here's to second chances!'

'To second chances,' said Ava and gave her a kiss.

The rest of the day passed by in a blur, seamlessly moving from receiving line to wedding breakfast and then on to toasts. Jackie sobbed buckets throughout the speeches, especially at Andrew's quietly dignified Father of the Bride moment. Ava had leant over and handed her a tissue, which she had immediately used to make sure her mascara didn't run. The minute the applause began Jackie grabbed Ava's hand and whispered, 'I'm so happy for you too, darling. So happy. And he has fabulous hair.'

Ava wasn't quite sure what the best response to this compliment would be, but before long she was rescued by the part of the day she had looked forward to most: the dancing. The music began and Rory and Lauren took to the dance floor for their first dance, a slow traditional Waltz. Then, before she had had a chance to look for him, Ava felt Gabe's arm snake round her waist.

'May I have this dance?' he whispered in her ear.

Ava saw her mother's eyes widen with excitement as she elbowed Andrew to pay attention.

'Darling, this dance is yours,' smiled Ava, for once not minding being the subject of such momentary scrutiny.

As the beat changed, he led her to the dance floor and took her in his arms. Almost immediately it began to feel as if no one else was in the room.

'I never thought I would learn so much from dancing,' she told him.

'Nor did I,' he smiled, 'but I never want to stop!